HOMESICK FOR
ANOTHER
WORLD

Ottessa
Moshfegh

JONATHAN CAPE
LONDON

1 3 5 7 9 10 8 6 4 2

Jonathan Cape, an imprint of Vintage Publishing,
20 Vauxhall Bridge Road,
London SW1V 2SA

Jonathan Cape is part of the Penguin Random House group of companies
whose addresses can be found at global.penguinrandomhouse.com.

 Penguin
Random House
UK

First published by Jonathan Cape in 2017

penguin.co.uk/vintage

A CIP catalogue record for this book is available from the British Library

ISBN 9780224101349

Printed and bound by Great Britain by Clays Ltd, St Ives Plc

Penguin Random House is committed to a sustainable future
for our business, our readers and our planet. This book is
made from Forest Stewardship Council® certified paper.

 MIX
Paper from
responsible sources
FSC® C018179

CONTENTS

HOMESICK FOR
ANOTHER
WORLD

My classroom was on the first floor, next to the nuns' lounge. I used their bathroom to puke in the mornings. One nun always dusted the toilet seat with talcum powder. Another nun plugged the sink and filled it with water. I never understood the nuns. One was old and the other was young. The young one talked to me sometimes, asked me what I would do for the long weekend, if I'd see my folks over Christmas, and so forth. The old one looked the other way and twisted her robes in her fists when she saw me coming.

My classroom was the school's old library. It was a messy old library room, with books and magazines splayed out all over the place and a whistling radiator and big fogged-up windows overlooking Sixth Street. I put two student desks together to make up my desk at the front of the room, next to the chalkboard. I kept a down-filled sleeping bag in a cardboard box in the back of the room and covered the sleeping bag with old newspapers. Between classes I took the sleeping bag out, locked the door, and napped until the bell rang. I was usually still drunk from the night before. Sometimes I had a drink at lunch at the Indian restaurant around the corner, just to keep me going—sharp wheat ale in a squat, brown bottle. McSorley's was there but I didn't like all that nostalgia. That bar made me roll my eyes. I rarely made my way down to the school cafeteria, but when I did, the principal, Mr. Kishka, would stop me and smile broadly and say, "Here she comes, the vegetarian." I don't know why he thought I was a vegetarian. What I took from the cafeteria were prepackaged digits of cheese, chicken nuggets, and greasy dinner rolls.

I had one student, Angelika, who came and ate her lunch with me in my classroom.

"Miss Mooney," she called me. "I'm having a problem with my mother."

She was one of two girlfriends I had. We talked and talked. I told her that you couldn't get fat from being ejaculated into.

"Wrong, Miss Mooney. The stuff makes you thick in the middle. That's why girls get so thick in the middle. They're sluts."

She had a boyfriend she visited in prison every weekend. Each Monday was a new story about his lawyers, how much she loved him, and so forth. She always had the same face on. It was like she already knew all the answers to her questions.

I had another student who drove me crazy. Popliasti. He

was a wiry, blond, acned sophomore with a heavy accent. "Miss Mooney," he'd say, standing up at his desk. "Let me help you with the problem." He'd take the chalk out of my hand and draw a picture of a cock and balls on the board. This cock and balls became a kind of insignia for the class. It appeared on all their homework, on exams, etched into every desk. I didn't mind it. It made me laugh. But Popliasti and his incessant interruptions, a few times I lost my cool.

"I cannot teach you if you act like animals!" I screamed.

"We cannot learn if you are crazy like this, screaming, with your hair messy," said Popliasti, running around the room, flipping books off window ledges. I could have done without him.

But my seniors were all very respectful. I was in charge of preparing them for the SAT. They came to me with legitimate questions about math and vocabulary, which I had a hard time answering. A few times in calculus, I admitted defeat and spent the hour jabbering on about my life.

"Most people have had anal sex," I told them. "Don't look so surprised."

And, "My boyfriend and I don't use condoms. That's what happens when you trust somebody."

Something about that old library room made Principal Kishka keep his distance. I think he knew if he ever set foot in there, he'd be in charge of cleaning it up and getting rid of me. Most of the books were useless mismatched sets of outdated encyclopedias, Ukrainian bibles, Nancy Drew. I even found some girlie magazines under an old map of Soviet

Russia folded up in a drawer marked SISTER KOSZINSKA. One good thing I found was an old encyclopedia of worms. It was a coverless, fist-thick volume of brittle paper chipped at the corners. I tried to read it between classes when I couldn't sleep. I tucked it into the sleeping bag with me, pried open the binding, let my eyes roll over the small, musty print. Each entry was more unbelievable than the last. There were round-worms and horseshoe worms and worms with two heads and worms with teeth like diamonds and worms as large as house cats, worms that sang like crickets or could disguise them-selves as small stones or lilies or could stretch their jaws to accommodate a human baby. What is this trash they're feed-ing children these days? I thought. I slept and got up and taught algebra and went back into the sleeping bag. I zipped it up over my head. I burrowed deep down and pinched my eyes closed. My head throbbed and my mouth felt like wet paper towels. When the bell rang, I got out and there was Angelika with her brown-bag lunch saying, "Miss Mooney, there's something in my eye and that's why I'm crying."

"Okay," I said. "Close the door."

The floor was black and piss-colored checkerboard lino-leum. The walls were shiny, cracking, piss-colored walls.

I had a boyfriend who was still in college. He wore the same clothes every single day: a blue pair of Dickies and a paper-thin button-down. The shirt was Western style with opales-cent snaps. You could see his chest hair and nipples through it. I didn't say anything. He had a nice face but fat ankles and a soft, wrinkly neck. "Lots of girls at school want to date me," he said often. He was studying to be a photographer, which I didn't take seriously at all. I figured he would work in an office after he graduated, would be grateful to have a real job like that, would feel happy and boastful to be employed, a bank account in his name, a suit in his closet, et cetera, et cetera. He was sweet. One time his mother came to visit from South Carolina. He introduced me as his "friend who lives downtown." The mother was horrible. A tall blonde with fake boobs.

"What do you use on your face at night?" is what she asked me when the boyfriend went to the toilet.

I was thirty. I had an ex-husband. I got alimony and had decent health insurance through the Archdiocese of New York. My parents, upstate, sent me care packages full of postage stamps and decaffeinated teas. I called my ex-husband when I was drunk and complained about my job, my apartment, the boyfriend, my students, anything that came to mind. He was remarried already, in Chicago. He did something with law. I never understood his job, and he never explained anything to me.

The boyfriend came and went on weekends. Together we drank wine and whiskey, romantic things I liked. He could handle it. He looked the other way, I guess. But he was one of those idiots about cigarettes.

"How can you smoke like that?" he'd say. "Your mouth tastes like Canadian bacon."

"Ha-ha," I said from my side of the bed. I went under the sheets. Half my clothes, books, unopened mail, cups, ashtrays, half my life was stuffed between the mattress and the wall.

"Tell me all about your week," I said to the boyfriend.

"Well, Monday I woke up at eleven thirty a.m.," he'd start. He could go on all day. He was from Chattanooga. He had a nice, soft voice. It had a nice sound to it, like an old radio. I got up and filled a mug with wine and sat on the bed.

"The line at the grocery store was average," he was saying.

Later: "But I don't like Lacan. When people are so incoherent, it means they're arrogant."

"Lazy," I said. "Yeah."

By the time he was done talking we could go out for dinner. We could get drinks. All I had to do was walk around and sit down and tell him what to order. He took care of me that way. He rarely poked his head into my private life. When he did, I turned into an emotional woman.

"Why don't you quit your job?" he asked. "You can afford it."

"Because I love those kids," I answered. My eyes welled up with tears. "They're all such beautiful people. I just love them." I was drunk.

I bought all my beer from the bodega on the corner of East Tenth and First Avenue. The Egyptians who worked there were all very handsome and complimentary. They gave me free candy—individually wrapped Twizzlers, Pop Rocks. They dropped them into the paper bag and winked. I'd buy two or three forties and a pack of cigarettes on my way home from school each afternoon and go to bed and watch *Mar-ried . . . with Children* and *Sally Jessy Raphael* on my small black-and-white television, drink and smoke and snooze. When it got dark I'd go out again for more forties and, on occasion, food. Around ten p.m. I'd switch to vodka and would pretend to better myself with a book or some kind of music, as though God were checking up on me.

"All good here," I pretended to say. "Just bettering myself, as always."

Or sometimes I went to this one bar on Avenue A. I tried to order drinks that I didn't like so that I would drink them more slowly. I'd order gin and tonic or gin and soda or a gin martini or Guinness. I'd told the bartender—an old Polish lady—at the beginning, "I don't like talking while I drink, so I may not talk to you."

"Okay," she'd said. "No problem." She was very respectful.

Every year, the kids had to take a big exam that let the state know just how bad I was at doing my job. The exams were designed for failure. Even I couldn't pass them.

The other math teacher was a little Filipina who I knew made less money than me for doing the same job and lived in a one-bedroom apartment in Spanish Harlem with three kids and no husband. She had some kind of respiratory disease and a big mole on her nose and wore her blouses buttoned to the throat with ridiculous bows and brooches and lavish plas-tic pearl necklaces. She was a very devout Catholic. The kids made fun of her for that. They called her the "little Chinese lady." She was a much better math teacher than me, but she had an unfair advantage. She took all the students who were good at math, all the kids who back in Ukraine had been beaten with sticks and made to learn their multiplication tables, decimal places, exponents, all the tricks of the trade. Whenever anyone talked about Ukraine, I pictured either a stark, gray forest full of howling black wolves or a trashy bar on a highway full of tired male prostitutes.

My students were all horrible at math. I got stuck with the dummies. Popliasti, worst of all, could barely add two and two. There was no way my kids could ever pass that big exam. When the day came to take the test, the Filipina and I looked at each other like, Who are we kidding? I passed out the tests, had them break the seals, showed them how to fill in the bubbles properly with the right pencils, told them, "Try your best," and then I took the tests home and switched all their answers. No way those dummies would cost me my job.

"Outstanding!" said Mr. Kishka when the results came in. He'd wink and give me the thumbs-up and cross himself and slowly shut the door behind him.

Every year it was the same.

I had this one other girlfriend, Jessica Hornstein, a homely Jewish girl I'd met in college. Her parents were second cousins. She lived with them on Long Island and took the LIRR into the city some nights to go out with me. She showed up in normal jeans and sneakers and opened her backpack and pulled out cocaine and an ensemble suitable for the cheapest prostitute on the Vegas strip. She got her cocaine from some high-school kid in Bethpage. It was horrible. Probably cut with powdered laundry detergent. And Jessica had wigs of all colors and styles: a neon blue bob, a long blond Barbarella-type do, a red perm, a jet black Japanese one. She had one of those colorless, bug-eyed faces. I always felt like Cleopatra next to Opie when I went out with her. "Going clubbing" was always her request, but I couldn't stand all that. A night under a colored lightbulb over twenty-dollar cocktails, getting hit on by skinny Indian engineers, not dancing, a stamp on the back of my hand I couldn't scrub off. I felt vandalized.

But Jessica Hornstein knew how to "bump and grind." Most evenings she bid me adieu on the arm of some no-face corporate type to show him "the time of his life" back at his condo in Murray Hill or wherever those people lived. Occasionally I took one of the Indians up on his offer, stepped into an unmarked cab to Queens, looked through his medicine cabinet, got some head, and took the subway home at six in the morning just in time to shower, call my ex-husband, and make it to school before the second bell. But mostly I left the club early and got myself on a seat in front of my old Polish lady bartender, Jessica Hornstein be damned. I dipped a finger in my beer and rubbed off my mascara. I looked around at the other women at the bar. Makeup made a girl look so desperate, I thought. People were so dishonest with their clothes and personalities. And then I thought, Who cares? Let them do what they want. It's me I should worry about. Now and then I cried out to my students. I threw my arms in the air. I put my head on my desk. I asked them for help. But what could I expect? They turned around at their desks to talk to one another, put on their headphones, pulled out their books, potato chips, looked out the window, did anything but try to console me.

Oh, okay, there were a few fine times. One day I went to the park and watched a squirrel run up a tree. A cloud flew around in the sky. I sat down on a patch of dry yellow grass and let the sun warm my back. I may have even tried to do a cross-word puzzle. Once, I found a twenty-dollar bill in a pair of old jeans. I drank a glass of water. It got to be summer. The days got intolerably long. School let out. The boyfriend graduated and moved back to Tennessee. I bought an air conditioner and paid a kid to carry it down the street and up the stairs to my apartment. Then my ex-husband left a message on my machine: "I'm coming into town," he said. "Let's have lunch, or dinner. We can have drinks. Next week. No big deal," he said. "Talk."

No big deal. I'd see about that. I dried out for a few days, did some calisthenics on the floor of my apartment. I borrowed a vacuum from my neighbor, a middle-aged gay with long, acne-scarred dimples, who eyed me like a worried dog. I took a walk to Broadway and spent some of my money on new clothes, high-heeled shoes, silk panties. I had my makeup done and bought whatever products they suggested. I had my hair cut. I got my nails polished. I took myself out to lunch. I ate a salad for the first time in years. I went to the movies.

I called my mom. "I've never felt better," I said. "I'm having a great summer. A great summer holiday." I tidied up my apartment. I filled a vase with bright flowers. Anything good I could think to do I did. I was filled with hope. I bought new sheets and towels. I put on some music. "*Bailar,*" I said to myself. Look, I'm speaking Spanish. My mind is fixing itself, I thought. Everything is going to be okay.

And then the day came. I went to meet my ex-husband at a fashionable bistro on MacDougal Street where the waitresses wore pretty dresses with white lace–trimmed collars. I got there early and sat at the bar and watched the waitresses move around gingerly with their round, black trays of colored cocktails and small plates of bread and bowls of olives. A short sommelier came in and out like the conductor of an orchestra. The nuts on the bar were flavored with sage. I lit a cigarette and looked at the clock. I was so early. I ordered a drink. A Scotch and soda. "Jesus Christ," I said. I ordered another drink, just Scotch this time. I lit another cigarette. A girl sat down next to me. We started talking. She was waiting, too. "Men," she said. "They like to torture us."

"I have no idea what you're talking about," I said and turned around on my stool.

Then it was eight o'clock and my ex-husband walked in. He spoke to the maître d' and nodded in my direction and followed a girl to a table by the window and just waved me over. I took my drink.

"Thank you for meeting me," he said, removing his jacket.

I lit a cigarette and opened the wine list. My ex cleared his throat but said nothing for a while. Then he did his usual hem and haw about the restaurant, how he'd read about the chef in whatever magazine, how the food on the plane was awful, the hotel, how the city had changed, the menu was interesting, the weather here, the weather there, and so on. "You look tired," he said. "Order whatever you want," he told me, as though I were his niece, some babysitter character.

"I will, thank you," I said.

A waitress came over and told us the specials. My ex charmed her. He was always kinder to the waitress than he was to me. "Oh, thank you. Thank you so much. You're the best. Wow. Wow, wow, wow. Thank you, thank you, thank you."

I made up my mind to order, then pretend to go to the bathroom and walk out. I took off my dangly earrings and put them in my purse. I uncrossed my legs. I looked at him. He didn't smile or do anything. He just sat there with his elbows on the table. I missed the boyfriend. He'd been so easy. He'd been very respectful.

"And how's Vivian?" I asked.

"She's fine. She got a promotion, busy. She's okay. Sends her regards."

"I'm sure. Send her my regards, too."

"I'll tell her."

"Thanks," I said.

"You're welcome," he said.

The waitress came back with another drink and took our order. I ordered a bottle of wine. I thought, I'll stay for the wine. The whiskey was wearing off. The waitress went away and my ex got up to use the men's room, and when he got back he asked me to stop calling him.

"No, I think I'll keep calling," I said.

"I'll pay you," he said.

"How much money are we talking?"

He told me.

"Okay," I said. "I'll take the deal."

Our food came. We ate in silence. And then I couldn't eat anymore. I got up. I didn't say anything. I went home. I went back and forth to the bodega. My bank called. I wrote a letter to the Ukrainian Catholic school.

"Dear Principal Kishka," I wrote. "Thank you for letting me teach at your school. Please throw away the sleeping bag in the cardboard box in the back of my classroom. I have to resign for personal reasons. Just so you know, I've been fudging the state exams. Thanks again. Thank you, thank you, thank you."

There was a church attached to the back of the school—a cathedral with great big mosaics of people holding up a finger as though to say, *Be quiet.* I thought I'd go in there and leave my letter of resignation with one of the priests. Also, I wanted a little tenderness, I think, and I imagined the priest putting his hand on my head and calling me something like "my dear," or "my sweet," or "little one." I don't know what I was thinking. "My pet."

I'd been up on bad cocaine and drinking for days. I'd roped a few men back to my apartment and showed them all my belongings, stretched out flesh-colored tights and proposed we take turns hanging each other. Nobody lasted more than a few hours. The letter to Principal Kishka sat on the bedside table. It was time. I checked my reflection in the bathroom mirror before I left the house. I thought I looked pretty normal. That couldn't be possible. I put the last of the stuff up my nose. I put on a baseball cap. I put on some more ChapStick.

On the way to church I stopped at McDonald's for a Diet Coke. I hadn't been around people in weeks. There were whole families sitting down together, sipping on straws, sedate, mulling with their fries like broken horses at hay. A homeless person, man or woman I couldn't tell, had gotten into the trash by the entrance. At least I wasn't completely alone, I thought. It was hot out. I wanted that Diet Coke. But the lines to order made no sense. Most people were huddled in random patterns, gazing up at the menu boards, eyes glazed over, touching their chins, pointing, nodding.

"Are you in line?" I kept asking them. Nobody would answer me.

Finally I just approached a young black boy in a visor behind the counter. I ordered my Diet Coke.

"What size?" he asked me.

He pulled out four cups in ascending order of size. The largest size stood about a foot high off the counter.

"I'll take that one," I said.

This felt like a great occasion. I can't explain it. I felt immediately endowed with great power. I plunked my straw in and sucked. It was good. It was the best thing I'd ever tasted. I thought of ordering another one, for when I'd finished that one. *But that would be exploitive,* I thought. *Better let this one have its day. Okay,* I thought. *One at a time. One Diet Coke at a time. Now off to the priest.*

The last time I'd been in that church was for some Catholic holiday. I'd sat in the back and done my best to kneel, cross myself, move my mouth at the Latin sayings, and so forth. I had no idea what any of it meant, but it had some effect on me. It was cold in there. My nipples stood on end, my hands were swollen, my back hurt. I must have stunk of alcohol. I watched the students in their uniforms line up for the Eucharist. The ones who genuflected at the altar did it so deeply, wholly, they broke my heart. Most of the liturgy was in Ukrainian. I saw Popliasti play with the padded bar you knelt on, lifting it up and letting it slam down. There were beautiful stained-glass windows, a lot of gold.

But when I got there that day with the letter, the church was locked. I sat down on the damp stone steps and finished my Diet Coke. A shirtless bum walked by.

"Pray for rain," he said.

"Okay."

I went to McSorley's and ate a bowl of pickled onions. I tore the letter up. The sun shone on.

Every day at noon Mr. Wu walked through the back alley, past the stinking ravine and the firecracker salesman and the old temple now used as a kind of flophouse for the farmworkers who came in from the country to these outskirts to sell at the market, and down past the rows of little stores that were mostly barbershops and brothels and pharmacies and little clothing stores and cigarette shops, and found a seat at the little family restaurant, under the great, hard-whipping fan sticky with dust from the road, and ordered dishes of pork and potato and whatever fresh vegetable was on display, and sat and watched cartoons and smoked while the food cooked, and the dogs walked by, and the dust rose and fell behind the small trucks and bikes and scooters.

He was in love with the woman at the video-game arcade. She was about his age, in her mid-forties, and had a daughter in high school. He knew her both from the arcade and from around the neighborhood, as she and her daughter lived just a few doors down from him in an apartment with her sister and her sister's retarded son. The woman ignored Mr. Wu when they passed each other on the busy road. But when he ran into her in the narrow pathways of the market, she'd smile politely and ask after his health. "Never better" was the answer he always mumbled. He knew his breath was bad, and because her eyes wandered away so quickly, he knew she had no interest in him.

Mr. Wu dared not visit the local prostitutes. He took a bus into the city and spent the extra money for that bit of privacy. Besides, he thought, it's better not to know where these girls come from, who else they are working on, and so forth. He was bashful about sex and insisted on getting underneath the sheets to take off his clothes. During the act he kept his hands placed lightly on the girl's shoulders and averted his eyes but did not close them. He had learned somewhere that closing your eyes meant that you were in love. He imagined closing his eyes with the woman from the arcade. He wondered if she had the same kind of body as these prostitutes: soft, scentless, and wan. He thought it was quite standard to hate himself a little after visiting a prostitute, so he was never startled when the thought came to him: I am disgusting. On the bus home, he ate an ice cream and looked out the window and thought of his woman at the arcade and of what she might be doing at just that moment, and his heart hurt.

He lived alone in the tallest house in the neighborhood. The downstairs neighbors were a young couple with a big, fat baby and a pet sow. The husband made a living collecting bribes for a local councilman. The woman had one flaccid hand that reminded Mr. Wu of a large prawn. He shuddered and gagged whenever he saw it. He felt sorry for the child, held and fed by that twisted, thin, limp, and red-skinned tentacle. The woman from the arcade had small, gentle, bronze-colored hands. Strong and muscled, not bony and not fat. Just right, he thought. Perfect hands. He went to the arcade at least once a day and stayed for three to four hours at a time, usually in the late evenings. Sometimes he went in the mornings, too, when it was free of children. Days he did not go, he felt sick to his stomach, and his heart growled like a trapped animal, brooding and useless. So he went as often as he could.

The arcade was not really an arcade. It was a room full of computers with games loaded onto them and access to the Internet. He bought a daily pass from the woman. He handed her a large bill so that she would have to make change and he could stand there longer, watching her count the money, feeling her near to him across the counter.

"How are you today, Mr. Wu?" she said. She said this every day.

He mumbled something unintelligible. He never knew what to say around her. Everything he wanted to say was "You are beautiful" and "I'm in love with you." There was, in his mind, nothing else for him to say.

"Thank you," he said instead, taking his change and the little card with his log-in information on it.

"Enjoy," said the woman.

He walked to the computer with the best view of her. He peered out from over the monitor all evening, watching her greet the teenage boys, take their money, hand them their cards. When there were no customers, she played games on her cell phone. She likes games, he thought. That's wonderful, so light of heart, so free. He loved the stiff, thick shiftiness of her hair, which she most often wore down and boxy at her shoulders. Her face was tan and shiny, with big cheeks and a small, round nose. Her eyes were small and clear and bright. She wore lipstick and blue eye shadow. Every day she was more beautiful, he thought. He watched her look in her compact. He wondered what she thought when she looked in the mirror, if she knew her own beauty.

One day he got an idea. He would ask for her phone number so that they could be texting pals. He got the idea from a conversation he'd overheard at his lunch spot. Two men were talking about an article they'd read about technology and dating. He thought it was a risk to ask for her number and knew that asking straight out would give him away. He did not want her to know that he was in love with her. He wanted to divulge that information slowly, in increments, step by step as he wooed her into his arms. Or better yet, he would keep his love for her a secret their entire lives and allow her to think it was she who had seduced him. She the one hopelessly in love, so lucky to have him. He imagined himself across from her at the dinner table, years later. She gazes at him with almost nauseating devotion. He eats his rice straight backed, unconcerned, secretly enraged with happiness.

He decided he could not do it. Asking for the woman's cell-phone number was like asking for her hand in marriage. He knew he would be rejected. He went to the arcade and stood in line and paid for his time and smelled her hair and watched her count the money and his heart ached. Her phone was lying on the counter. If only he could snatch it for a moment, he thought. But there was no chance. He took his seat behind the computer and pined. He watched her work. He watched her use her phone. On his way out he saw what he couldn't believe he had missed before. The arcade had a flyer with a coupon for one free hour of playtime between midnight and six a.m. on weekdays. The arcade phone number was on it. He took a flyer. He would call the number later. If the woman didn't answer, he'd know it wasn't her cell-phone number. But he could pretend to be a policeman, or some higher-up statesperson demanding to speak to the arcade manager. He could say she was in violation of a code, and that he'd need to speak to her immediately. He could call when he knew she wasn't there. He had a plan. He practiced over and over again what to say.

"This is Lieutenant Liu. Give me the manager."

"Give me the manager's direct number."

But the next morning he went to the arcade and stood in

line and paid for his time and watched her fiddle with her earring and make change and his heart nearly broke in half. He was impatient. He went and sat behind a computer in the far corner and called the number on the flyer.

"Wei?" answered the woman.

She had answered on her cell phone.

He nearly jumped for joy. He had her, he felt, in arm's reach.

"Wei?" he heard again. She was behind the counter, scribbling on a pad, phone to her ear, undisturbed. He waited a few more seconds, then hung up. He quickly e-mailed his brother, who was a military man in Suizhou. He wrote that he'd met the most amazing woman in the world, and that he'd probably make her his wife within a year. Then he wrote, "She is old, and not very pretty." He wrote that because he knew that it was bad luck to boast.

He left the arcade and made his way down the back alley, past the ravine, toward the restaurant where he would have a special lunch that day. Everything looked so beautiful. The sun, the sky, the dry brown brittle roads. A red banner announcing the opening of a new grocery store lit his heart on fire as he crossed the little footbridge. He bought a pack of the most expensive cigarettes. He bought a can of orange soda and a small bottle of *baijiu*. At the old temple flophouse he dropped to his knees and said a prayer of thanks for the woman's cell-phone number.

Now that he had the woman's cell-phone number, he would send her a text. But he didn't know how to start off the exchange. "Who's this?" he considered texting. "I just found your number saved in my phone. But I don't know who you are."

But that was no way to begin the romance of his life. He racked his brain for a good opener.

"I've seen you at the arcade."

"I see you around and think you're beautiful."

"I think you're beautiful and would like to get to know you better."

"I find you attractive."

"I like watching you count money."

"You have nice hair and nice hands," he thought of texting.

None of these were good openers. He decided to wait until the perfect line struck him, rather than to rush into a sloppy exchange that might trip him up. More than anything in the world, perhaps more than winning her heart, he did not want to appear awkward.

"I will go to the brothel," said Wu to himself and went out and walked to the bus and waited.

Now, he knew full well that any normal man in his position would simply ask her out to dinner. But that seemed to him to be the worst possible tactic to employ. If he gave her an opportunity to reject him, he was sure she'd take it. "You have seen my face," he considered texting.

His downstairs neighbor was also waiting for the bus.

"Brother Wu," he called to him. "What's your direction?"

"I am going into town to speak with some higher-ups," lied Wu. "We are working on hiring a cleaning crew for Hu Long Road. It will take some real convincing to allocate more funds for this project. It is not my job, but someone has to speak up."

"You're an asset to our community," said the neighbor. He looked despondent. His wife's prawn claw must be getting him down, Wu thought, at once sympathetic and cruel.

"How is the wife, the baby?" he asked.

"The baby is sick. My wife cannot nurse, and the baby food we give it makes it shit water. I've done something to anger the gods," said the neighbor. He held up his hands, palms up to the sky. Wu hadn't been around this sort of superstitious type for a while. He'd forgotten they existed. His own prayer earlier that morning had not really been one of gratitude, but like a child's birthday wish. He'd wished to one day hold the woman naked in his arms and lay her across a moonlit bed.

"Where are you headed?" Wu asked his neighbor.

"To the doctor," he said. "To buy more medicine."

Wu had run out of things to say. He looked at his phone, as though already expecting a reply from the woman at the arcade. He still hadn't thought of what to text her. He thought, Maybe the neighbor knows.

"Tell me, neighbor," he began. "How did you get your wife to marry you?"

"We sat beside each other in grade school," the neighbor said simply. "We lived nearby, and our mothers played mah-jongg at night, so we played together, we were friends. We were friends first. And then the rest," he said. "She has a sick hand, you know." He looked at Wu out of the corners of his eyes.

"I hadn't noticed," lied Wu.

"It made her desperate, I think, to settle for any man."

This gave Wu an idea.

He turned to the neighbor. "I wish you both the best, and your little boy," he said.

"The child is a girl," said the neighbor.

But Wu was not listening. He was thinking of the woman at the arcade.

He thought hard on the bus and performed distractedly with the little prostitute. To stave off his shame, afterward he took himself to a Western restaurant for dinner, ordered steak, a fresh cabbage salad, a glass of red wine.

He took a taxi home.

He knew what to text the woman at the arcade. He would text, "How does it feel to be a middle-aged divorcée living with your retarded nephew and working in a computer café? Is it everything you ever dreamed?"

He took a long time to type all the letters in pinyin and to select the right characters in the phone. He read it over and over again until the taxi stopped in front of his door. He pressed Send and paid the driver.

He went to the arcade. The woman was not there. He paid for his time and got a computer in the corner, out of sight of anyone else, and sat and played video games, pausing to check his phone every minute or two, until the sun came up.

As he walked home, he stopped in the courtyard of the old PLA camp to watch a group of high schoolers practice their sword postures. They looked very elegant and upright in their pea green uniforms, he thought. A bird warbled somewhere in a flowering tree. He walked beneath a curved cement archway and through the badminton courts and out through the tall wrought-iron gates and up the road to the morning market under the bridge and bought a bowl of hot dry noodles and brought it home to his apartment and ate it by the open window.

He was awakened by his phone that afternoon. It was a text from the woman.

"Actually, I am a very sad person. I am very lonely and troubled. Who are you?"

He couldn't believe his attack had produced such a vulnerable, honest reply.

"I am an admirer," he wrote back. "I think you are beautiful."

And then he sent another text: "I am in love with you."

He lay back down and waited for her to text him back. He waited twenty minutes. Then he couldn't wait anymore.

"When I said I was in love with you, I meant I admire

you very much. I'd like to get to know you better. But I'm not sure that you'll be attracted to me."

Still, that wasn't good enough.

"I don't know what type of man you like. What type do you like?" Now he had made a big mistake. He had said too much. He felt he had ruined everything. He knew he had just ruined his entire life.

"I like a man who isn't afraid to try new things," she wrote back.

He did not want to ruin what he had left. He thought carefully of how to reply. But she sent another text.

"Let's meet," she wrote. "I want to see what you look like."

"When?" he wrote back. "I am free anytime."

"Tonight," she wrote. "Meet me at the back gate by the market at midnight. I will wear a rose in my hair."

The man's heart stopped for a moment and then started back up again very slowly. He lay back down and caressed himself beneath the sheet. He had not caressed himself in a long time, he realized. He thought of their meeting, her face, the rose, the striped shadows from the iron gate falling across her bosom in the moonlight. He would watch her for a few moments before emerging from the shadows. He would be a long dark figure, he thought. He would be smoking a ciga-rette. No, that might disgust her. He would keep his hands in his pockets, his chin down. He thought of the American movie *Casablanca*. He would be like in *Casablanca*. He would touch her face lightly with the back of his hand. She would blush and turn her face away, but then she would look up at him again, into his eyes. They would fall in love, and he would kiss her. Not a long kiss on the mouth, but small kisses on the cheeks and neck and forehead. Mr. Wu thought long kisses on the mouth were disgusting. When they happened in movies, he averted his eyes. The thought kept him from caressing himself any further. He read all her texts again. It was only two o'clock. He dressed and went to the arcade.

The woman at the arcade looked worried and unkempt. Her hair was tied in a ponytail and she wore a stained trench coat over her dress. He tried not to pay attention to her disarray. Once she was his, he could dress her any way he liked.

"How are you, Mr. Wu?" she asked. She barely looked up from her wad of bills.

"How are you?" he replied searchingly. He put his arm up on the counter, tried to smile. She turned and yelled to one of her employees in the back room, counted out his change, and handed him his card.

"Enjoy," she said gruffly and picked up her phone.

He took a computer directly in front of the counter so that if he sat to the side of it and crossed his legs as though he were reading articles online and smoking, he could look at her out of the corner of his eye. He watched her take out her compact and pat down her hair. She took down her ponytail and tried to comb it out with her fingers. It only made her hair look worse. She tied it back up again and drew down the corners of her eyes. She seemed to clean out some gunk from her eyes. Mr. Wu gagged a little and stubbed out his cigarette. He looked at the time. It was three thirty. She powdered her face, and as he watched he noticed that her powdering was a little heavy-handed, that she was powdering a little too quickly, with too much gusto. He thought she looked the wrong color. He thought she looked very strange. Now she took out some rouge and spread it on her wide cheeks. That's not so bad, he thought. But then she licked her fingers and wiped some of the rouge off. He thought of all the money and cards she'd handled with those fingers. He thought, Would I kiss those fingers? He thought of the fingers of the prostitute from the day before and wondered where they'd been, how much money they'd handled, and what sticky knobs of doors they'd pulled on. Then the woman put on some blue eye shadow and red lipstick. Wu could not help having the thought that the woman looked like a prostitute. She looks worse than a prostitute, he thought. She looks like a madam. He wondered if he still loved her. He took out his phone and reread all her texts again.

"I am very lonely and troubled. Who are you?"

She sounded desperate, he thought.

He had made a grievous mistake, he thought.

He logged off his computer, got up, walked to the counter, and handed her his card.

"Thank you," she said. He felt sick.

There was a karaoke bar above the dry-goods store on the corner. He went up the stairs. The woman there gave him a large beer and a bowl of peanuts. He ate them quickly and drank the beer and looked out the window and smoked and remembered the woman smearing on that greasy lipstick. He imagined her as the manager of a team of teenage prostitutes. He imagined her yelling at one of them for not pleasing a customer. He had a horrible vision. He envisioned the woman from the arcade washing the prostitute's private parts with the hose from a latrine. He imagined her hand in the prostitute's private parts. He ordered another beer. He could not believe his own mind. He imagined the woman's mouth on the prostitute's private parts. He imagined her cleaning all the little pockets of this prostitute's private parts with her tongue, using her tongue like a bar of soap. "I like a man who is not afraid of trying new things." What if these new things were disgusting things like what he was imagining? What if she wanted him to lick her private parts like that? Could he do it? What if she wanted to use the latrine on his hand? And what if she wanted to lick his fingers after she'd used the latrine on his hand? He couldn't possibly go through with something like that. What if she wanted to clean herself after moving her bowels without toilet paper, lick her fingers and then ask to kiss him on the mouth? He might have no idea that she'd cleaned herself after moving her bowels without toilet paper and licked her fingers. She might want to kiss him tonight, at midnight. His eyes filled with tears. He put out his cigarette.

"Sing a song?" said the woman behind the bar.

But Wu was too disgusted. He went down the stairs and

took a walk by the ravine. He imagined the woman from the arcade swimming in the refuse. He imagined her sucking the dirty water into her mouth and then spurting it out like a fountain. I will never kiss that woman on the mouth, he decided. That is one thing I'll never do.

But he still loved her, he tried to think. I could still love her.

He went back up past the ravine and past the shops and bought a bottle of *baijiu* and another pack of cigarettes and went and sat on the steps of the temple flophouse and drank and smoked for a while. A dog came and sniffed his leg. He drank and drank and spat and flicked his cigarettes at the passing dogs. "Ha ha ha ha ha," he cackled. He looked at his watch: five o'clock. He had plenty of time before his date. At the little family restaurant he ate a soup made of mutton and spicy peppers. He shoveled the rice into his mouth like a peasant, let it fall all over his lap and onto the floor. My last day of freedom, he thought. He decided to take a taxi to the city and visit his little prostitute. He bought another bottle of *baijiu* for the road.

His little prostitute was not at work that day.

"Sorry," said the fat, gray-haired madam. "We have other nice girls for you." He looked at the teenagers sitting on the stained couch. They barely lifted their heads from their phones. One of them had stiff shifty hair like the woman at the arcade, but her face was covered in hard little pimples.

"I'll take the one with the pimples," he said.

"Wan Fei!" yelled the madam. The girl got up. She was extraordinarily tall, he saw.

"Never mind," he said. "Just give me the dumbest one you have."

"Zhu Wenting!" yelled the madam. A fat-faced, pale, short-haired girl got up, eased her phone into the back pocket of her pale yellow jeans. He followed her into the back room and watched her undress in the red light. She had small, hard, pointy breasts. He went over to her and pinched them. She had no reaction.

"Does that hurt?" he asked her.

She pinched his cheek like a little child's. "Does that hurt?" she asked him. He found her delightful. He got undressed. Although he was drunk, he was still shocked by his own actions. He reached down and caressed himself while the prostitute walked to the bed and pulled back the sheets. Her bottom was round and dimpled and the color of polished brass.

"Let me kiss you," he said and pushed her face down into the pillows.

As he swiveled his tongue around her privates, he fell in love with the woman at the arcade again. He reached down and caressed himself. The prostitute laughed and put her butt in the air.

"Put your finger in it," she said.

He was aghast.

"In what?" he wanted to ask. But he did not ask. He put

his finger in his mouth—he did that—and put it up the prostitute's bottom. She made a squeaking noise and wriggled and squeezed on his finger and squeaked again.

"Wrong one," she said.

He was not embarrassed. He put a second finger in there. She made a bigger noise. He pushed them deeper in. He decided he would make love to her this way—in her bottom, with his fingers. This was living, he thought. He reached down and caressed himself as he did it. She wriggled and squealed.

"Be quiet," he said. He took his fingers out of her bottom and pushed her head into the pillow to muffle her squeaks. That gave him an idea. He squished his fingers between her face and the pillow and hooked them in her mouth. He felt around her mouth for her tongue and did his best to wipe his fingers off on her tongue. Then he went back to making love to her behind with his fingers. He continued to caress himself. He thought of the woman at the arcade.

"Enjoy," she'd said.

He laughed. The prostitute's muffled squeals excited him. He took his fingers out of her behind and put them in his mouth. He could not believe what joy he'd brought himself. His eyes filled with tears.

Around eleven forty-five he passed the ravine and stood and took in the moonlight. He felt nervous and yet very serene and tired. Along the road were just a few cars and a few people and a few cows led on ropes and a few dirty children throwing Pop-its at the side of the bridge. He walked toward the road but then stopped abruptly. The woman from the arcade had turned the corner and walked, a rose in her hand, in his direction. They could not possibly walk together to their rendezvous. That would defeat the entire purpose of their meeting, he thought. He hung back and waited for her to pass, then continued, watching the steadiness of her gait. She twisted off the stem of the rose and began to put it in her hair.

He walked several yards behind her, then watched as she fixed the collar of her coat and smoothed out her skirt as she waited, looking around nervously in the dark for him. She did not look as garish as she had earlier that day in the arcade. She curled the end of a strand of her hair around her finger, then let it go. She looked beautiful. It was almost just as he'd imagined, only the striped shadows of the iron bars did not fall across her bosom, for she was standing on the wrong side of the gate. The faint light that was cast down on her was from the neon sign across the road. It made her look intelligent, he thought, wise, savvy, in a way.

He was not sure he could approach her.

He decided to send her a text.

"Go stand behind the gates. I will stand under the neon sign. If you like me, clap your hands. If you don't, whistle."

He took a deep breath and lit a cigarette and went and stood in the light. He looked at his phone, then up, looking straight in her direction. He turned to the side, to the back, then to the front again. He waited for a clap, a whistle, but heard nothing. He waited five minutes. He had his answer.

Mr. Wu went back down the road and bought an armful of fireworks and took them up to the karaoke bar over the dry-goods store and up onto the roof and started sending them off into the ravine. They made a delightful wheezing and whipping noise before they exploded. He watched the white and green and red and yellow lights fizzle out and extinguish in the dirty ravine sludge. He decided to send one higher up into the sky. It sailed over the ravine and hit the banner announcing the opening of the new supermarket. The banner lit on fire. He quickly ducked back into the doorway and went down into the bar, said good night, and stumbled down into the road. He walked home under the burning banner and down the dark and quiet road, pausing now and then to raise his arms in victory.

n order to collect unemployment benefits, I had to fill out this log of all the jobs I'd applied for. But I wasn't applying for any jobs. So I just wrote down "lawyer" and made up a phone number. Then I wrote down "lawyer's assistant" and put down the same phone number. I went on like that. "Law-firm janitor." I looked at the number I'd made up. I tried calling it. It rang and rang. Then a woman got on the line.

"Who's this?" is how she answered the phone.

"I'm doing a study," I said. "How do you feel about people seeing you naked?"

"I was a nude model for an art school," she said, "so I have no problem."

She said her name was Terri and that she lived out in Lone Pine with her mother, who had Parkinson's. She said she wanted to get pregnant so she'd have something to think about all day.

"I'm an Indian," she said next. "Chumash. What are you?"

"I'm regular," I told her.

"Good. I like regular men. I wish I wasn't an Indian. I wish I was black or Chinese or something. Well," she said, "how about you come out here and we see what we can do? I'm not after your money, if that's what you're thinking. I get checks in the mail all the time."

It sounded like a vulture was squawking in the background. I thought for a minute.

"One thing," I said. "I have pimples. And a rash all over my body. And my teeth aren't great either."

"I'm not expecting much," she said. "Besides, I don't like perfect-looking men. They make me feel like trash, and they're boring."

"Sounds good," I said.

We made a date for dinner the next day. I had a good feeling about it.

It was true: I had pimples. But I was still good-looking. Girls liked me. I rarely liked them back. If they asked me what I did for fun, I told them lies, saying I Jet Skied or went to casinos. The truth was that I didn't know how to have fun. I wasn't interested in fun. I spent most of my time looking in the mirror or walking to the corner store for cups of coffee. I had a thing about coffee. It was pretty much all I drank. That and diet ginger ale. Sometimes I stuck my finger down my throat. Plus I was always picking at my pimples. I covered the marks they made with girls' liquid foundation, which I stole from Walgreens. The shade I used was called Classic Tan. I guess those were my only secrets.

My uncle lived out in Agoura Hills. I called him sometimes out of desperation, but he only ever wanted to talk about girls.

"I don't like anybody right now," I told him over the phone. I was looking in the mirror over the bathroom sink, doing some one-handed picking.

"But women are good," he said. "They're like a good meal."

"I can't afford a good meal," I said back to him. "Anyway, I go for quantity over quality."

He told me to go ask if Sears or T.J.Maxx was hiring, or Burger King. For someone else, maybe that was fine advice. He himself didn't need to work. He was on disability for having a gimp leg. Also, he had a colostomy bag he didn't care for properly. He used a lot of peach-scented air freshener around the house to cover the smell. He rarely left the living room and liked to order in large Mexican dinners or whole pizzas. He was always eating something and dumping out the colostomy bag right afterward.

"I don't feel very well," I told him. "I'm too sick to find a job."

"Go to a doctor," he said. "Look in the phone book. Don't be a fool. You need to care for your health."

"Can I borrow some money?" I asked him.

"No."

I found a cheap doctor in a Korean shopping mall on Wilshire.

The mall was basically empty, just a lot of fake brass and cloudy windows and orange fake-marble floors. I looked up into the galleria. The glass ceiling was cracked all over. A pigeon soared around, then rested on a strand of unlit Christmas lights. Someone had spread newspapers around the floor. There was a luggage store, a place to get your photo taken, a hair salon. That was it—all the other stalls were empty. A homeless Korean lady padded by me in dirty, quilted long underwear, pushing a baby carriage full of trash. I took a long whiff.

I found the clinic down a dim hallway of unmarked offices. On the door there was a poster of all the services the doctor offered. I found my symptoms: weight gain, hair loss, rash. I went inside. A fat lady stood at the counter in front of the receptionist.

"This prescription is for the yellow kind and I need the pink kind. The Percodan," she was saying.

I had a thing about fat people. It was the same thing I had about skinny people: I hated their guts. After a few minutes, a nurse told me to follow her through the office. We passed an unframed poster of hot rods and another poster of kittens inside a top hat. The nurse pointed to a man in a flannel shirt holding a yellow legal pad. He resembled a retired WWF wrestler. His eyes hid behind folds of skin and raised moles and eyebrows badly in need of plucking. He needed a shave too. Most men have no idea how to groom themselves. From where his shirt puckered between the buttons, I could tell he wasn't wearing anything under the flannel. Wiry black hairs lay across his gut. He smelled like old food.

"Are you a real doctor?" I asked him.

He steered me onto a greasy examination table.

"So you've got something wrong with you," he said, looking at the form.

"I try to throw up all the food I eat, but I'm still fat," I said. "And the rash." I pulled up my sleeve.

The doctor took a step back. "You ever wash your sheets?"

"Yes," I lied. "So what's wrong with me?"

"I'm not one to judge," he said, placing his hand over his heart.

As good-looking as I was, I was scared nobody would ever marry me. I had small hands. They were like a girl's hands, but with hair. Nobody marries men with hands like that. When I fit my fingers down my throat, it's easy. My fingers are thin, soft. When I put them down there, it's like a cool breeze. That's the best way I can explain it.

"Uncle," I said on the phone. "Can I do some laundry at your place?"

"Sure," he replied. "Come on over. But bring your own laundry detergent. And some Diet Coke!"

My uncle lived off the 101. I stopped at Albertsons for the detergent and Diet Coke. I also bought a cheesecake and a carrot cake. I used my EBT card. I never had any shame about that damn EBT card. I got a large coffee and some cigarettes from the gas station next door, too. I didn't really smoke. I just lit the cigarettes and carried them around my uncle's house. It covered the smell decently.

"Look at my boy," hollered my uncle, wobbling up out of his recliner. He had a pair of spruce green leather recliners about a foot away from a gigantic television. It was the kind of television they put in hotel lobbies. All he did was watch TV or talk on the phone or eat. He loved game shows and cooking shows. I'm not saying he was an idiot. He was just like me: anything good made him want to die. That's a characteristic some smart people have.

"Hi," I said.

My uncle's robe was hanging open. I could see that damn colostomy bag.

"Tell me," he said as I took out the cakes. "You seeing anybody these days?"

"Maybe, but I don't want to jinx it," I said. "I don't want to talk about it."

"You always let me down."

We sat in the recliners. I ate the cheesecake and my uncle ate the carrot cake. We watched the end of a movie called *While You Were Sleeping*. My uncle emptied his colostomy bag, and then I sent that cheesecake down the toilet. I put the laundry in. I drank some coffee and went back to the toilet to throw up some more. When I was done, I picked up my uncle's razor and shaved the hair off my knuckles. I showed them to my uncle.

"Somebody should rub my feet with those hands, but not you," he said.

I sat down, sniffed the air, and lit a cigarette.

"I'm still not feeling well," I said. "And I'm broke."

"I won't give you any money," he answered. "But if you cut the grass, I'll pay you for your time."

"How much time?"

"Twenty bucks' worth."

"I'll consider your offer and get back to you," I said. My uncle liked official talk like that.

"Looking forward to it," he replied. Then he reached under his robe and shuffled the bag around. My eyes rolled.

We watched *Law & Order,* then *Oprah,* then *Days of Our Lives.*

I cut the grass.

I'd gone out on dates before. Nothing really spectacular ever happened. One girl had been a nun when she was younger. I liked her, but she was always talking about herself. It was like she was waiting for something in my face to light up, and nothing ever did.

"I am not a character in a television show," I explained. "All I want to do is see your naked body, then reevaluate."

She followed me to the restroom. We were at an Asian bistro in Century City. The bathroom was polished concrete. The lighting was cold and dim. She revealed herself one half at a time. First the shirt off, then back on, then the skirt down, then back up. We dated for a few weeks—just heavy petting, nothing in and out. Finally I lied and told her I had contracted cat scratch fever from a neighbor's kitten and needed time to recover, alone. She stopped calling eventually.

Only once did I pick up a prostitute. I found her sitting on the curb outside the Super 8 near Little Armenia. She had a clear plastic bag for her belongings: a small makeup case, a pair of running shoes, two bananas, and a plastic flower.

"How do I seem to you?" I asked up in the motel room. "How do I smell?"

"You smell like air freshener," she said. "You smell like nothing."

"Great," I said. I took my shirt off. "Am I fat?" I asked her. She squinted her eyes and smushed her lips together.

"You're not skinny, and you're not fat," she said. The way she pointed her finger reminded me of my high-school principal.

"Does my face look swollen?" I asked her.

"What do you mean?" she said.

She pulled a banana out of her plastic bag and started to peel it.

"Can you see my pimples from there?" I asked. She was sitting on the linty bedspread. I went and stood by the window.

"Yeah, anybody can," she said.

I took a few steps away into the shade. "How about now?"

"I can still see them," she said.

I drew the blinds and asked again. She nodded.

Then I sat down next to her and splayed my hands out on the bed.

"What do you think about these?" I asked.

Nobody ever gave me the answer I wanted. Nobody ever said, "Oh, so beautiful!"

The next day back at my apartment, I still had the rash. There was nothing I could do about it before my date that night with Terri. I lay on my bed and reached down to the floor and picked little crumbs and hairs out of the carpet. My stomach ached. I hadn't moved my bowels in days. I drank a gallon of salt water and flipped on the radio. I listened to some hip-hop songs. I liked hip-hop songs because they stirred up my spirit without messing with my mind. Forty minutes later, I moved my bowels. If I ever write a book, it will be filled with tricks and tips for men. For example, if your face is puffy, fill your mouth with coffee grounds. If you have a weak jaw, grow a beard. If you can't grow a beard, wear colors lighter than your skin tone. If you want something and can't have it, want something else. Want what you deserve. You'll probably get it. Above all, control yourself. Some days, to keep myself from eating, I'd hit my head against a wall or sock myself in the stomach. Sometimes I hyperventilated or strangled myself a little with a towel. I used a permanent marker to draw dotted lines around the bulges of fat around my sides, my thighs. I did calisthenics on the kitchen floor. Instead of shaving cream, I used moisturizer. Instead of soap, two-in-one shampoo plus conditioner.

Then the phone rang.

"I'm writing my will," said my uncle. "I'm leaving every-thing to you, including the television," he said.

"Thanks," I said. "Think I could get two hundred bucks in advance?"

"On one condition," he said. "I want my ashes sprinkled in outer space. I saw a commercial once. I think it costs more than it's worth, but I'd feel better knowing for sure nothing bad will happen to me after I'm dead. You might have to sell some of the furniture, and the TV."

"That's a lot to ask," I said. "Would you settle for a moun-taintop by the beach?"

"I'd have to see the place first," he said after a long pause.

"If we could set up a meeting for this afternoon, I'd pre-fer it."

"You got a date tonight?" he asked excitedly. "Who with?"

"Pick you up in an hour," I said.

I had a really good feeling about Terri. I was thinking she might be the one. When I imagined her, I pictured an Indian with long braids and a feather tied to her forehead. I pictured her in a tepee, wearing a scrap of deerskin. I pictured her naked, watching TV in my uncle's recliner and yawning. I pictured her using the toilet, reading an old book about spirituality. Maybe we could go to a casino together. Maybe we could find an all-you-can-eat buffet. She said she had money, af-ter all.

"Do you have cash?" I yelled at my uncle from inside the car as he wobbled out of the house.

"You call this mowing the lawn?" he cried, waving his cane at the grass.

"Did you bring cash?" I needed to know. "Did you?"

"Yes," said my uncle, zipping up his Windbreaker and patting down where the colostomy bag fit. He knocked on the car window with the top of his cane.

"Let me see the money," I said.

He pulled out his wallet and fanned the twenty-dollar bills. I unlocked his door.

When we got to the foot of the mountain, my uncle shook his head. "I don't like it here," he said. "Too much sunshine. Where are we, anyway? What kind of a place is this?"

"Malibu," I said.

The parking lot was nearly empty, and there were picnic tables and a carved wooden sign and a trail that led into a valley of small trees. My uncle craned his neck and squinted out the window up at the top of the mountain.

"There must be animals up there," he said. "Mountain lions, coyotes. Look at all those birds!" He looked around nervously, fumbling his hands in his lap. "And there's dirt everywhere."

"You have a point," I said, rolling my eyes.

He crossed his arms and shook his head again. "I don't want animals pissing all over my ashes."

"I'll spray poison on your ashes, if you want," I said. "I promise."

"You go up there and check it out," he said. "I'm too old. I'm tired. I'll stay in the car. If you can find a place in the shade, with no animals, I guess we've got a deal."

And so I got out and started walking. But I wasn't about to walk the whole way up the mountain. I found a flat patch of grass between the trees and did some sit-ups and lunges and lay back down, and I thought of Terri. I pictured her posing nude in the desert—quiet, still, her long slippery black hair spilling across her perfect breasts. When I kissed her, her mouth was like strawberry ice cream. "You're so handsome," she'd say to me. "You're so fit." Life was wonderful, I thought, walking toward a rock jutting out from the hillside. I could see the ocean and the hills and the highway. It seemed like a fine spot to spend all of eternity. The place was full of chipmunks.

"Pretty good," I told my uncle when I got back to the car. "Pay up."

When I looked at his face, it was gray and drawn. "I was just thinking," he began. His voice was choked and high, and I could hear the phlegm in his throat clicking. "How many more times will I see you? A few dozen?" He seemed to be having trouble breathing. I slapped his back.

"Are you having a heart attack?" I asked him. "Do you need an ambulance?"

"Take me home," he said squeakily. He took out his wallet and handed me the cash.

On the drive to Lone Pine to meet Terri that night, I couldn't stop thinking about my uncle. When I'd dropped him off at his house, he hadn't invited me in or asked about my date or said anything at all. He'd just gotten out of the car and stood on the sidewalk, leaning on his cane and staring at the lawn. It was true that I hadn't mowed it properly. There were long, triangular patches that I'd missed, and I'd left the lawn mower sitting out by the driveway instead of wheeling it back to the garage. But what did he expect for twenty dollars? How could he be upset with me after everything I'd done for him?

"You made it," said Terri, standing out on the porch.

The place was a cheap ranch-style house with an old gray dog sleeping in the yard. It was evening. Birds circled around. I had a headache.

"I made us dinner," Terri said. She was short and big hipped and seemed shy standing there in jeans and a blouse with frills around the throat. I walked up the porch steps and took a good look. She had blue eye shadow on and a necklace with long red stones dangling on it. Her chest was large but looked like it would just sag and splay all over the place if it wasn't hoisted up into a bra. I tried to imagine what those art students ever saw in her. I looked around her face. It was round and brown and had a scar running down from her left eye. I had a not-so-good feeling. Her hair was thick and pulled back in a ponytail. Her nose was squat and wide and had little pimples around the nostrils. I tried not to stare at them. "Are you hungry?" she asked, smiling. She had yellow, nubby teeth. I tried to see past her teeth into the inside of her mouth. "I've got cookies, too," she said. She pointed into the house through the screen door.

I didn't know what to say to her. The house smelled like garlic and laundry. She led me through the living room, where the sofa was covered in plastic and the furniture was white and gold and tacky. She pulled a chair out from the kitchen table and turned off the small black-and-white TV on the counter. I guessed she sat in front of it and ate cookies all day. I thought maybe she'd be okay looking if I put her on a diet, bought her some workout DVDs, got her teeth fixed. She was not the girl I'd been picturing, but there was something sweet about her.

"Do you have a family?" she asked me, setting down a plate of Nutter Butters. I put one in my mouth and nodded. "Brothers and sisters?" Terri asked. I shook my head. She got up and poured me a glass of water from the tap. The glass was from Disneyland.

"I have an uncle," I said, taking another cookie.

"I just have my mom," she said. "She's sleeping. All she really does is sleep."

Terri's face looked puffy and sad. I figured she'd improve after a course of diuretics, some benzoyl peroxide. I ate a few more cookies.

"Are you hungry?" she asked again. I tried to imagine getting on top of her. I imagined it would be like resting on a water bed.

"Better we do it before we eat," I said, pushing the plate of Nutter Butters away. Terri blushed. I knew I was better looking than her. I knew she would be grateful no matter what I did to her. She stood and led me to her bedroom. I watched her struggle with her jeans. Her thighs swung around as she crawled onto the bed. She kept her bra on, thank God. "You're so handsome," she said. I stood above her and took my shirt off. Terri reached up to touch me. I wasn't all that interested in being touched. I didn't want her to feel my rash. What I wanted was to put my fingers in her mouth. I closed my eyes and felt around her face and stuck my index finger inside. She used her tongue on it and sucked it, and I put another finger in. She kept sucking on my fingers. It was such a good feeling. It was like coming out of the cold and stepping into a cozy room with a fire going. It was like stepping into a hot bath. I wanted to put my whole hand in her mouth. I held the back of her head with one hand and reached down her throat with the other. She choked and tried to speak, but I just kept shoving my hand down there. I could see my hand bulging in her throat from the outside. Eventually she stopped struggling. "Good girl," I wanted to say but didn't. When I looked down, I could see something twinkle in her eyes.

Afterward I didn't kiss her or pet her or anything. It wasn't like that. We got up and ate the food she had made: spaghetti and meatballs and chocolate pudding. Then I threw up and said good-bye. I told her I'd call her. She stood on the front porch in a pink robe and watched me drive away.

o———o

Later, when my uncle asked me how the date went, I told him all the details.

"Terri is the most beautiful woman in the world. Luscious brown hair, little button nose, eyes like a baby deer. She's classy, you know. Not like all these sluts down here. And she's fun, too. We really did it up. We had a great time."

My uncle grumbled and adjusted the seat-back angle of his recliner.

"Be careful with women," he told me. "All they want is love and money."

"Terri's different," I said. "Can't you just be happy for me?" I put my hands in prayer position and held them up to my uncle, as though I were making a plea. Ever since Malibu he acted like everything I did was stupid, like everything I did rubbed him the wrong way. He wouldn't look at me. He just stared straight ahead at the television.

"If she's so great," said my uncle, "why isn't she here spooning us up some Neapolitan ice cream? Where is she, anyway?" He took a handful of peanuts from the container in his lap and let them trickle down from his fist into his mouth. I watched him chew and poke at the colostomy bag. I never answered his questions.

Later we watched *The Maury Povich Show* and *One Life to Live* and a movie about people who live in the New York City subway tunnels.

I mowed the lawn again.

On our first date, he bought me a taco, talked at length about the ancients' theories of light, how it streams at angles to align events in space and time, that it is the source of all information, determines every outcome, how we can reflect it to summon aliens using mirrored bowls of water. I asked what the point of it all was, but he didn't seem to hear me. Lying on the grass outside a tennis arena, he held my face toward the sun, stared sideways at my eyeballs, and began to cry. He told me I was the sign he'd been waiting for and, like looking into a crystal ball, he'd just read a private message from God in the silvery vortex of my left pupil. I disregarded this and was impressed instead by the ease with which he rolled on top of me and slid his hands down the back of my jeans, gripping my buttocks in both palms and squeezing, all in front of a Mexican family picnicking on the lawn.

He was the manager of an apartment complex in a part of town where the palm trees were sick. They were infested with a parasite that made them soft like bendy straws, and so they arched over the roads, buckling under the weight of their own heads, fronds skimming the concrete surfaces of buildings, poking in through open windows. And when the wind blew, they clattered and sagged and you could hear them creaking. "Someone needs to cut these trees down," my boyfriend said one morning. He said it like he was really sad about it, like it really pained him, like someone, I don't know who, had really let him down. "It's just not right."

I watched him make the bed. His sheets were a poly-cotton blend, stained, faded, and pilly pastel landscapes. What was supposed to keep us warm at night was a spruce green sleeping bag. He had an afghan he said his grandmother had knit—a matted brown and yellow mess of yarn that he laid asymmetrically over the corner of the bed as a decorative accent. I tried to overlook it.

I hated my boyfriend but I liked the neighborhood. It was a shadowy, crumbling collection of bungalows and auto-body shops. The apartment complex rose a few stories above it all, and from our bedroom window I could look out and down into the valley, which was always covered in orange haze. I liked how ugly it all was, how trashy. Everyone in the neighborhood walked around with their heads down on account of all the birds. Something in the trees attracted a strange breed of pigeon—black ones, with bright red legs and sharp, gold-tipped talons. My boyfriend said they were Egyptian crows. He felt they'd been sent to watch him, and so he behaved even more carefully than ever. When he passed a homeless person on the street, he shook his head and muttered a word I don't think he could have spelled: "ingrate." If I turned my back during breakfast he'd say, "I noticed you spilled some of your coffee, so I wiped it up for you." If I didn't thank him profusely, he'd put down his fork, ask, "Was that okay?" He was a child, really. He had childish ideas. He told me he "walked like a cop," which scared off criminals on the street at night. "Why do you think I've never been mugged?" He made me laugh.

And he explained something he thought most people didn't understand about intelligence. "It comes from the heart," he said, beating his chest with his fist. "It has a lot to do with your blood type. And magnets." That one gave me pause. I took a better look at him. The texture of his face was thick, like oiled leather. The only smile he ever gave was one where he lowered his head, stuck his chin out, and pulled the corners of his mouth from ear to ear, eyes twinkling up idiotically through batting eyelashes. He was, after all, a professional actor. "I've been laying low," he explained, "waiting for the perfect time to break out. People who get famous quick are doomed." And he was superstitious. He carved a scarab beetle out of Ivory soap and mounted it with putty over the door of our apartment, said it would protect us from home invasions and let the aliens know that we were special, that we were on their side. Every morning he went out front and blasted the bird droppings, which were green and fluorescent, off the front stoop with a high-pressure hose. He hated those birds. They circled overhead, hid in the palm fronds when a cop car passed, screeched and cawed when a child dropped a lollipop, stood in thick lines on the electric wires, stared into our souls, according to my boyfriend.

"And also," he went on, putting his hands in his pockets, a gesture meant to let me know that he was defenseless, that he was a good boy, "I have to pick up a package at the post office." He made it sound like he was going on a secret mission, like what he had to do was so difficult, so perilous, required so much strength of character, he needed my support. He slid the pick-up slip from the postman across the counter as proof.

"You'll do great" is what I said, trying to belittle him.

"Thanks, babe," he said and kissed my forehead. He looked down at the kitchen tile, shrugged his shoulders, then lifted his chin to show me a brave grin. I left him alone to clean the floor, which he did by picking up each little crumb with his fingers, then rubbing out stuck-on dirt with squares of paper towel he wet in the sink. He had a theory about how to stay in shape. It was to tense your body vigorously during everyday activities. He walked around with buttocks clenched, arms rigid, neck and face turning red. When I first moved in, he ran up the stairs with my suitcase, then stared down at me as though I would applaud. And once, when he saw me glance at his arm, he said, "I'm basically an Olympic athlete. I just don't like to compete." He had a crudely drawn tattoo of a salivating dog on his shoulder. Underneath it was written COMIN' TO GETCHA!

And he was short. I had never dated a short man before. The thought crossed my mind: Perhaps I am learning humility. Perhaps this man is the answer to my prayers. Perhaps he's saving my soul. I should be kind. I should be grateful. But I was not kind and I was not grateful. I watched with disgust as he unpacked a box of books he'd found in the trash, squatting down rhythmically to place each one on the shelf. These were his constant calisthenics. His legs were iron, by the way. His hamstrings were so tight he could barely bend at the waist. When he tried, he made a face like someone being penetrated from behind.

"When I get paid," he said, dusting the mantel, "I'm going to wear my yellow sports jacket and take you out on the town. Did I show you my yellow sports jacket? I bought it at a vintage boutique," he said. "It was really expensive. It's awesome."

I'd seen it in the closet. It was a contemporary, size 8 woman's blazer, according to the label.

"Show me," I said.

He ran, tucking his shirt in, licking his palms to slick his hair back, and came back with it on. His fingers barely poked out from the cuffs. The shoulder pads nearly hit his ears, as he had basically no neck. "What do you think?" he asked.

"You look very nice," I said, masking my lie with a yawn.

He grabbed me, picked me up, pinning my elbows, twirled

me around, making pained faces from the effort, despite his Olympic strength. "Soon, babe, I'm gonna take you to Vegas and marry you."

"Okay," I said. "When?"

"Babe, you know I can't really do that," he said, putting me down, suddenly grave and uncomfortable, as though the idea had been mine.

"Why not?" I asked. "You don't like me?"

"I need my mother's blessing," he said, shrugging, frowning. "But I love you so much," he confirmed, stretching his arms demonstratively above his head. I watched the plastic yellow button on the blazer strain and pop. He gasped, went on a mad search for the button on his knees, smushing his face against the base of the couch while he grasped blindly with his short arms under it. When he stood up, his face was bright red, his jaw was clenched. The look of sincere frustration was refreshing. I watched as he sewed the button back on with blue thread, grinding his teeth, breathing hard. Then I heard him in the bathroom screaming into a towel. I wondered who had taught him how to do that. I was slightly impressed.

He came back from the post office two hours later with a large, oblong cardboard box.

"I got hit by one of those birds," he said, turning his head to the side to reveal a bright green smear of bird shit along his face. "It's a sign," he said. "For sure."

"You better get cleaned up," I said. "Your agent called."

"Did I get an audition?" he asked. He came toward me with open arms. "Did she say what it was for?"

"A beer commercial," I said, backing away. "Your face," I pointed.

"I'll fix it," he said. "Babe, we're gonna be rich." I watched him peel off his clothes and get into the shower. I sat on the toilet and clipped my toenails.

"The trick to acting," he said from the shower, "is you really need to give it one hundred fifty percent. Your average actor gives maybe eighty, at most ninety percent. But I go all the way and then some. That's the secret."

"Uh-huh," I said, flushing my toenails down the toilet. "Is that the secret to success?"

"Yeah, babe," he assured me, whipping open the shower curtain. His body was a freckled mess of jerking muscles and stubble. He shaved his chest almost daily. He had a scar on his rib cage from where he'd been stabbed in a bar fight, he told me. He had all kinds of stories. He said back home in Cleveland he used to hang around with gangsters. He spent a night in jail once after beating up a pimp who he'd seen kick a German shepherd—a sacred animal, he explained. Only his story of burning down an abandoned house when he was sixteen had the ring of truth.

"And you know what else?" he said, squatting in the bathtub and slathering the towel between his legs. His towels were all stenched with mildew and streaked with rust stains, by the way. "I'm handsome."

"You are?" I asked innocently.

"I'm a total stud," he said. "But it creeps up on you. That's why I'm good on TV. Nonthreatening."

"I see." I stood and leaned against the vanity, watched him wrap the towel around his waist, pull out his bag of makeup.

"I'm a face changer, too," he went on. "One day I can look like the boy next door. The next day, a stone-faced killer. It just happens. My face changes overnight on its own. Natural-born actor."

"True enough," I agreed, and watched him dab concealer all over his nose.

While he was at his audition I walked around the apartment complex, kicking trash into corners. I sat in the concrete courtyard. There were birds everywhere, pecking at trash, lining the balconies, purring like cats between the succulents. I watched one walk toward me with a candy-bar wrapper in his beak. He dropped it at my feet and seemed to bow forward, then extended his wings wide, showing me the beautiful rainbow sheen of his jet black chest. He flapped his wings gently, with subtlety, and rose from the ground. I thought maybe he was trying to seduce me. I got up and walked away, and he continued to hover there, suspended like a puppet. Nothing made me happy. I went out to the pool, skimmed the surface of the blue water with my hand, praying for one of us, my boyfriend or me, to die.

"I nailed it," he said when he came home from the audition. He shrugged the yellow blazer down his stiff arms, laid it on the back of the barstool at the kitchen counter. "If they don't hire me, they don't know what's good for them. I really hit a home run." I kept stirring the spaghetti. I nodded and tried to smile a little. "And I saw the other guys that were auditioning, and man," he said, "they were all the worst. I'm a shoo-in. My agent call yet?"

"No," I said. "Not yet."

"I should go rub my crystal skull," he said. "Be right back."

I had a bad feeling about what my boyfriend had brought back from the post office. The box sat on the couch, unopened. He stood at the sink, vigorously scrubbing the plates from dinner, buttocks clenched and vibrating. "What's inside?" I asked.

"Open it up, babe," he said, turning slightly to make sure I caught sight of his devilish grin. It was the same grin he gave in his head shots. "Check it out," he said.

I licked my knife clean and cut through the packing tape. The box was full of Styrofoam peanuts. I fished around inside and found a long shotgun padded in bubble wrap.

"What's it for?"

"To shoot the crows," my boyfriend said. He held a plate up to the light and polished it frenetically with a paper towel. I thought for a moment.

"Let me take care of it," I said. "You need to focus on your career."

He seemed stunned, put down the plate.

"You do enough around here," I said. "Unless you would actually enjoy shooting those birds?"

He picked up the plate and turned his back to me.

"Of course not," he said. "Thanks, babe. Thanks for your support."

He slept that night with his phone next to his ear on the pillow and didn't touch me or say anything at all except "Good night, Skully" to his crystal skull on the bedside table. I put my head on his shoulder, but he just rolled onto his side. When I woke up in the morning, he was staring at the sun through the smog on the balcony, holding his eyes open with his fingers, crying, it seemed, though I wasn't sure.

I still hadn't cleaned the vacant apartment by the time the couple showed up to see it in the afternoon. I found them wandering around in back by the pool, sharing a huge bag of Utz potato chips. The man was younger, maybe midthirties, and wore a button-down shirt much too big for his wiry frame. The shirt had rectangular wrinkles in it, as though it had just been taken out of its packaging. He wore jean shorts and sneakers, a red Cardinals hat. The woman was older, very tanned and fat, and had long salt-and-pepper hair parted in the middle. She wore a lot of turquoise jewelry, had something tattooed on her forehead between her eyes.

"Are you here to see the apartment?" I asked. I had my clipboard with the requisite forms, the keys.

"We love it here," said the woman frankly. She wiped her hands off on her skirt. "We'd like to move in right away."

I walked toward them. That tattoo on her forehead was like a third eye. It looked like a diamond on its side with a star inside of it. I stared at it for a second too long. Then her boyfriend chimed in.

"Are you the manager?" he asked, thumbing his nose nervously.

"I'm the manager's girlfriend. But don't you want to see the place first?" I jangled the keys for them.

"We already know," the woman said, shaking her head. She moved gently, like dancing to soft music. She seemed sweet, but she talked mechanically, as though reading off cue cards. She stared resolutely at the stucco wall above my head. "We don't need to see it. We'll take it. Just show us where to sign." She smiled broadly, revealing the worst set of teeth I'd ever seen. They were sparse and yellow and black and jagged.

"These are the forms to fill out," I said, extending the clipboard toward her. The man continued to eat the chips and walked to the edge of the pool, stared up at the sky.

"What's with the birds?" he asked.

"They're Egyptian crows," I told him. "But I'm going to shoot them all."

I figured they were weirdos and nothing I said to them mattered. From the way the man nodded and dove his squirrel-like hand back into the bag of potato chips, it seemed I was right.

"Now listen," said the woman, squatting down with the clipboard on her knees, breathing heavily. "We're selling our estate up north and we want to pay for a year's rent in advance. That's how serious we are about renting this apartment."

"Okay," I said. "I'll tell the owners." She stood and showed me the form. Her name was Moon Kowalski. "I'll let you know," I said.

The man wiped his palms off on his shorts. "Hey, thanks a lot," he said earnestly. He shook my hand. The woman swayed from side to side and rubbed her third eye. When I got back to the apartment, there was a message from my boyfriend's agent saying he'd gotten a callback. I went back to bed.

"I got you some ammo," said my boyfriend. He put the box right in front of my face on the pillow. "So you can shoot the birds." He seemed to have turned a corner. He seemed in high spirits.

"Call your agent," I told him. Then I turned my head. I could not stand to see him roar and pump his fist and dance excitedly, thrusting his crotch in celebration.

"I knew it, babe!" he cried. He pounced on me in the bed, flipped me faceup, and kissed me. His mouth had a strange taste, like bitter chemicals. I let him peel my shirt up to my throat, twist the fabric until he could use it like a rope to pull me up toward him. He unzipped his shorts. I looked up at his face just to see how ugly it was and opened my mouth. It's true I relished him in certain ways. When he was done, he kissed my forehead and knelt by the bedside table, index finger on his crystal skull, and prayed.

I picked up the box of slugs. I'd never fired a gun before. There were instructions on how to load and fire the shotgun in the box it came in, with diagrams of how to hold the butt against your shoulder, little birds floating in the air. I listened to my boyfriend on the phone with his agent.

"Yes, ma'am. Yes, ma'am. Thank you very much," he was saying. "Uh-huh, uh-huh."

I really hated him. A crow came and sat on the sill of the window. It seemed to roll its eyes.

There were people I could have called, of course. It wasn't like I was in prison. I could have walked to the park or the coffee shop or gone to the movies or church. I could have gone to get a cheap massage or my fortune told. But I didn't feel like calling anyone or leaving the apartment complex. So I sat and watched my boyfriend clip his toenails. He had small, nubby feet. He collected the clippings in a pile by dragging his pinky finger neurotically across the floor. It pained me to see him so pleased with himself. "Hey, babe," he said. "What do you say we go up on the roof, try the gun out?" I didn't want to go up there. I knew it would make him happy.

"I'm not feeling well," I said. "I think I have a fever."

"Oh, man," he said. "You sick?"

"Yeah," I said. "I think I'm sick. I feel terrible."

He got up and ran to the kitchen, came back chugging from a carton of orange juice. "I can't get sick now," he said. "You know this commercial is gonna be huge. After this, I'll be famous. You want to hear my lines?"

"My head hurts too much," I said. "Is that your new hairstyle?" He was always putting gel in his hair and he was always squinting, pursing his lips. "Is that gel?"

"No," he said, lying. "My hair's just like this." He went to the mirror, sucked in his cheeks, pushed his hair around, flexed his pectorals. "This time when I go in," he said, "I'm gonna be sort of James Dean, like I just don't give a shit, but sad, you know?" I couldn't stand it. I turned and faced the wall. Out the window the palms hovered and shimmied and cowered in the breeze. I didn't want him to be happy. I closed my eyes and prayed for a disaster, a huge earthquake or a drive-by shooting or a heart attack. I picked up the crystal skull. It was greasy and light, so light I thought it might be made of plastic.

"Don't touch that!" my boyfriend cried breathlessly, leaping over the bed and grabbing the skull out of my hands. "Great. Now I need to find a body of water to wash it in. I told you, don't touch my stuff."

"You never said I couldn't touch it," I said. "The pool's right outside."

He put the skull in a pocket of his cargo shorts and left.

The buzzer rang the next evening. I got on the intercom.

"Who is it?" I asked.

"It's the Kowalskis," the voice said. It was Moon's voice. "We couldn't wait. We're here with cash and a moving truck. Buzz us in?"

My boyfriend hadn't come home yet from his callback. He'd called to say that he was staying out late to watch the lunar eclipse and not to wait for him, and that he forgave me for touching his crystal skull and that he loved me so much and knew that when we were both dead we'd meet on a long river of light and there'd be slaves there to row us in a golden boat to outer space and feed us grapes and rub our feet. "Did my agent call yet?" he had asked.

"Not yet," I'd told him.

I put on my robe and went downstairs, propped open the gate with a brick. Moon stood there with a manila envelope full of money. I took it and handed her the keys.

"Like I said, we couldn't wait," said Moon. Her husband was unloading their moving truck, lugging black garbage bags off the back and placing them in rows on the sidewalk. Those damned crows flew across the violet sky, perched on top of the truck, cawed quietly to one another.

"It's late," I said to Moon.

"This is the perfect time to move," she said. "It's the equinox. Perfect timing." Her husband set down a moose head mounted on a shield-shaped piece of plywood. "He loves that moose," said Moon. "You love that moose, huh?" she said to her husband. He nodded, wiped his forehead, and ducked back into the truck.

I went back upstairs and started packing, stuffed the

money Moon had given me at the bottom of my suitcase, cleared out my drawer, my boyfriend's makeup case, wrapped the shotgun in that terrible afghan, zipped it all up. Watching from the mezzanine as Moon carried in a large potted tree, her husband slumped behind her under a bag of golf clubs, I felt hopeful, as though it were me moving in, starting a new life. I felt energized. When I offered to help, Moon seemed to soften, flung her hair back and smiled, pointed to a woven basket full of silverware. I helped Moon's husband carry the old mattress out to the curb. We set it up against a tree trunk and watched the tree veer back precariously toward the apartment complex. A cluster of crows sprang out from its leaves. "Gentle souls," the man said and lit a cigarette.

When the truck was empty, Moon told me to sit down in the kitchen, rubbed the seat of a chair with a rag. I sat down.

"You must be tired," she said. "Let me find my coffee pot."

"I should get going," I said.

"No, you shouldn't," said Moon. Her voice was strange, pushy. When she spoke it was like a drum beating. "Be our guest," she said. "Want saltines?" That third eye seemed to wink at me when she smiled. She found a plate and laid out the crackers. "Thank you for your help," she said.

I looked around at the walls, which were mottled and scratched and dirty.

"You can paint the place, you know," I told Moon. "My boyfriend was supposed to have painted already. Of course he didn't."

"The manager guy?" the husband called out from the brown velour sofa they'd set in the middle of the living room.

"How long have you two been a couple?" Moon asked. She laid her hands down flat on the kitchen table. They were like two brown lizards blinking in the sun.

"Not long," I said. "I'm leaving him," I added. "Tonight."

"Let me ask you one thing," Moon said. "Is he good to you?"

"He beats me," I lied. "And he's really dumb. I should have left him a long time ago."

Moon got up, looked over at her husband.

"I've got something for you," she said. She disappeared into the bedroom, where we'd piled all the garbage bags full of stuff. She came out with a black feather.

"Is that from the crows?" I asked.

"Sleep with this under your pillow," she said, rubbing her third eye. "And as you drift off, think of everyone you know. Start off easy, like with your parents, your brothers and sisters, your best friends, and picture each person in your mind. Really try to picture them. Try to think of all your classmates, your neighbors, people you met on the street, on the bus, the girl from the coffee shop, your dentist, everybody from over the years. And then I want you to imagine your boyfriend. When you imagine him, imagine he's on one side and everybody else is on the other side."

"Then what?" I asked her.

"Then see which side you like better."

"You need anything," said her husband, "you know where to find us."

I went home and put on the yellow sports jacket. It didn't fit me any better than it fit my boyfriend. I put the feather under the pillow.

That night I had a dream there was a monkey in the tree outside my window. The monkey was so sad, all he could do was cover his face and weep. I tried handing him a banana but he just shook his head. I tried singing him a song. Nothing cheered him. "Hey," I said softly, "come here, let me hold you." But he turned his back to me. It broke my heart to see him crying. I would have done anything for him. Just to give that little monkey one happy moment, I would have died.

My boyfriend came home the next morning with a black eye.

"I can't talk to you," he said to me, rubbing the skull in his small, rough hands. I sat on the bed and watched him. His brow was furrowed like an old man's. "I can't even look at you," he said. "They're saying you're a scourge. A bad scourge."

"They?" I asked. "Do you know what a scourge is?"

He cocked his head. I watched his wheels grind. "Um," he said.

"You love me, remember?" I said.

"'Scourge' means you're going to ruin everything," he answered after a long pause.

"What happened to your eye?" I asked him, reaching a hand out. He blocked my arm with a swift karate chop. It didn't hurt. But I could see his heart beating through his shirt, sweat leaking down his arm.

"It's not good for me to talk to you," he said. He went into the bathroom. I heard the door slam, the shower run, and, after a moment, the nervous tapping of the razor against the tile. I sat on the bed for a while. The sun flickered harmlessly through the swaying palms.

I got my suitcase and lugged it up the two flights to the roof. I'd been there only once before, one night soon after I'd moved in, when I couldn't sleep. My boyfriend had come up and found me sitting on the ledge. We had talked for a while and kissed. "If you get torches and wave them up to the sky, it's like a signal to the aliens," he had said. He'd gotten up and twirled his arms around like propellers. "It's the light that calls them." He'd looked deep into my eyes. "I love you," he'd said. "More than anyone else on Earth. More than my own mother. More than God."

"Okay," I'd told him. "Thanks."

Up on the roof I unzipped my suitcase, pulled out the shotgun. It was easy enough to slide the round into the magazine tube, as they called it, pull the action back. That's what the instructions said to do. But there were no birds around. I tried firing off a round, hoping it would startle the Egyptian crows, hoping something, anything, would leap up in front of me, but my hand shook. I got scared. I couldn't do it. So I sat for a while and stared down at all the concrete, the palms flapping to and fro between the electric wires, then lugged the suitcase back down to our apartment.

After that he'd disappear a lot, call me from some windy alleyway, talk fast, explaining his regret, ask me to marry him, then call back to tell me to go to hell, that I was trash, that I wasn't worth his time on Earth. Eventually he'd knock on the door with huge scabs all over his arms and face, body thrumming with methamphetamine, head bent like a naughty child's, asking to be forgiven. He always hid his shame and self-loathing under an expression of shame and self-loathing, swinging his fist back and forth, "Shucks," always acting, even then. I don't think he ever experienced any real joy or humor. Deep down he probably thought I was crazy not to love him. And maybe I was. Maybe he was the man of my dreams.

A DARK AND WINDING ROAD

My parents kept a small cabin in the mountains. It was a simple thing, just four walls, and very dark inside. A heavy felt curtain blotted out whatever light made it through the canopy of huge pines and down into the cabin's only window. There was a queen-size bed in there, an armchair, and a wood-burning stove. It wasn't an old cabin. I think my parents built it in the seventies from a kit. In a few spots the wood beams were branded with the word HOME-RITE. But the spirit of the place made me think of simpler times, olden days, yore, or whenever it was that people rarely spoke except to say there was a storm coming or the berries were poisonous or whatnot, the bare essentials. It was deadly quiet up there. You could hear your own heart beating if you listened. I loved it, or at least I thought I ought to love it—I've never been very clear on that distinction. I retreated to the cabin that weekend in early spring after a fight with my wife. She was pregnant at the time, and I suppose she felt entitled to treat me terribly. So I went up there to spite her, yes, and in hopes that she would come to appreciate me in my absence, but also to have one last weekend to myself before the baby was born and my life as I'd known it was forever ruined.

The drive to the cabin is easy to imagine. It was a drive like any drive to any cabin. It was up a dark and winding road. The last half mile or so was badly paved. With snow on the ground, I would have had to park in a clearing and walk the rest on foot. But the snow had melted by the time I got there. This was April. It was still cold, but everything had thawed. Everything was beautiful and dark and powerful the way nature is. I brought all my favorite things to eat and ate them almost immediately upon arrival: cornichons, smoked trout, rye crackers, sheep feta, cured olives, dried cherries, coconut-covered dates, Toblerone. I also brought up a nice bottle of Château Cheval Blanc, a wedding gift I'd hidden and saved for three years. But I found no corkscrew, so I resorted to the remnants of a bottle of cheap Scotch, which I was surprised and relieved to discover on a shelf in the closet next to a dried-out roll of fly tape. Later, after dozing in the armchair for quite a while, I went outside in search of firewood and kindling. Night had fallen by then and I had no flashlight, hadn't even thought to bring one, so I sort of grappled around for sticks in the glare from my headlights. My efforts amounted to a very brief but effective little fire.

I've never been outdoorsy. My parents rarely brought us

up to the cabin as children. There was barely room enough for a young couple, let alone bickering parents and two bickering sons. My brother was younger than me by just three years, but those three years seemed to stretch to a wide chasm of estrangement the older we got. Sometimes I wondered if my mother had strayed, we were that different. It wouldn't be fair to call me a snob and my brother trash, but it wouldn't be far from accurate. He called himself MJ, and I went by Charles. As a child I played clarinet, chess. Our parents bought MJ a drum set, but he wasn't interested. He played video games, made messes. At recess I'd watch him throw fake punches at the smaller kids and wipe his snot on his sleeve. We didn't sit together on the bus. In seventh grade I won a scholarship to an elite private high school, started wearing ties, played rugby, read newspapers, and spent all my time at home in my room with my books. I turned out successful, but nothing special. I became a real-estate lawyer, married my law-school girlfriend, bought a pricey condo in Murray Hill, nothing close to what I hoped I'd do.

MJ was a different type of man. He had zero ambition. His friends lived in actual trailer parks. He dropped out of the public high school his junior year, shot dope, got a job in the warehouse of an outlet store, I think, unpacking boxes all day. I'm not quite sure how or if he makes a living now. He used to show up at Christmases unshowered in a ratty hooded sweatshirt, would pass out on the couch, wake up and eat like a wild boar, burping and laughing, then disappear at night. He was talented physically, could easily lift me up and spin me around, which he did often just to taunt me when we were teenagers. He had terrible cystic acne in high school—big red boils of pus that he squished mindlessly in front of the television. He didn't care how he looked. He was a real guy's guy. And I was always more my mother's type. We shared a certain refinement, which I'm sure was annoying to my brother: he called me a faggot every chance he got. In any case, I hadn't seen him in several years, since my wedding, and I hadn't been up to the cabin since my wife and I first started dating. We'd spent an awkward night up there together one spring, a lifetime ago, but that's not a very interesting story.

I rolled a joint in my car with the lights on and smoked it sitting in the armchair, in the dark. There was no cell-phone service up there, which made me nervous. I don't know why I continued to smoke marijuana as long as I did. It almost always sent me into an existential panic. When I smoked with my wife, I had to feign complete exhaustion just to excuse myself from going out for a walk, which she liked to do. I was so paranoid, so deeply anxious. When I got high, I felt as though a dark curtain had been pulled across the world and I was left there alone to waver in its cold, dark shadows. I never dared to smoke by myself at home, lest I throw myself from our twelfth-story window. But when I smoked that night at the cabin, I felt fine. I whistled some songs, tapped my feet. I whistled one difficult tune in particular, a Stevie Wonder song, which is melodically complicated, and after a few rounds I could really whistle it beautifully. I remembered what it was like to practice and get good at something. I thought of how great a dad I would be. "Practice makes perfect," I'd tell my child, a truism maybe, but it now seemed suddenly endowed with great depth and wisdom. And so I felt wonderful about myself, forgetting the strange world outside. I even thought that after my child was born, I'd still come up to the cabin once or twice a month, just to keep the secret of how great I was. I whistled some more.

Around nine o'clock, I pulled my sleeping bag out and unrolled it on the bed, which was covered in old blankets and dust and mouse poop, and slept with no trouble at all. In the morning I guzzled a liter of mineral water and drove on the dark and winding road back to Route 11, where there was a Burger King. I ate breakfast there. In addition to my breakfast sandwich and coffee, I purchased several Whoppers that I figured I could heat on the wood-burning stove for lunch and dinner, should I decide to stay another night. I also bought a six-pack of beer, a family-size bag of Cool Ranch Doritos, and a pound of Twizzlers from the gas station. And I bought the local newspapers and a magazine called *Fly Tyer* to stare at while I chewed. On my cell phone I found one missed call from my wife. I happily ignored it.

Back at the cabin I shook the dust off the blankets covering the bed because I wanted to lie down in the light from the window and read *Fly Tyer* and eat Twizzlers. Something flesh colored caught my eye amid the blankets. At first I thought what I'd seen was my wife's old diaphragm—a Band-Aid–colored thing that I'd always hated looking at. Then I thought it might be an old prosthetic arm, or a doll. But when I pulled another blanket back, I saw it was a dildo. A large, curved, Band-Aid–colored rubber dildo. My first instinct, of course, was to pick it up and smell it, which I did. It only smelled faintly of rubber, anonymous. I set it on the sill of the window and went outside to collect more firewood. I was determined to start a real fire. Was I perturbed to find the dildo? It only peeved me the way one is peeved when one hears his neighbors banging pots through the walls. And it seemed at the time more like vandalism than evidence of any kind of sexual activity. It seemed like a prank. Outside I was happily surprised to find a large store of dry logs in the crawl space under the cabin.

Once I'd gotten the fire roaring, I sat down and cursed myself for having forgotten to buy a corkscrew from the gas station, since late morning by the fire seemed like the perfect time to sip my wine. I swore aloud. The friend who had given me that bottle was an old college classmate. I'd slept with his girlfriend one weekend senior year while he was visiting his parents, and I'd never told him. His girlfriend's name was Cindy and she was half Pakistani and liked poppers and farted in her sleep. She was the last girl I slept with before my wife. So that bottle meant more to me than good wine. There was no way I was sharing it with my wife. I considered driving back down to the gas station, but there was no guarantee they'd have a corkscrew. Plus I was too scared to leave the fire burning unattended. There was no fire extinguisher, and the plumbing was shot. Not being able to wash my hands was the only real drawback to the place. I relieved myself outdoors, watching the smoke puff out of the metal chimney like a choo-choo train. Afterward I used sanitizing gel on my hands and sat in the armchair again.

I'd gotten lucky the night before, but after I smoked another joint that morning and saw my fire burning, heart still banging with fury about the impenetrable wine, Cindy's brown legs hanging off the bed, I knew I was in trouble. My thoughts turned to the primitive longings of early man, and I searched in my heart for some remnant of primal wantonness, and because I was looking, I found it. I rolled another joint and smoked it and removed my shirt and fed the fire apprehensively and sat on the bare floor of the cabin and growled and rocked like a baby and crawled around on my hands and knees. But the floor of the cabin was filthy. I found a broom and swept. Whoever was going up there and doing the dildoing had no regard for cleanliness, I thought to myself. I cleaned until I was hungry and fed the fire again and put one of the Whoppers on the iron stove. The special sauce melted and the bun burned on the bottom, but when I bit into it, it was all just chewy and lukewarm and reminded me of my elementary-school cafeteria and that low-quality food that I'd so desperately wanted to comfort me but hadn't.

The cabin hardly looked any cleaner after all that sweeping. In fact, I probably stirred up more dust than I swept out the door. I sneezed and drank a few beers and relieved myself again and used more hand-sanitizing gel and sat in the armchair. I smoked another joint. That last one was a mistake, because after just a few minutes I was picturing my unborn son crying over my grave fifty years into the future, and I felt the gravity of his woe and resentment toward me, and I despised him. Then I imagined everything bad he'd say about me to his own children after my death. I imagined my grandchildren's bitchy faces. I hated them for not worshipping me. Had they no idea of my sacrifice? There I was, perfectly wonderful, and nobody would see that. I looked up and saw a bat hanging from the rafters. I went to a very dark place. The oceanic emptiness in my gut churned. I pictured my old body rotting in my coffin. I pictured my skin wrinkling and turning black and falling off my bones. I pictured my rotting genitals. I pictured my pubic hair filling with larvae. And after all that, there was infinite darkness. There was nothing.

Just as I considered hanging myself with my belt, there was a knock on the door of the cabin, and a girl's voice called out, "MJ?"

The only girlfriend of MJ's I'd ever met had the odd name of Carrie Mary. I always thought Carrie Mary must have been slightly retarded because she had that kind of fat double chin and weak smile and the sort of waddle that some retarded people have, and she wore her hair in small pigtails all over her head, fixed with childish bows. I think my parents were too polite to question the relationship, but when MJ brought her home one Thanksgiving, I confronted him. "Are you taking advantage of Carrie Mary because she's mentally disabled?" My brother did not answer me. He simply took the log of goat cheese I was spreading on melba toast and threw it at the floor and stepped in it with his dirty tennis shoe. He tracked that goat cheese all around the house, and later that night I heard my brother fucking Carrie Mary. He sounded like a growling bear when he fucked her. I'd never heard anyone grunt like that before. It was so authentic. It scared me. I couldn't look him in the eye for days.

But the woman at the door was not Carrie Mary. I composed myself and received her in a manner I thought was perfectly casual. "How do you do? I'm Charles." I was very high. Shirtless, I folded my arms across my belly like a straitjacket.

"He here?" she asked, seeming to notice neither my greatness nor my awkwardness. She was a local—long, dyed, purplish hair, big gray sweatshirt, tight jeans, dark lipstick, no coat on. She looked like the kind of girl who works at a Store 24 or some pizza parlor or bowling alley, takes a lot of flak from the patrons, eleventh-grade education. "Is MJ around?" she asked, sniffling from the cold. A chilling perfume, like vodka and honey, cut through the air. I thought I'd die.

"No," I said. It seemed imperative that I come off casual. "Haven't seen him."

She bit her lips in disappointment, rubbed her hands together. I could see she was wearing a full face of makeup. Chalky powder caked over her cheeks, rouge, blue eye shadow. She looked young, twenty maybe. I tried to ask for her name.

"And to whom do I have the pleasure?" is what I said, and immediately I heard my voice echo through the trees like some nervous pervert or dweeb, like someone who's never had a conversation before.

"Is he coming back soon?" she asked. "MJ?"

"Yes, MJ," I said before I could even understand her question.

"Cool if I wait for him? My brother can't pick me up till four."

I nodded. She stepped closer to me, and for a moment I thought she wanted me to embrace her, so I lifted my arms awkwardly, then put them down. She was generous not to stare at my gut, my nipples.

"Can I come inside?" she asked.

"Sorry," I said and turned to give her room to walk through the doorway. I don't know why I kept up the lie about MJ. I certainly wasn't in the mood to entertain this young woman, whose name I soon learned was Michelle, but spelled somehow with an *x* because, as she put it, her family was European. Perhaps somewhere in me I felt that keeping her company would be a further affront to my wife, which was the entire point of my trip, after all. I admit I was grateful to have something come in and disturb the journey of my thinking. The first thing she did was light a cigarette and pace around and point to the dildo and blow a ring of smoke and say to me, as though she were asking me the time of day, "You a fag?"

"No," I replied, disgusted. And then for some reason—maybe I wanted to school her, blow her mind—I said, "I'm not a fag—I'm a *homosexual*." I pronounced the word very carefully, elongating the vowels and punctuating the *u,* which I thought was a pretension quite in keeping with my statement.

"For real?" she said, flicking her cigarette and gazing down at my crotch. "How do you know MJ?" she asked. I put my shirt back on.

"A friend," I said.

"What kind of friend?" she asked.

"A very *dear* friend," I replied. The words just came out of me. I sat in the armchair and crossed my legs. Michelle seemed to read my mind and offered me a cigarette. She looked at me suspiciously. I smoked as faggily as I could, bringing the cigarette to my puckered lips, sucking my cheeks in, then flinging my arm out, hyperextending the elbow as I exhaled to the side. I had her fooled, I knew. I was like a purring cat.

"You come up here a lot?" she asked. "To see MJ?"

"From time to time," I replied, swinging my foot. "When we can both get away."

The girl kept sniffling. She threw her cigarette out the open door and closed it, went and knelt by the fire, warmed her hands.

"Where'd he go?" she asked. She was uneasy, but she wasn't the type of girl to get offended. I was familiar with girls like her—tough, blue-collar teenagers. They were around when I was an undergrad, off campus. There was one like Michelle who worked as a bartender in a small pool hall my friends and I went to because we thought it was quaint.

That girl was beautiful, could have been a movie star if she'd wanted to, but she just chewed gum and had dead eyes and seemed immune to all manner of flattery or abuse. That's what Michelle was like. She seemed immune. And for that reason, I felt impelled to hurt her.

"He went out," I said, "to buy a corkscrew." I pointed to the Château Cheval Blanc on the floor next to my overnight bag.

She picked up the bottle, smeared her nose on her sleeve. She was pretty. A cold face with small features like a child's, no wrinkles, no expression. She held the bottle by its neck and swung it around, squinted at the label. "You like wine?" she asked. She was being polite, making conversation. I was afraid she'd drop the bottle and break it. I tried to sound relaxed.

"I love wine. Red, white," I said, "rosé." I tried another word. "Blush."

"MJ didn't tell me you were going to be here," she said, putting the wine down. "We'd had a time set and everything." She shrugged, flipped her hair.

"He'll be back," I said. "We'll sort it out."

She nodded and sniffed and crossed her arms and looked down.

"Are you hungry?" I asked her. The second Whopper was still in the bag on the counter by the sink. I pointed.

"No, thanks," she said.

"I'm a vegetarian myself," I said. "MJ likes that kind of food." I was feeling very clever, very bold. "That's what I love about him -childish tastes." With this statement I felt I had surpassed a misrepresentation and graduated to fraud, from novice to expert. "He just likes to play. Play and play. I suppose that's what you two do together?"

She sat on the bed, folded her legs up Indian style. "We smoke," she said. "Crystal?" She pulled a small glass pipe from her pocket, a crumpled ball of foil, displayed them to me on the palm of her hand like a fortune-teller or a blackjack dealer, then laid them on the blanket beside her.

"Aha," I said. I must have looked like a grandfather to her. She was perched on the bed there like a bird, hair flipping magically with a flick of the wrist in the quivering light from the small window. We passed a minute or two of long, dramatic silence. I felt I was in the presence of some great power. Then it suddenly occurred to me that MJ might show up.

"Maybe I should go," I said. "Leave you two to it." She didn't try to stop me. I collected my things. I put my boots on. But I couldn't leave the girl in there alone. This was my cabin, after all. I sat back down. She looked at her phone for a while.

"No reception," she mumbled, biting her lips. She yawned.

There was one thing about my brother I loved. He was loyal. He would punch me, and he would insult me, but he would not betray me. Despite all our differences, I believe he understood me. When we were younger, seven and ten, I suppose, our mother worked at an after-school day care at a church and would let us play in the backyard, where there was a swing set and a sandbox and a bush with berries on it we were warned not to touch. But I liked to collect the berries. I filled my pockets with them and flushed them down the toilet when I got home. MJ and I barely spoke all afternoon. He was a little kid. He dug in the sand and pissed in it, spat, threw rocks at squirrels, shimmied up the posts of the swing set, threatened to throw a shoe at my head. I mostly sat on a swing or under a tree. I was too smart to play any games.

As the weeks passed, we got bored and started taking walks through the neighborhood. It was a wealthy suburb— pretty Dutch Colonials, some big Victorians. Those houses are worth in the millions now. We just strolled around, peering into windows. MJ liked to rifle through mailboxes or ring doorbells, then run away, leaving me standing there with my hands in my pockets. But nobody ever came out of those houses. MJ must have known nobody would. He dared me to do things, stupid things, but I was a coward. "Pussy brains" is what MJ called me. I barely cared. He could say what he liked. He could do whatever he wanted to me. I knew, when the time was right, I would get back at him.

One afternoon we found an empty house and hoisted each other in through an open window. MJ went straight to the basement, but I just stood frozen in the kitchen, waiting, afraid to call out to him, heart tearing through my chest. When MJ came back up, he had a hammer in his hands. "For squirrels," he said. He opened the refrigerator. Inside it were the most delicious foods I'd ever seen. There was a roasted ham in there, an assortment of cheeses, and there was a pie—

blueberry, I think. Something came over me in that moment.
I pulled the poisonous berries from my pocket and smushed
them inside the pie, up under the crust. MJ gave me the
thumbs-up. That was the first time we broke into a house together. I stole a chip of Roquefort that day. We went back
the next day and I stole the rest of it. This went on, I think,
for months until our mother enrolled us in the aftercare. I
still have a buffalo nickel that I stole from inside an old roll-
top desk in one of those houses. Many other things we stole
and threw away—scribbled notes, address books, a fork, a
pack of cards, a toothbrush, things like that. Sometimes I'd
sit at one woman's vanity, smell all her perfumes and lotions,
stare at my face in the mirror while MJ mucked around in
the kid's room. I'd douse my cheeks with a powder puff. I'd
lie on the unwieldy water bed. I'd sniff things, lick things,
then put everything back in its place.

Twenty years later, I still felt that the good things, the
things I wanted, belonged to somebody else. I watched the
waning light play in Michelle's somber eyes. She returned
my gaze for a moment. It was clear the curtain had fallen
for her, too. We shared a moment of recognition, I think,
alone there in the darkening cabin.

"I don't think MJ's coming," she said finally. She looked
at me straight in the face, shrugging. "If he does come—"
she began.

"We'll say we couldn't wait. We'll say, 'You snooze, you
lose,'" I agreed as she uncrinkled the foil.

We shared a wonderful afternoon together. We seemed to

be playing our roles, the two scorned lovers. When she picked it up off the windowsill, I had the sense we were accomplishing great things. I let her do whatever she wanted to do to me that day in the cabin. It wasn't painful, nor was it terrifying, but it was disgusting—just as I'd always hoped it to be.

A year after my wife died, I took a job at Offerings, a residential facility for adults with moderate developmental disabilities. They all came from wealthy families. They were slow, of course. You can call them "retarded"—that word doesn't offend me as long as it's used the proper way, without pity. I was already sixty-four when I took the job. I didn't need the money, but I had the rest of my life on my hands and I wanted to spend it among people who would appreciate me. Of course I'd gone through the requisite training over the summer and was stable and willing, so there I was.

I was responsible for the daily care of three grown men. They were reasonable enough people, kind and conversational and generally decent, and they seemed to benefit from my attention and company. Each day I guided them as loosely as possible toward whatever activities the facility had planned and away from things that could be harmful or self-destructive. Most evenings we ate dinner together in the dining hall, a room designed to look something like a country club—pastel tablecloths, dark floral wallpaper, waiters in white dress shirts and burgundy aprons refilling wineglasses. The place had a well-stocked bar. Smoking was even allowed in certain areas. The residents were adults, after all. We weren't there to discipline them, change them, improve them, or anything like that. We were merely being paid to help them live as they pleased. The official title of my post was "daytime companion," though I stayed at Offerings later and later into the evenings as time went on.

Paul, the eldest of my charges, had a real enthusiasm for food and fire. He liked to make jokes, mostly bad puns, and he had a few catchphrases that never failed to draw laughs at the dinner table. "The poop is in the pudding," he'd say every Thursday, wide-eyed, mouth hanging open in anticipation. Thursday was pudding day, of course. Paul's IQ was up in the high sixties. He could have lived independently with occasional help shopping and cleaning, but he said he liked it at Offerings. He enjoyed himself.

"Larry," Paul said one day, motioning for me to follow him. His room smelled of Christmas all year round. He was permitted to light candles, so he burned cinnamon- and pine-scented ones constantly, almost religiously. I'd often find him spaced out at his desk, staring at the flickering flames, his hand moving robotically between a bag of chips and his mouth.

"Check this out," he said, pulling a cardboard box full of *Penthouse* and *Hustler* and *Playboy* magazines out from beneath his bed. He looked up at me and opened to a full-page spread of a blonde in soft light lying in a bed of autumn leaves, knees wide. She wore little leather moccasins on her feet and a feather tied around her neck, and nothing more— Miss November. Paul put a finger from one hand down on the page right over the girl's private parts, then pressed a finger from the other hand against his pursed lips and grinned. He put the magazine back in the box and stood looking at me, beaming.

"That's very good, Paul," I said, punching him lightly on the shoulder. I hadn't received much training in how to handle those types of situations. I did the best I could.

There isn't much to say about Claude. He was younger and more on the folksy side. He had his heart set on being a father one day, as though it were a status he could earn simply by being considerate and well liked, and so he tried to be kind, cute even. He had an aunt who came to visit him every now and then, brought him stuffed animals and picture books and French pastries. "Is he happy?" she'd ask me while Claude picked crumbs from his pale goatee. I'd just nod and put my arm around his shoulders. Each time I did, he'd rest his head against my chest and close his eyes. It was hard to have any respect for Claude.

I had an even harder time with Francis. He was only nineteen, a fearful guy with nervous habits like picking at his skin and biting his nails and patting his hair down, habits

I was supposed to try to curtail by handing him a Slinky or a Rubik's Cube to keep his hands busy, but I rarely did. I just smiled when he got agitated, tried to say something soothing, did my best not to condescend.

"It's all right, Francis," I'd tell him. "Nobody's going to bite you."

But he was rarely soothed. I had to hold my tongue when he'd caution me not to drive too fast in the Offerings van on field trips or stir too much sugar into my coffee. "Rots your teeth," Francis said, wiggling a finger. The others cast him as a party pooper, a wet blanket. "Fwancis," Paul called him. Francis looked like the runt of a litter—small shouldered, pale, with blackheads and pimples around the corners of his mouth and nostrils. His anxiety was ridiculous sometimes. "When I die, will somebody eat me?" he once asked.

Most days they were all happy. Like children, the residents seemed to have the wonderful ability to forget themselves in simple activities. They could be moody, but rarely did a worry or care transfer from one day to the next. Each night I stopped by Marsha's office to hand in my report. She and I shared a sense of humor about our work there, how an entire day could be spent playing tiddledywinks or watching cartoons or marathon episodes of *Family Feud,* a show that had a cultlike following among the residents at Offerings. Marsha was a kind and thoughtful woman, and troubled in a way I could never figure out. I tried to be friendly, compliment her on her earrings, wish her a good night, what have you. She was married and twenty years my junior, so of course nothing ever happened between us.

Not long after my wife had died, Lacey, my daughter, had come and emptied the house of its finer furniture. It was my wife's stuff—her eye, her taste—and looking at all of it just sitting there collecting dust disturbed me. I was glad to see it go. I never cared much for nice things or money anyway. It had been my wife's idea for me to go into business with her father. The man had started a company renting out construction equipment, built himself up, succeeded. I cared nothing for that business. He kept me on the in-house end of things, which protected me from the gritty details. The worst I ever had to do was fire one of the cleaning ladies in the office for stealing food from the break room. "It came from upstairs," I told her. "If it were up to me, none of us would work here." She took it well enough, and I went back to my files, literally pushing papers around on my desk until I could go home. The best part of my day was the drive home at sunset on the freeway—the silhouettes of high pines black against the pastel sky, the sun smoldering as it disappeared.

It went on like that for decades, me twiddling my thumbs behind that desk, my wife at home filling the house with antiques and fake flowers, dipping her fingers into cheesecakes and frostings and hollandaise and gravy. She died young of a heart attack, out of the blue. She wasn't as fat as other women I've seen, and she was never crass or inarticulate, but I hadn't found her attractive for years. Sometimes I feel I barely even knew her. The only times she seemed truly joyful were when she was on her way out to go shopping or to get her hair and nails done. My poor wife. I didn't know how little I loved her until she was dead.

Once it was emptied of all my wife's things, the house felt as though it had returned to the earth, some natural state of being. Maybe that is why, when Marsha Mendoza gave me a small succulent in a terra-cotta plastic pot for Easter, I stopped off at the public library and picked up a book about the species. They're such hardy little bastards. Stick a leaf of one in a cup of dirt and it will sprout roots all on its own. Its ability to regenerate, to thrive, is astonishing. By mid-May I had propagated a dozen new plants in china teacups and platters and little soup bowls that my wife had kept in a display hutch. My daughter had taken the hutch and left the dinnerware in piles on the hardwood floor. I wasn't going to use the dishes for food. I ate everything off paper plates, a bachelor in the classic sense. It filled me with great pride to watch those succulents grow. I got in the habit of giving them out as presents whenever there was an occasion. I even gave one to Paul for his thirtieth birthday.

"Fuck-you-lent," he said, setting the little plant on the table. He spread his palm and held it out to me for a high five. We had all gathered around to watch him blow out the candles on his birthday cake.

"What if it dies?" Francis asked. "What if he kills it?"

"Those plants are almost impossible to kill," I said. "Their Latin name is *Sempervivum*. Live forever. Don't worry about it."

Claude distributed huge chunks of cake around the table. I helped Paul up out of his chair and hugged him. He was about sixty pounds overweight. His parents lived in Florida, visited him rarely, took issue with the incidental costs he incurred at Offerings, mostly from extra food. At least once a week, a delivery guy would wander into the foyer looking for Paul with a satchelful of pizzas and chicken wings. Paul could sit contentedly for hours in front of the television with bags of yogurt-covered pretzels and caramel popcorn. Occasionally he overate to the point of being sick. "Gotta throw up now, Larry," he'd say. Fifteen minutes later he'd be at it again. What could I do? I wasn't there to keep him on a diet. Besides certain rules for safety within the facility, the residents could do whatever they wanted. The handbook stipulated only that a resident's contract at Offerings could be terminated if he or she violently attacked a staff member or another resident. And overnight visits were not permitted.

I often wondered whether Paul understood what it meant to make love to a woman, just the basic practicality of what goes where, what it would mean to begin and finish. Perhaps he'd had some experiences with women he didn't care to share with me, though I think if he'd had any, he'd have bragged about them plenty. "Sex o'clock, Larry," he said daily before waddling over to his room, shutting the door, and pulling out his box of pornography, I assumed. A birthday trip to Hooters had been his idea. He'd gone to a Hooters once in Las Vegas, he claimed, and had the time of his life.

"Las Vaginas," he joked. "Food and girls, girls and food. Mm," he said. He licked frosting off his fingers. "Hooters has everything."

"I've got money," said Claude, though I don't think Claude had much sexuality.

"They've got food *here*," Francis reminded us, poking at the cake with his pinkie.

"Larry will take us to Hooters," Paul announced, smiling proudly. "Girls," he said. "Ooh." He shut his eyes and lifted his arms, twisting invisible knobs as though they were a woman's nipples. He gyrated, licked his palm. I hid my revulsion behind a cough. "Girls," he cried again, his eyes rolling back in ecstasy. "Girls, girls, girls."

Lacey and I had never been close. We never bonded. She loved me no more than I'd loved her mother, I guess—the sort of strained affection captured best in stiff family portraits taken at the mall, a hand cupping a shoulder, a benign tilt of the head, eyes wide and vacant for the camera. My wife had insisted on posing for those photos every Christmas, and I had complied until I couldn't stand to anymore.

"Take the photo without me," I said to her one year. "Mother and daughter." I expected her to put up a fight, but she simply stirred the cream into her coffee, a smudge of bright pink lipstick on the porcelain rim. I watched her sip and squint as though she were imagining it—mother and daughter.

"You're right, Larry," she said. "It's better without you."

We talked like that. She bought herself expensive jewelry with her father's money—gold tennis bracelets, heart-shaped pendants, something called chocolate diamonds—and wrapped them up and signed my name on the gift cards. "To my dear wife, with love, Larry."

"Oh, honey, you really shouldn't have," she'd say after dinner, pulling the box out from under her seat cushion. She put the bracelet on, held her wrist out admiringly. Of course it felt awful. "I love you, Larry," she'd coo, getting up to kiss me on the cheek. Her lipstick was always thick and greasy. It took cold cream and a shave to get it off my face the next morning. Her jewelry sat in towering stacks of little boxes on her dressing table until she was dead and Lacey came and swept them into a plastic laundry basket along with a few items from the closet—a fur coat, a few purses, some fancy shoes. Everything else got donated. Her makeup and perfume I threw in the garbage, much of it unused, unopened.

Francis decided to stay behind while we went to Hooters. He joined a group in the TV lounge to watch *Les Misérables*. All the residents at Offerings loved Broadway shows. There must have been two dozen VHS cassettes of musicals on the shelf—*Annie Get Your Gun, Bye Bye Birdie, The Sound of Music, West Side Story, The Wizard of Oz. Grease* was the big favorite. Everyone knew all the songs by heart.

"Les Jizz," said Paul, cackling.

"How much money should I bring?" asked Claude, fingering through his wallet.

"Bring it all," said Paul.

I did nothing to rein in their excitement. Claude put on a clip-on tie. Paul paced in the hallway as I filled out the form to borrow the van.

"Going out?" asked Marsha Mendoza as she walked past.

"Birthday dinner," I answered, gesturing toward Paul and smiling as best I could. Marsha gave Paul a hug. He groaned as they embraced, eyes widening lecherously. I looked away.

"Hooters, huh, Paul?" I asked after Marsha had left.

"Hooters," he said and chuckled, wiping his mouth with his hairy forearm.

On the way there, stopped at a red light in the Offerings van, I watched all the regular people mill down the sidewalk. I rarely interacted much with anyone back then who wasn't retarded. When I did, it struck me how pompous and impatient they were, always measuring their words, twisting things around. Everybody was so obsessed with being understood. It made me sick. I glanced up at Paul in the rearview mirror as he touched his fat, chapped lips. His hands always smelled of butane and the powdered cheese and spices that coated his favorite corn chips. I could hear Claude breathing from the backseat. He was always congested, his nose always whistling like a drafty window. I checked my reflection in the vanity. I sprayed my mouth with Binaca.

"What's that?" Claude wanted to know, but I didn't answer.

"Hoot hoot," said Paul, slicking his hair back with sweat when the light turned green.

I had been to Hooters once before. With all the nice restaurants in town, my father-in-law had taken me there for lunch on my fiftieth birthday.

"No disrespect to my daughter," he'd said, swinging the door open to that nauseating aroma of french fries and cigarette smoke and beer. My birthday falls around Christmastime, so all the waitresses wore stockings with one green leg and one red leg under their tiny orange shorts, little red Santa hats with big white pom-poms, a tuft of fake mistletoe tied with silver twine like a pendant around their necks. Their "wifebeater" tops left very little to the imagination. I tried to hide my concern, but it was impossible. Hooters was no place for good people.

"Be a man, Larry," my father-in-law had said, punching the menu I was holding with his fist. This was years before my wife died. "Life is short. Happy birthday, son," he said.

He was in his early seventies by then, with a gut that strained the buttons of his work shirts, his belt on its last hole. He loosened his tie, took a look around. "Not as good as the Hooters in Galveston," he said, "but they've got a few good-looking girls. That black gal?" He nodded. The booth was brightly lit, the oblong, pale wood table lined with paper place mats showing large owls with huge, dilated pupils, as though the birds were watching us, probing some deep sub-conscious level of our minds, priming us to be charmed. I turned my place mat over. I would not be hypnotized.

"What can I get you?" asked our waitress a moment later. She was a lanky blond teen with fake eyelashes, teeth like porcelain, nails and mouth a strange, neon purple. My father-in-law ordered for us both—an assortment of appetizers, burgers. "We'll hang on to the menus," he said, "in case the birthday boy here wants dessert." I tried to smile politely as the blonde's jaw dropped.

"You're kidding me," she said. "Well, aren't we lucky to have you come and see us on your special day? Now, let me guess," she cocked her hip, tapped her chin with a finger, looked skyward, up at the gypsum ceiling. "Thirty-eight." She stabbed the air. "Am I right?"

"A clean fifty," my father-in-law answered for me, smiling.

"Someone's been taking care of himself," she went on. Where did young women learn to speak that way? I wondered. What school had she gone to? What did her parents do?

"It's nothing," I said awkwardly.

"It is most certainly not nothing." She pretended to be mad for a moment, then softened, looked down on me with a conspiratorial wink. "You hang on to that menu and let me know what dessert strikes your fancy, and it'll be on me. A birthday treat. And me and the ladies will do a little some-thing special."

"Please," I said, putting up my hands. "Don't sing."

"Don't sing?" she said.

"Larry, let them sing," my father-in-law protested.

"Don't bother," I said. "It's nothing. Thank you," I said. I could feel my face burning. I gulped my ice water. She stood there pretending to look displeased at my self-denial. I said thank you a few more times.

"Well, okay," she said finally, voice lilting, and then she leaned toward me. I thought she might be trying to rub her bosoms in my face, but then she said, "Looky here." The charms on her bracelet jangled as she shook the mistletoe above my head. Her breath smelled like candy.

"Aren't you sweet," said my father-in-law.

Then the girl kissed me on the lips. It was terrible. I should have stopped her, but I didn't want to embarrass the poor girl. I wiped my mouth with my napkin.

"Happy birthday," said my father-in-law, slapping the table and chuckling as the girl rose, sweeping her hair back and fixing her Santa hat.

"Want some more water?" she asked, not an eyelash out of order. She looked pleased, as though she'd just petted a dog. "You okay, honey?" She put a hand on my shoulder.

"Yes," I said. "Fine. Thank you."

Truth be told, I'd lost my enthusiasm for women some-where along the line. Later, as a widower, I was relieved to be celibate, continent, out of the sex game for good. After my wife died, my daughter encouraged me to date, find some gentle but sporty senior citizen to wine and dine. As if I'd ever had any interest in wining and dining. "Or find someone young enough and you could even have another kid," she said.

"What would I want with a kid?" I replied. "What are you getting at?"

"Mom wouldn't mind," she said next. "Trust me." They'd had plenty of secrets between them.

"I'm happy," I told my daughter. "Don't worry about it. I'm fine here all alone."

When Paul and Claude and I arrived, we found that the Hooters had been closed and turned into a Friendly's. Paul took it badly. "Friendly's is for kids," he complained as we walked through the parking lot. I couldn't imagine the decor or menu at Friendly's would differ very much from Hooters'. They both had a lot of cream-colored plastic and tacky people, bright lights and bad food, I presumed.

"It's all the same," I told Paul, swinging the door open.

"They have a gumball machine," Claude pointed out as we walked in. He fingered his tie, smiling politely. The place was full of fat ladies and their men, who looked wrinkled and haggard, heaps of mashed potatoes disappearing under the crooked awnings of their thick mustaches. There was one table of pug-nosed young women, bored and stirring their milkshakes with their straws, a half-eaten plate of fries split between them. A few children fussed and lolled around in their high chairs. The air was humid, the lighting bright and fluorescent, the carpet gray and stained. It was not a happy place. As we waited for someone to greet us, an Asian family passed us on their way out.

"Ching chang China," Paul sang, tugging at the corners of his eyes. I ignored it. Then he turned to me and crossed his arms over his fat belly. "I hate it here, Larry. What happened to Hooters?"

"Maybe a city ordinance. No idea," I answered. Claude took my arm as though to comfort me. Paul shook his head and picked at his lips and stared out over the tables.

We followed a short Latina woman to a booth. "This okay?" she asked, her smile wavering slightly as she registered that Claude and Paul were retarded. One must make certain adjustments—that's normal. Paul squeezed in on one side of the booth, and Claude sat next to me on the other. The woman slapped down huge, laminated menus on the table from under her arms. I thought of Marsha Mendoza, her dark lipstick, the furrowed sadness of her mouth at rest. But our waitress looked nothing like Marsha. She bore no resemblance to any Hooters girl, either. She was heavy. Her lips and eyes were rimmed with dark liner, her hair maroon and stiff. Her hands were small and meaty. She looked like a hardworking woman, someone's stern mother, eyebrows raised high in expectation. She left us to peruse the menus.

"You see, Paul? Nice lady like that's going to be our waitress. Now pick what you want to eat before she comes back."

"She's not that nice," Paul said, opening the menu. "Hooters got nicer ones."

I doubted that Paul could tell the difference. He had no clue what real beauty was.

"I'm having ice cream for dinner," Claude said, "because it's Paul's birthday. Happy birthday, Paul."

"Paul, what are you getting?" I asked, trying to sound chipper.

"Chicken shit," he said, laughing despite his disappointment. Then he banged at the table with his fat hands. "This place sucks," he whined.

Claude frowned in sympathy.

When the Latina woman came back, I straightened Paul's silverware. His pouting did not discourage her. She had her pad out, pen poised, smiling. Only those eyebrows—which now I realized were just painted on in two wide arcs across her forehead—seemed to quiver. She wore a red shirt and black trousers. Her figure was not very good, breasts and gut melded into a solid tub of fat under her cinched apron. The pouch at her waist bulged with straws. Her skin was dark and pitted and silvery with makeup. Still, there was kindness in her eyes. She looked at Paul and nodded.

"This," he said, smudging his finger over a picture of a large platter of BBQ ribs.

After Claude ordered his ice cream, the woman clicking and unclicking her pen during the pauses in his litany of requested toppings, I ordered the meat loaf. It was an item in the Seniors section.

"That comes with a Happy Ending Sundae," the woman told me.

"Sounds fine," I said and thanked her. When she'd gone, Paul promptly resumed his laments. I couldn't blame him for being disappointed, but it seemed ridiculous for a grown man to sit whimpering at the table, blowing his nose into napkins and stuffing them in the pockets of his cargo shorts. I couldn't look at him at all. His face became so apish and gross when he was upset. The sight of him, I felt, would ruin my appetite.

"They sell hats at Hooters," he sniffed. He stared at me and moaned.

It was clear that my succulent wasn't a good enough gift for Paul. He was materialistic, like my wife. How many blouses and bracelets does a woman need? How many terrible framed watercolors, throw pillows, little silver things shaped like birds or cats, or ceramic hearts filled with potpourri, or crystal ashtrays does a human being require? My wife had filled the house with that kind of nonsense. And she was a snob, on top of it. She would have rolled her eyes if she'd seen me eating at a Friendly's with a couple of retards. She would never have understood why I was there. She had no idea what it meant to expand one's horizons.

I put my arm around Claude, hoping we could change the subject. "Excited for ice cream?" I asked. Our waitress stopped off to deliver sodas and small packets of colored crayons for Paul and Claude. Claude tore into them immediately, scribbling on the back of his paper place mat. Paul opened the packet and snapped each crayon in half, let the broken pieces roll across the table toward me. Claude collected them, herding the pieces into a pile, then continued to draw.

"You can have my sundae, Paul, if it makes you feel any better," I told him.

"I don't want your stupid sundae," he said. "Ice cream melts, Larry. You eat it and it's gone. You can't take it with you." He took another napkin, rubbed his eyes, blew his nose.

"You can take your crayons with you," I said. "I could ask for a new pack. Should I?"

He grunted, wiping the tears off his face with the hairy backs of his hands. Then he turned to the window and began to peel the paper off his straw very slowly, like someone plucking a flower, lost in thought. "I hate life," Paul said and quickly sucked down his glass of Coke.

"Guys. Ice cream," said Claude, watching his silver dish float through the air, high on the huge tray our waitress carried. She set the tray down on a little stand next to our table, then distributed our plates, smiling. She seemed undeterred by the awkward tension in our group, which I took as a testament to her strong character. She was very professional. Nothing like the girls at Hooters. I caught her attention by staring into her eyes, which were big and black and set deeply under the fat, shining ridge of her brow bone.

"Okay?" she asked.

"It's his birthday," I said, pointing at Paul.

"You wanna cake?" she asked, addressing Paul directly. "You wanna candle?" Paul said yes, licking his fingers morosely, his face already covered in BBQ sauce. He was not ashamed.

Those strange painted eyebrows crimped and settled.

When she brought the plate of cake, her grubby hand cupped around the lit candle, Paul pushed himself up and scooted out from the booth and stood next to her, staring down at the flame, and she sang to him in Spanish, softly, beautifully, glancing bashfully up into his small, swollen eyes.

At home that night, I sank deep into a bath, played a cassette tape of golden oldies, watched the water turn milky and still between my knees. I got wistful remembering how my wife would stand at the vanity in a pink satin robe, fixing her hair as though I'd care what she looked like when we got into bed. She wasn't a beautiful woman, but she dressed well and had small, sparkling eyes. Emerald eyes, I called them when we first started dating. "Honey" was what she called me. When she first started calling me that, I felt it was dismissive, that she was using the pet name as a way to blanket over everything that was good and distinctive about me, that by calling me "honey" she might as well have been addressing a servant or a dog. But after a while I began to hear the love in it, to yearn for it, and eventually it felt so good, so soothing, that when she used my name, Lawrence, it sounded dry and cruel, and my heart would flinch as though it were being pinched and gouged by her long, cherry-colored fingernails. I slept on the couch that night, the TV flickering like a flame over my shoulder, the succulents creeping in cups and saucers across the mantle, the coffee table, all the window sills, the whole house full of them, my perfect little children.

You could tell just by looking—grape-soda stains on their kids' T-shirts, cheap dye jobs, bad teeth—the people of Alna were poor. Some of them liked to huddle on turnouts or thumb rides up and down Route 4, sunburned and tattooed, but I never thought to stop and pick one up. I was a woman alone, after all. And I didn't want to have to talk to them, get to know them, or hear their stories. I preferred to keep the residents of Alna as part of its scenery. Wild teens, limping men, young mothers, kids scattered on the hot concrete like the town's lazy rats or pigeons. From a distance I watched the way they congregated, then dispersed, heads hung at midlevel, neither noble nor disconsolate. The trashiness of the town was comforting, like an old black-and-white movie. Picture an empty street with a broken-down car, a child's rusty tricycle abandoned on the curb, a wrinkled old lady scratching herself while watering her dun-colored lawn, the hose twisting perversely in her tight fist. Crumbling sidewalks. I played along when I went up there, slipping pennies in and out of the dish on the counter of the Gas Plus on State Street as though a few cents could make or break me.

I made an abysmal living back home teaching high-school English, and my ex-husband rarely paid his alimony on time. But by Alna's standards, I was rich. I owned my summerhouse up there. I'd bought it from the bank for next to nothing, full of cobwebs and tacky wallpaper. It was a one-and-a-half-story bungalow overlooking the Omec River, a sloshy milelong tributary to a lake twice the size of Alna itself. The real-estate taxes were negligible. The cost of living was a joke. The teenage boys in the sandwich shop in town remembered me from summer to summer because I tipped them the fifty cents change they tried to give me. Otherwise I didn't mingle. I'd made the acquaintance of a few of the neighbors—mostly single moms whose teenage children smoked and strollered their own babies around the graveled driveways. An old man across the street had a long beard stained brassy from cigarette smoke. "Hey, neighbor," he'd say, wheezing, if I saw him out walking his dog. But I never felt I was anybody's neighbor. I was only ever just visiting Alna. I was slumming it up there. I knew that.

Clark supplied a steady stream of coeds to occupy the house during the school year. He taught computer programming at the community college ten miles away, in Pittville. I paid him to look after my place. I sometimes got the sense he was overcharging me, inventing problems and costs to inflate his monthly bills, but I didn't care. It was worth the peace of mind. If something went wrong—if the pipes froze or the rent was late—Clark would handle it. He'd wrap the windows once it got cold, fix a leaky faucet, a short circuit, a broken step. And I was glad I never had to deal with any of the tenants. Each summer I drove up to Alna, I'd find the house altered—a new perfume lacing the humid air, menstrual stains on the mattress, hardened bacon grease splattered on the kitchen counter, a fleck of mascara on the bathroom mirror like a squashed fly. I mostly didn't mind these remnants. Having a tenant kept the vagrants out of what would otherwise be an empty shelter from September to June. The street people of Alna were notorious for taking up residence wherever they could find it and refusing to leave, especially during the winters, which were, in Alna, deadly.

There was no scenic hike or museum to visit, no guided tour, no historic monument. Unlike where my sister summered, Alna had no gallery of naive art, no antique shop, no bookstore, no fancy bakery. The only coffee to buy was at the Gas Plus or the doughnut shop. Occasionally I drove to Pittville to see a movie for two dollars. And sometimes I visited the deluxe shopping center on Route 4, where the fattest people on Earth could be found buzzing around in electronic wheelchairs, trailing huge carts full of hamburger meat and cake mix and jugs of vegetable oil and pillow-size bags of chips. I only shopped there for things like bug spray and batteries, clean underwear when I didn't feel like doing laundry, an occasional box of Popsicles.

Monday through Friday I kept to my summer diet of one footlong submarine sandwich per day—the first half for lunch, the second half for dinner. I got these sandwiches from the deli downtown, around the corner from the bus depot at the hilltop crossing of Riverside Road and Main Street, where the vagrant townsfolk dressed like zombies and kept wolf dogs on rope leashes. The town was rife with meth and heroin. I knew that because it was obvious and because I dabbled in both when I was up there. Unless it was raining, I walked the two miles back and forth up Riverside every weekday morning, got a soda and my sandwich, and more often than not hit the bus-depot restroom to buy ten dollars' worth of whatever was for sale—up or down.

On the weekends, I took myself out to eat. I had lunch either at the doughnut shop, where you could get an egg-and-cheese sandwich for a dollar, or at the diner on 122. I liked to sit at the counter there and get a platter of chopped iceberg smothered in ranch dressing and a bottomless Diet Coke and listen to the waitress greet the regulars—big men in T-shirts and suspenders, left arms brown as burned steak. Half the time I couldn't understand what anyone was saying. For Saturday-night dinners I hit the Chinese buffet for sautéed broccoli and free box wine, or I went to Charlie's Good-Time, a family-style bar serving french fries and pizza. The bar was attached to a combination arcade and bowling alley. I didn't talk to anybody when I went out. I just sat and ate and watched the people talk and chew and gesture.

The Good-Time was where I met Clark my first summer in Alna. Through the haze of cigarette smoke and steam from the bar's kitchen, he was the only person who looked remotely educated. I was inclined to brush him off at first because he was nearly bald and wore a knotted hemp necklace. His hand was limp and clammy when I shook it. But he was persistent. He was kind. I let him pay for a pitcher of beer and try to impress me with his knowledge of literature. He told me he didn't—couldn't—read fiction written after '93, the year William Golding died, and he claimed to know the editor of a well-known literary journal in the city, one I'd never heard of. "Stan," Clark called him. "We go way back." I overlooked all the glaring errors in his personality—his arrogance, his airs, his bony, hairy hands. I still remember the humility it took for me to agree to take him home, then the appalling ease with which I accepted his pathetic overtures of gratitude and affection. He wore a cheap white dress shirt and blue jeans, brown leather sandals, and a small gold hoop earring in one ear, and when we undressed in the dark in my empty upstairs bedroom, me crouching under the sloped ceiling, his genitals swung in my face like a fist. Afterward he said I was a "real woman," whatever that was, asked if I had any children, then shook his head. "Of course you don't," he said, cradling my pelvis. I ran my fingers through his soft, thinning hair.

For the next few weeks he helped me sand the kitchen

counters, peel off wallpaper, paint, scrub, fix the old stove. He rubbed my back at night while we watched videos we rented from the Gas Plus. He liked to blow into my ear—some high-school trick, I supposed. We talked mostly of the house, what needed to get done and how to do it. Things started to feel serious when he got a friend of his with a truck to help move in furniture I bought for pennies from the secondhand store in Pittville. My sister would have called it all "shabby chic," not that I cared. Nobody was judging me in Alna. I could do whatever I wanted.

Clark was the one to introduce me to the submarine-sandwich diet and to the zombies at the bus depot. One morning he held out his long pinkie fingernail. "Sniff it up," he said. The stuff threw sex and romance under an immediate dark and meaningless shadow. It blotted out all our "feelings for each other," as Clark had described our rapport. We didn't sleep together again after that first high, but we did spend a few more weeks in each other's company, nibbling the sandwiches and snorting the stuff from the zombies. Depending on what stuff they'd given us, we'd spend the days either cleaning or passed out on the brittle wicker daybed or on loose cushions on the porch, overlooking the Omec. The day I left to drive back down to the city that summer was a strange parting. We hugged and everything. I cried, sorry to say good-bye to my narcotic afternoons, my freedom. Clark offered to keep the house up while I was away, find me tenants, act as "property manager," as he called it. I generally don't like to hold on to loose ends, but I made this exception. If the house burned down, if the pipes burst, if the vagrants made a move, Clark would let me know.

Half a dozen years had passed since that first summer in Alna, and almost nothing had changed. The town was still full of young people crashing junk cars, dirty diapers littering the parking lots. There were *X*'ed-out smiley faces spray-painted over street signs, on the soaped-up windows of empty storefronts, all over the boarded-up Dairy Queen long since blackened by fire and warped by rain. And the zombies, of course, still inhabited Alna's shadowy, empty hilltop downtown. They slumped on the curb, nodding, or else they rifled through Dumpsters for things to fix or sell. I often saw them speed-walking up and down the slopes of Main Street with toasters or TV sets under their arms, ghost faces smeared with Alna's dirt, leaving a trail of garbage in their wake. If they ever left Alna, cleaned up, shipped out, the magic of the place would vanish. Monday, Wednesday, Friday—I figured three times a week was a sane frequency—I visited that bus-depot restroom, my ten-dollar bill at the ready.

Nobody ever asked me any questions. The zombie in charge just handed me my little nugget, my little jewel, kept his face hidden under the hood of his raggedy sweatshirt, sweat dripping off his chin and plinking down onto the dirty bathroom tiles. There was no logic to what was kept in stock on a given day. Each time I got home and tried what they'd given me, it was always the right stuff. It was always a revelation. Never once did those zombies steer me wrong.

Clark never got that about the zombies—their supernatural wonder. He was too concerned with his own intelligence to see the bigger picture. He thought that the drugs we bought in the bus-depot restroom were intended to expand his mind, as though some door could be unlocked up there and he would greet his own genius—some glowing alien in glasses and sneakers, spinning planet Earth on its finger. Clark was an idiot. We saw each other once or twice each summer. I'd take him out to eat in Pittville to thank him for his help with the house, and I'd listen to him gripe about how hard the winter had been, the state of affairs at the college, budget cuts, local government, the health of his dog. He quoted Shakespeare too often. And "That's just life" was a common phrase he used to sound deep and wary—a perfect example of his laziness. Still, I didn't hate him. A few times we even tried to recapture whatever odd coincidence of lonesomeness and availability we'd found together that first summer in Alna, but inevitably one of our body parts would fail us—sometimes his, sometimes mine. It was always humbling when that happened. Time was passing, I was getting old, "middle-aged," my sister called it. The truth was undeniable: I'd be dead soon. I considered this every morning I walked home from the bus-depot bathroom, a little foil-wrapped turd of drugs stuffed in with the lint and pennies in the pocket of my pleated khaki shorts.

I missed Alna during the school year. I missed the zombies.

Grading papers, sitting in staff meetings, I wished I was sitting on my porch, looking down at the Omec and considering small matters—the little birds and where they found worms to feed their babies, the shifting shades of brown on the rocks as the water splashed them, the way the vines fell from the highest tree branches and got tangled tumbling in the rushing, sudsy water below. When the big city was covered in snow, my bones like ice, frozen air stabbing at my lungs, I told myself I'd go swimming in the lake that summer, get a real tan, frolic, so to speak. I owned a bathing suit, but it was pilly and stretched and the last time I'd worn it—at my sister's pool party a few years before—I'd felt droopy and pasty, like my mother. The freckles on my thighs, once adorable marks of health and frivolity, were now like spots of dirt or little bugs I kept trying to scrape away with my fingernail. My sister showed me pictures later on, pointing out how flat my breasts had gotten.

"Do some of these," she told me, pumping the air with her elbows in her stainless-steel kitchen. That was another thing I liked about Alna. Once I'd settled in each June, I could ignore my sister's phone calls, claiming bad reception. I needed a break from her. She had too much influence over me. She only wanted to discuss things and name things for what they were. That was her thing. "Melasma," she said, pointing to my upper lip. "That's what you call that."

One morning on my way home from the sandwich shop and bus depot, I passed a yard sale. It was the usual garbage: baseball caps, plastic kitchen utensils, baby clothes folded into tiny cubes spread out on stained floral bedsheets. The only books at Alna yard sales were convenience-store paperbacks or cookbooks for microwave ovens. I didn't like to read while I was in Alna anyway. I didn't have the patience. That day a tall, gray, metal sunlamp caught my eye. The scrap of masking tape stuck to its base was marked in red: three dollars. I didn't care if it worked. If it didn't, trying to fix it would occupy me for at least an afternoon. It was worth the trouble.

"Whom do I pay?" I said to the gaggle of women sitting on the front steps. They all had the same flat, long, brown hair, the same pinched eyes, bulbous mouths, and throats like frogs. Their bodies were so fat, their breasts hung and rested on their knees. They pointed to the matriarch, a huge woman sitting on a piano bench in the shade of a large oak. Her left eye was swollen shut, bruised yellow, black, and blue. I gave her the money. Her hand was tiny and plump, like a doll's, fingernails painted bright red. She stuffed the bill I gave her in the pocket of her worn cotton housedress, pulled a sucker from her mouth, and smiled, showing me—not without some hostility—a lone bottom row of teeth rotted down to stubs, like a baby's teeth. She was probably around my age, but she looked like a woman with a hundred years of suffering behind her—no love, no transformations, no joy, just junk food and bad television, ugly, mean-spirited men creaking in and out of stuffy rooms to take advantage of her womb and impassive heft. One of her obese offspring would soon overtake her throne, I imagined, and preside over the family's abject state of existence, the beating hearts of these young women pointlessness personified. You'd think that, sitting there, oozing slowly toward death with every breath, they'd all go out of their minds. But no—they were too dumb for insanity. "Rich bitch," I imagined the mother to be thinking as she plunked her sucker back into her mouth. I lugged the lamp up the street, thinking of her flesh spreading around her as she lay down on her bed. What would it feel like, I wondered, to let myself go? I was eager to get home, uncrinkle the little fortune in my pocket. If the sunlamp did work, I would bring it back down to the city with me. The light could soothe me in the winter and clean my dirty city soul each night.

It's not that I lacked respect for the people of Alna. I simply didn't want to deal with them. I was tired. During the school year, all I did was contend with stupidity and ignorance. That's what teachers are paid to do. How I got stuck teaching Dickens to fourteen-year-olds is a mystery to me. I'd never planned on working all my life. I'd had this fantasy that I'd get married and suddenly find a calling beyond the humiliating need to make a living. Art or charity work, babies—something like that. Each time seniors had me sign their yearbooks, I wrote, "Good luck!" then stared off into space, thinking of all the wisdom I could impart but didn't. At graduation, I'd take a few Benadryl to soothe my nerves, watch those tasseled caps float around, all the idiotic high fives. I'd shake a few hands, go home to load my car with musty summer clothes and a case of sparkling mineral water, then drive the five hours up to Alna.

When I got back to my house with the lamp that day, a girl was standing in my front yard. She had her back turned, and she seemed to be staring up at the windows, a hand held over her head to block the sun's glare. Nobody had ever come into my yard before. In all my time in Alna, nobody but Clark had ever even knocked on my door. I put the lamp down by my car and cleared my throat.

When the girl turned around, I saw that she was pregnant. The swell of her baby made a tent of her long black sleeveless shirt. She was thin otherwise, a scrawny young mother, the kind my sister abhorred. Her leggings were pastel purple, and her hair was short like a boy's, and blond. She approached me, her hands supporting the small of her back, wincing in the sunshine, trying to smile.

"Is this your house?" she asked. As she came closer, I thought I detected rose perfume. A raised mole on her chin glistened with sweat. I folded my arms.

"Yes," I stammered, "it's my house. I'm the owner." I guessed at who she was then—a former tenant. A Teri or Maxine or Jennifer or Jill, whatever their names were. Maybe she'd forgotten something in the house. Those girls always left things behind—a hairbrush, a bobby pin, empty boxes of crackers, tampons in the medicine cabinet, stray socks and underwear between the washer and dryer. I happily used up their leftover bars of vanilla- and floral-scented soaps, each laced with hairs and gouged by their fingernails in sharp half-moons. "Can I help you?"

The pregnant girl stood before me now, face gleaming,

and looked down at the sunlamp. She held up one hand to wave hello. In her other hand she carried a sheaf of flyers.

"I'm a housecleaner," she said. "I wanted to drop this off."

She handed me one of the flyers. It was a hazy photocopy of a handwritten ad that included her name and phone number and a long list of the services she provided. "I do laundry. I sweep and mop. I straighten up. I dust. I vacuum," I read aloud. She'd drawn stars around the page, a smiley face at the bottom, at the end of a line that read, "Ask about babysitting." Her hourly rate was less than what a person would make working at a fast-food restaurant. I considered pointing that out to her but didn't. I picked the lamp back up.

"Do you need help?" she asked. I ignored her tanned, outstretched arms and let her follow me across the yard. "I cleaned your house last year, actually," she said. "After you left, before the students moved in, I guess."

Clark hadn't told me he'd outsourced the cleaning.

"So you know Clark," I said, pulling out my keys.

"Yeah," she said, "I know him."

I didn't bother to wonder whether Clark might be responsible for her pregnancy. He didn't have it in him. Even with me he'd been fiercely dedicated to his fancy brand of condoms. But it burned me to picture him ogling the girl, counting out the cash to pay her for cleaning up my filth. Poor girl. She was pretty for Alna, and tough in a way that came through in her shoulders. They weren't wide, per se, but angular and taut with budding muscles like a teenage boy's. She must have thought I was old and ugly. I could have been her mother, I suppose. I struggled with the sunlamp as we climbed the few steps to my front door.

"Clark should hire you to clean before I arrive, too," I said, opening the door and putting the lamp down inside. "The bathroom especially is always yucky when I get here."

"I can usually do a house like this in an hour or two," she said, still standing out on the doorstep. "But I've been getting slower and slower, with this baby thing." She pointed down at her belly, then looked up at me, as if she would find some sympathy there. Her eyes were clear and blue but hooded and tired. She spoke with the grumbling, rhythmless lilt of Alna talk. Maybe she had a dragon or a devil tattooed on the small of her back, or a *Playboy* bunny on her lower abdomen, now stretched and mutated by her pregnancy, that "baby thing," as she called it. I studied her face as she peered over my shoulder into the darkened house.

"Want to clean now?" I asked her.

"Okay, sure."

Then, despite the information I'd just read on the flyer, I asked, "How much do you charge?"

She shrugged, those gleaming shoulders twitching, clavicles glistening in the sunshine. "Ten bucks?"

"For the whole house?"

She shrugged again.

"Come on in," I said and held open the door.

"Let me just call my mom."

I pointed to the phone on the wall by the fridge and watched her waddle past me toward it. She put the flyers down on the counter. Her belly was huge, nearly ready to pop. What kind of mother lets her pregnant teen wander around outside in the sweltering heat? I wondered. But I knew the answer. This was the Alna way.

I stared at the girl's face as she passed, her tiny pores, her small, upturned nose, oily purple makeup darkening into the crease of her heavy eyelids. She dialed the phone and lifted the collar of her shirt to wipe the sweat off her chin. I opened the cabinet under the sink and gestured toward the cleaning supplies down there. She nodded. "Hi, Momma," she said, turning away from me, coiling the cord around her thin wrist.

I left her there, went into the den, unwrapped my sandwich on the coffee table, and unscrewed my soda. I was a grown-up. I could sit on the sofa and eat a sandwich. I didn't have to call my mother. I didn't even have to clean my own house. I listened to the girl talk. "I'm fine, Momma. No, don't worry," she said. "I'll be home in time for dinner." After she hung up, I heard her rattling the bucket of sprays and cleaners from under the kitchen sink.

"You must be hungry," I said to her, eyeing her slim calves as she walked past me through the den. I held out half of my sandwich.

"I'm okay," she replied, one arm weighed down by the bucket, the other dragging a broom behind her. "I'll start upstairs," she said and lugged the stuff up the steps, her face flat and serious, the enormous bulge of her belly straining against her shirt, which was already darkened with sweat down the front. I chewed and watched her disappear up the stairs. Shreds of lettuce spilled out the sides of my sandwich. A slice of pickled jalapeño smacked the hardwood floor. I left it there and ate, happily. It was deadly quiet in that house without the television on. I could hear the toilet flush, the girl grunt and breathe, the scrub brush scrape rhythmically against the bathroom tile. I gulped my soda down, burped with my mouth open wide. I wrapped up the dinner half of my sandwich and set it aside.

Then I took out my zombie dust. I figured I could just test it to see what the zombies had chosen for me that day, a sneak preview of what I had in store. Later, once the girl was gone, it would be nice to take a shower, walk through the clean house, silent and fresh, and sit at the coffee table in my bathrobe with a rolled-up dollar bill. I'd let my soul fly wherever the stuff sent me until it got dark and I remembered the sandwich and the world down below. My mouth watered just imagining it. My hands got hot. That was the best part, that moment, anticipating miracles. But when I uncrinkled the foil and peeled back the plastic wrap, what I found was not magic powder but a cluster of clouded, butter-colored crystals. The hard stuff, I thought, agog. Upstairs there was a loud thud. I put the stuff down on the table and listened.

"You okay?" I hollered, still staring down at the crystals.

"Yeah, I'm all right," the girl answered. The scrub brush started up again slowly.

What was the meaning of those crystals? They had appeared only once before, with Clark that first summer in

Alna. I was still new to the zombies then, still afraid of them. My walks up Riverside with Clark were fraught with nervous thrills. The bus station had been out of operation for a few decades—fake-wood-veneer benches and an old soda-vending machine, empty windows, faded ads with Smokey Bear admonishing smokers and Hillside Church offering day care and asking for charity. Occasionally teenagers would skateboard around, hopping up with a frightening rumble and clack onto the counters at the old ticket windows. The men's toilets were in back, through a short maze of brick riddled with graffiti. A few zombies were stationed back there, sitting on sinks or squatting on the floor, their wolf dogs tied to a pipe in the wall, panting. The zombie in charge sat in a stall with the door swung halfway open. Silently he took our money and handed over the goods. His fingers were huge and cracked and red, black creases lining his palm, his nails thick and yellow. I hid my face under my hair, lurked and cowered next to Clark, masking myself in false subservience. The zombies saw through all that. They saw everything. But I was clueless still. I was a foreigner. I didn't know their customs. I got more comfortable as time went on, of course. And then once Clark was out of the picture, I was forced to go alone. The zombies rarely lifted their gaze above my waistline. Theirs was a solid, grounding, animal attitude. Each time I met them in the bathroom I felt I was walking in naked, as if I were some pilgrim approaching a saint. I offered ten dollars and I received my blessing.

When the crystals had appeared for me and Clark all those

years before, I had been honored, moved even. It felt like some kind of rite of passage, a sacrament. But when Clark saw the crystals, he crushed the foil back up and jammed the stuff down the front pocket of his jeans.

"What are you going to do with it, Clark?" I asked.

"Flush it, at my house" was his brilliant reply.

Whatever lame affection I had left for Clark was smashed in that instant—it was obvious he was trying to deceive me. I suppose those crystals worked to save me from really getting attached to the man. Such was the magic wisdom of the zombies.

"What's wrong with my house? Flush it here," I insisted.

"I could flush it here," he murmured.

"So flush it." But Clark just sat there, stroking his beard and staring at the television as if the opening credits of *Will & Grace* had hypnotized him, as if he'd become one of the zombies.

"Ahem."

"What?" he asked.

"Give it back," I said, elbowing him in the knees.

"Trust me," he whispered. "This stuff rots your brains." He stood up, scratching his head, his armpit a rat's nest of hair flecked with white gunk from his antiperspirant. "I'm going home," he said. "I'm tired."

I let him go then. I didn't argue. He tried to kiss me good-bye but I turned my face away. I spent the rest of the day bored in front of the television, pining, furious, confused. I tried to go upstairs and scrape the leftover wallpaper in the bathroom, but it was no use. The next morning I went to the zombies alone and received the usual stuff. When Clark called in the afternoon, I told him I needed some time to myself. I sniffed my magic powders while he blubbered an apology that sounded like all his lame professions—foolishly sincere.

After cleaning my bedroom, the girl trudged slowly down the stairs. I'd been lying on the sofa reading a teen magazine left behind by one of the tenants. I stared at articles that told me how to "live my dreams," "score total independence," and "make more $$$." I can't say exactly what I thought I'd do with the crystals. I'd seen movies about people smoking crack out of little glass pipes. I could fashion something, I thought, but I was scared I'd mess it up. I imagined dissolving the crystals like rock sugar in a mug of herbal tea, or grinding them like sea salt over a bowl of canned tomato soup. But I wasn't sure ingesting the stuff that way would work. And what if it did? I still had a life back down in the city, after all. There were certain realities I had to face. I couldn't handle real oblivion. I just wanted a vacation. So I had some doubts. I had some misgivings.

I'd been rolling the little nest of foil between my fingers, pondering all this, as I stared at the magazine. When I heard the stairs creak, I sat up and stuck the stuff back in the pocket of my shorts.

"Hot up there," I heard the girl say.

Her pretty, gleaming calves appeared between the rungs of the banister as she came down the steps. She'd folded the cuffs of her leggings up above her knees, which were red from kneeling on the floor. When her thighs appeared, I saw a black stain of blood at her crotch. She seemed not to know that she was bleeding. There was no way she could have seen the blood past the mountain of her belly, I suppose. She gripped the bucket with one hand and the railing with the other as she descended the stairs.

"Oh, shit," she said when she reached the landing. "I left the broom."

"I'll get it," I told her, folding the magazine shut.

"Shit," she said again, putting the bucket down and holding her face with her hands. "Head rush."

"I'll get you a glass of water," I offered. I wasn't good around blood.

"I'm okay," the girl said, bracing herself against the bookshelf. "Just dizzy." She turned toward the wall, leaned into it, said, "Whew."

I got up then, patting my pocket to make sure the ball of foil was safe inside. In the kitchen I let the tap run cold, got the ice from the freezer, took a glass from the drying rack.

"I'm really okay," the girl said.

I plunked the ice in the glass. The cubes cracked as the water ran over them. "See," the girl went on, "you're not missing anything."

"What?" I hollered back. But I'd heard her perfectly.

"You're not missing anything," she said again, louder.

"My mom says a baby is a blessing, but I don't know." I suppose it unnerved me that she could be so naive. She had no idea what her life was going to do to her.

"That baby's going to change your world," I said, walking back into the den. She was bent over with her face in front of the fan. I snuck a look at the bloodstain widening down her thighs. "My sister has a daughter," I said. "Gave up her career and everything." I handed the girl the glass. She pushed herself upright, took a long sip, set the glass down on the TV, and sighed. "Boy or girl?"

"Boy," she answered, blushing slightly.

"You sure you feel all right?"

She nodded.

I stood around watching her clean for a while, helping her here and there, moving furniture so she could mop. She seemed perfectly fine to me. "I love *The Matrix*," she said, straightening my shelves of VHS tapes. "I love old movies." She beat the sofa's cushions with her fist. She stacked the magazines on the end table. She straightened my framed poster of Monet's *Water Lilies*. Her eyes were clear and blue as ever under their thick, gleaming lids. I went upstairs to get the broom, then I retreated to the kitchen, put away the clean dishes, and did the dirty ones. I put the dinner half of my sub in the fridge and sponged off the counter. I took out the trash.

Outside my neighbors were filling a kiddie pool with water from their garden hose. I waved.

"Marvin died," one of the women said glumly.

"Who's Marvin?" I asked.

She turned to her sister, or mother—I couldn't tell—and rolled her eyes.

Clark had chained the lids of my trash cans to the plastic handles on the barrels. For some reason, the people of Alna liked to steal the lids and throw them in the Omec. That was one of their summer recreations, he'd told me. As I stuffed the garbage down, the pregnant girl threw open the screen door and walked stiffly down the front steps. She held one hand down under her belly and the palm of her other hand up in front of her face. When she saw me and the neighbors, she turned her palm around. It was covered in blood.

"Oh, honey!" cried one of the women, dropping the hose.

"Something's wrong," the girl stammered, stunned.

"Well, honey, what happened? Did you fall? Did you hurt yourself?" the women were asking. The girl caught my eye as they surrounded her. I put the lid on the trash and watched as the women guided the girl across the muddy grass. They made her sit down in a lawn chair in the shade. One of them went inside to call for help. I went back into the house and got the girl's flyers and twenty dollars from my wallet. When I got back outside, she was panting. I handed her the money, and she grabbed my forearm, smeared her blood all over it, squeezed it, shrieking, contracting her face in pain.

"Hang on, honey," the neighbor said, frowning at me, her fat hands stroking the girl's smooth, sweaty brow. "Help is on the way."

○———○

When the ambulance left that afternoon, I took a walk down to the Omec. Squatting by the edge of the river, I washed the blood off my arm. I took the crystals out and let them plunk down into the rushing water, threw the crumpled foil at the wind, and watched it hit the surface and float away. I looked up at the pale, overcast sky, the crows circling then gliding down to a nest of rotting garbage on the opposite bank. I sat on a hot rock and let the sun warm my bones. My thighs splayed out; my white skin tightened and burned. It was nice there with the cool breeze, the sound of the traffic through the trees, the earthy stench of mud. An empty Coke can tinkled a rhythm against the rock, shaken by the current. A toad hopped across my foot.

Later that evening I dragged the sunlamp out onto the curb, thinking maybe the zombies would find it. The next morning it was still there, so I dragged it back inside. I walked up Riverside Road. I got what I wanted. I walked back home.

They met one summer day through the high chain-link fence between their backyards. His yard was just plain dry brown dirt. Hers was full of dusty bags of fertilizer and tools haphazardly scattered where she'd started planting flowers in the tough soil. The man had seen neighbors come and go over the many years he'd lived there, in the dark corner of the cul-de-sac. "Through seven presidents," he told the girl, laughing nervously and swatting his neck as if to catch mosquitoes. He was only sixty but looked far older. Vitiligo had stripped his brittle hair of its color, made his face seem riddled with fat freckles. The girl was pretty, sturdy, in her early thirties. She had been living next door to the man for two months already. He had just been waiting for the proper moment to introduce himself.

"I'm Jeb," the man said.

"That's a long time, Jeb," the girl said to him. "That many presidents."

Jeb laughed again and sighed and looked at her through the fence. His shock of white hair gleamed in a single ray of light falling from the girl's yard into his. His strange, spotted face and bulbous nose made the girl look away. White strands of loose thread hung down from her jean shorts and fluttered around her thighs. Her breasts, Jeb noticed, were untethered—no bra. What color were her eyes? Jeb looked down at them, perplexed to find that they were of different colors, one a strange, violet shade of blue, the other green with flecks of black and honey. Coils of green rubber hose snaked through the mess in the yard behind her. He was glad, he told the girl, to have a new neighbor, and relieved that the property was being cared for after so long. The previous owners of the house had ripped out its walls, banged around all day, left busted garbage bags of broken plaster on the curb, chalking up the blacktop. The bank had taken it over in a terrible state of disrepair, then sold it to the girl for next to nothing.

"How are you and your husband liking the neighborhood?" Jeb asked through the fence. But he already knew that the boy was gone. Over the last few weeks, Jeb had watched the boy and the girl through the scrim of brown paper covering their den windows. He'd heard their spats and squabbles. The boy's motorcycle had been missing from its spot under the garage awning for days.

"Trevor left," the girl said, crossing her arms. She looked

down at the ground, hid her toes behind a tall tuft of crab-grass.

"He's at work," Jeb said, nodding, pretending to misinterpret her. "What is his profession, if I may ask?"

"No, I mean he's gone," the girl said. "For good this time."

"He's left you all alone?" Jeb hooked the fingers of one hand into the chain-link fence and took a step toward her. He placed his other hand over his heart and let his strange, sagging mandible soften into a deep frown. "That's just awful. Poor dear." He shook his head.

"Whatever, you know," the girl said. She made fists of her hands, then spread her fingers out like bombs exploding. "That's life."

"I *do* know," Jeb said gravely, his thick lips trembling in false sympathy. That was one way he knew to affect women—to seem overcome by his own unruly emotions, and then to apologize for them. "I'm sorry," he said, gasping and frowning again. Jeb saw that there was no ring on the girl's finger. She wasn't a widow or a divorcée; she was only newly single, and not for long, Jeb supposed. "I just know the feeling all too well," he said.

"Shit, don't cry," the girl said. Despite being pretty and soft of flesh, there was something harsh about her, Jeb thought. Something crude.

In the silence, he felt the girl's gaze shift across his narrow torso, the crepey, spotted skin on his thin arms. She was assessing him, he knew. He cleared his throat and brought his hands together, clapped them twice as though he'd just finished a difficult task. He corrected his slumped posture. "Our houses are mirror images, you know," he said. He held up his palms side by side in front of him. "*La destra*. And *la sinistra*, that's me. I know a little Italian," he added. "I took a class once, years and years ago." Then his voice took on a bright, folksy twang as he said, as if the girl had prompted him to, "Well, come on over sometime if you get lonesome. Have a cup of coffee with your old next-door neighbor. You're welcome anytime."

"Are you southern?" the girl asked, ignoring his invitation. She looked snooty. She looked distrustful.

"I'm an Alabama boy," Jeb answered. "But I've lived here forever. Too long. Seven presidents, if you can believe that," he said, laughing at the repeated joke as though to cheer her with his senility. When he smiled he exposed the deep rot of his clawlike teeth. They were nearly black along the gums. "Nice to meet you," he said. He put out his hand to mime a handshake through the chain link. The girl sniggered.

"We can shake *E.T.* style," she said and extended her index finger through the fence. Jeb met the tip of it with his. He marked the moment in his mind, the feel of her finger— hot, dry, resilient. "Bye," she said.

Jeb watched her round bouncing calves, brown from summer and flecked with mud, as she crossed the yard and went up her steps. "If you ever need a hand," he began, but the girl didn't hear him. Her silhouette passed behind the gray screens of the back porch, and then she was inside and her kitchen door was shut and her radio was on. She'd had the radio on a lot, Jeb had noticed, since the boy had left her. Jeb could hear almost everything that went on in her house, he'd figured out, if he listened carefully from his basement window.

That night, Jeb ate his dinner in the basement, listening to the sounds the girl made alone in her house. Her radio was tuned to old folk singers. Women's music, Jeb thought, spearing his food with a heavy silver fork. He chewed thoroughly, now and then gagging on the tough, pan-fried steak, the few raw strands of carrot and green bell pepper. He thought that drinking while you ate diluted the stomach's acids, so he rarely drank more than his morning coffee and an occasional tumbler of Kenny May whiskey when he had something to celebrate or mourn. Otherwise he was dumb to the pleasures of consumption. He did, however, enjoy the thrill of frugality in stocking large quantities of meat, purchased on sale, in his storage freezer, which he now used as a dinner table in the basement. He liked to buy his vegetables at a discount, too, usually off the sale rack in the supermarket. He'd been doing it for so long that the very sight of that neon orange discount sticker could make his mouth water.

He was glad the girl didn't try to emulate the singer's flourishes when she sang along. He would have been embarrassed to hear that. She sang a sad song—clearly she knew all the words—and in the rests he thought he detected the faint swish of a magazine. He imagined her sitting on a colorful quilt, yellow lamplight glazing her bare arms and glinting off the vertebrae of her neck as she peered down at the pictures of everything she coveted. He felt that he was getting to know the girl by the sounds she made—her foul mouth on the phone with her girlfriends, the violent slams of her bureau drawers as she dressed, her quick steps up and down the stairs in the morning, her slow steps up and down at night. Jeb had even heard her passing gas a few times, and he hoped one day to tell her so. "And yet my affection for you did not diminish," he imagined saying. "In fact, it only endeared you to me more."

Before Trevor left, Jeb hadn't liked to listen very closely. The two were always yelling at each other. "Where're my shoes?" "Ready?" "What?" "Babe?" And then there was "Babe, come talk to me" and "Babe, look at this" and "Babe, get down here." And the worst, "I love you, babe." Babe. No one in Jeb's life had ever called him that. "Jeb" was as sweet a name as he'd ever gone by, and still it had an ugly, rubbery ring to it, like a name for dishwashing detergent or soap used to mop prison floors. Jeb. It was short for Jebediah. But nobody ever asked him to explain it. Nobody could bear to look at him, he thought, much less sit and listen to him talk.

Sunday morning, Jeb's nephew parked his black sedan in the driveway and threw his cigarette butt at the parched dirt yard. Jeb fried some eggs and bacon, made toast, poured coffee, peeled the waxed paper off a fresh stick of butter. He'd spent the past hour listening to the girl plodding around her house, scrubbing the floors, filling buckets of water with the nozzle from the kitchen sink, hammering nails into the walls. The occasional cry of "shit" or "ouch" or "motherfucker" punctuated the radio news broadcast that blathered on from her kitchen. There were protesters in Egypt getting killed. There were scientists discovering new planets. There were fires in a national park, a flood in India, a spree of robberies across the river. Poor people and immigrants liked the president. A storm was coming. High winds, they warned. Keep your pets safe inside. "Whatever," the girl muttered, and turned the dial to jazz.

"My new neighbor's nice," Jeb said to his nephew once they'd sat down to eat in the breakfast nook. Jeb took for himself only one strip of bacon, one dry piece of toast. "Single gal," he went on, "right next door. I'm sure she could use a friend her own age."

The nephew ate a forkful of eggs. His face was thin and bearded. He wore a small gold hoop in one ear. "What's she look like?" he asked, head tilted skeptically. "Truthfully. Head to toe."

"Oh, please," Jeb said. "You're not one to be picky. Looks a bit like Lou Ann." Lou Ann had been the nephew's high-school girlfriend. "She has that kind of tan."

"I'll meet her," said the nephew. "But I'm not saying I'll take her out. I don't need any drama."

"What drama? You should be so lucky," Jeb said. "A sweet gal. Comes with baggage, of course, as they all do."

"Kids?" the nephew asked. "Forget it."

"No, no kids. Emotional issues, more like," Jeb said. "You know women. Stray cats, all of them, either purring in your lap or pissing in your shoes."

"Amen to that," said the nephew.

"She *is* pretty. Something special about her. A gal who might be worth suffering for, if you ask me. Anyway, you'd be so lucky," he repeated. He pulled the nephew's empty plate away. "Go over there and introduce yourself. Or better yet, bring her this piece of mail." He put the plate in the sink and went to the kitchen drawer, where he'd been saving a letter the postman had misdelivered. It was a notice from a university library across the river. The girl was late in returning a book and the fee was multiplying day by day. "I meant to give it to her yesterday," Jeb said.

"But it's Sunday morning," the nephew said.

"Never mind," Jeb said. "She's up. I'm sure she'll be happy to have a visitor." He put a hand on the boy's muscled shoulder as they walked to the front door. "When you see her, tell her I send my regards."

The nephew skipped through the front yard, kicking up dust, and jogged across the crumbling sidewalk onto the girl's front lawn. Her yard had no fencing around it, just thick, overgrown grass, small evergreen bushes, piles of damp mulch spread sloppily around two crooked saplings. A few empty flowerpots sat on the stoop. The nephew rang the doorbell, then knocked, his chest heaving with impatience. When the girl answered, Jeb ducked back into the house to watch the scene through his living room window.

She wore her frayed denim shorts and a black T-shirt with the sleeves cut off. The nephew stood agog for a moment, then handed her the letter. As they spoke, the girl flapped the letter in her hand. She dug her finger under the seal of the envelope, failing to notice that it had been opened and reglued by Jeb. The nephew looked expectant, scratched his ear, put his hands in and out of his pockets. The girl shrugged and flipped her hair and smiled. Finally he backed down off her front steps. The girl waved the letter, then shut the door. Jeb watched her silhouette through her papered windows. He kneaded his shoulder with his hand. It was all gristle and sinew. He peeled a soft brown banana. He listened to his nephew drive away.

In the early afternoon, Jeb was in the backyard, dragging a rusted lawn chair across the dirt. He sat in a spot from which he could see the girl doing dishes through her open kitchen door.

"Beware the storm!" he yelled when she finally walked out to the porch and sat on the warped wooden back steps. "I love this time, the calm before."

She looked at Jeb through the chain-link fence. He was just sitting there, facing her yard as if it were a TV set. "Hey," she said. The soft, warm wind tousled her long, loose hair. She gathered it in her fingers, then turned her back to Jeb to light a cigarette.

"Say," Jeb said, dragging the chair closer to the fence. "I don't mean to pry, but may I say how pleased I was to hear you made a new friend in my young nephew. Been a while since he had someone special in his life." He winked. "I wish you both well."

"It's not a big deal," the girl said, picking a fleck of tobacco from her tongue. "We're just having a drink together."

"Now, now," said Jeb. "I don't want to poke my head in. I respect y'all's privacy."

The girl stood. "There's nothing to be private about," she said. "It's not a date or anything. You could come with us if you wanted. It's the same to me either way."

"Oh, no, I couldn't intrude like that." Jeb furrowed his eyebrows, shook his head. The girl looked so beautiful in the wind and the strange pink light of the sun through the pale clouds. He watched her shirt flatten against her body in the wind. "You don't need an old man getting in your way," he said.

Holding the cigarette in her teeth, she wrestled her hair down again and twisted it into a braid. Her armpits were gritty with tiny hairs and flecked with white clumps of de-odorant. "If you want to join us, I don't mind. I don't care," she said flatly.

"If you insist," Jeb said. "Come over to my side, why don't you? We'll toast you the Alabama way, and then y'all can go off wherever young folks go. You do drink whiskey, don't you?"

"Who doesn't?" she answered, dragging her cigarette against the doorframe.

"See you at eight, then," Jeb said and watched her walk across her yard, pitched forward in the wind. She picked up a small potted sapling and carried it back to the porch. "It'll pass quick!" Jeb shouted, pointing up at the churning, rose-colored sky, but the girl couldn't hear him. The first thunder clapped. A flash of lightning. Jeb went back into the house and sat on the couch, listening and counting, waiting for the storm.

By eight o'clock the rains had arrived in lazy, side-sweeping sheets battering Jeb's windows. The sky was black now, but lightning turned it amethyst and smoky each time it cracked overhead. Jeb had showered, put on a clean shirt, combed his hair with pomade, shaved, slapped his jowls with cologne. His dinner had been a boiled chicken drumstick, a small can of sauerkraut, a few tart early-summer cherries. Through the concert of the storm, nothing from the girl's house had been audible at the basement window. Jeb's own radio now reported downed power lines, flooding on the interstate. Fallen branches had forced some roads to close. It wasn't safe to drive over the bridge, they said. The nephew called to convey a message to the girl. "Tell her I'm stuck. I can't come tonight."

"What a shame," Jeb said. "I'll tell her." In the living room, he tidied a pile of clipped coupons on the end table by the couch, set out the bottle of Kenny May. From the kitchen cabinet he chose two crystal-cut tumblers, licked the rims of both, and set them next to the whiskey. He tuned the radio to easy listening.

A few minutes past eight, his front buzzer rang. The girl was there in black rubber boots and a glossy yellow raincoat, its hood hovering stiffly over her darkened face.

"Is he here yet?" was how she greeted Jeb.

"Welcome, welcome," Jeb said, holding the door open. The girl stepped inside and took off her raincoat. Water dripped all over the floor. Jeb took a step back. The girl's dress was disappointing—not quite a housedress, but pastel, floral, cheap cotton, with short sleeves. He happily noted the appearance of earrings—small silver hearts. She smelled of coconuts, of fruity cocktails, tropical breezes, white-sand beaches. He took the girl's raincoat and hung it on the rack by the door.

"I guess I should take these off too," the girl said and bent over to loosen her foot from her boot. When she lost her balance, Jeb caught her forearm in his hand. She hardly seemed to notice. Jeb blushed at the sensuousness of her flesh—soft around the bone, like the arm of a baby. He tried not to squeeze her too tightly. When she righted herself, he let go. Then she bent and balanced and pulled the other boot off, giving the old man a glimpse of her hanging cleavage.

"I'm sorry to report that my nephew is running late," Jeb said, locking the front door. "He has been detained due to the rain." He inhaled the smell of her, searching his mind for the words. "Piña colada," he exclaimed, waggling a finger. "Your perfume. Am I right?"

"It's only moisturizer," the girl said, straightening her dress. "How late will he be?"

"Just a few minutes," Jeb said. "He says we shouldn't wait on him."

It was dim inside the house. Only small flame-shaped bulbs glowed faintly in the sconces in the front hall. Jeb showed her into the living room. The ceiling lamp there gave off a sputtering, weak light. Jeb's eyes were two black shadows when he stood under it. His face looked like a skull. "Come sit," he said, coaxing the girl with a hand at the small of her back. She allowed him that, to be hospitable, it seemed. She was thicker than she looked, Jeb thought. Strong but small, like a bulldog puppy. Tough bitch, he said to himself. "Kick back a bit."

The girl sat on the couch, holding the hem of her dress down as she crossed her legs. "Your house is just like mine, only in reverse," she said.

Jeb went to the end table, picked up the Kenny May, and poured them each a few fingers of whiskey. "I don't have any ice, I'm afraid," he said, holding a glass out to the girl.

Outside, the storm churned. Over the love song on the radio they could hear twigs and branches snapping, the rush of the wind through the leaves, rain splashing against the house.

"To new neighbors, new friends," Jeb said.

They raised their glasses and drank. The girl made a face and sniffed her whiskey. Jeb looked out the window, grinning. He was well aware that when he felt jubilant, he acted strangely. He could seem too eager, too effusive. He could disclose too much. He tried to hold himself upright, rigid, but he couldn't keep himself from speaking what was on his mind. "Pump and dump. You're familiar with the expression?" he asked. "That's what my nephew calls it. That's what he likes to do. The storm may have saved you from that humiliation. Thank God for Mother Nature."

"Jesus," the girl said, snorting. Men never ceased to amaze her—sly dogs, all of them, nasty creatures. "Christ," she said. She drank more whiskey. "The kid just asked me out for a drink. I'm no whore."

Jeb bent at the waist, lowered his head. "I guess your enthusiasm had him fooled," he said, and winked. Then he straightened himself again and tried to keep from smiling.

The girl tapped her fingernails against her glass and let herself sink back against the old plaid couch. Its springs had been flattened over the decades. The upholstery smelled of Jeb—bitter, like dry rot, and slightly chemical. The rough fabric of the cushions scratched the girl's arms. She closed her eyes, and sipped her drink. She was tired. It was hard work to get her house in order, and she was doing it by herself now.

She was glad to have the distraction, away from her thoughts, the cold jabs each time she longed for Trevor's hand to touch her, his lips to kiss her neck, her cheeks, her thighs. Sinking deeper into the couch, she thought that if Trevor were to come back she'd let him do whatever he wanted. Maybe she'd even let herself get pregnant. But the idea was like a bad taste in her mouth. She made a sour face. Jeb watched her diaphragm rise and fall under the thin fabric of her dress. She seemed edgy, irritated, her eyes twisted and barbed.

"I'm sorry, dear. Did I offend you?" he asked.

The girl looked straight up at him. "You're trying to get to me, aren't you?" she said. Jeb's eyes cowered and darted back and forth between her crossed, luminous knees and the rumbling windowpane. "I see your game. You're trying to shame me for being young and pretty. You want to make me apologize for all the other girls who didn't like you. You just can't stand that I'm right next door reminding you of all that. That's it, isn't it? Pump and dump," she scoffed. "Nothing you say can hurt me. See if you can do it. I dare you." She chuckled and sipped her whiskey, then placed the glass on the coffee table.

"You never know with young women these days," Jeb said. "It's a rough, wild world out there, and girls, women"— he knew the distinction was an important one to make for the girl to feel respected—"they just give themselves away for free. It breaks my heart. Low self-esteem, they call it." He clucked his tongue, shook his head, then brought his hand to his chest. "I'm sorry," he said, speaking softly, as though he were about to cry. He stooped forward over the coffee table, picked up the girl's glass, and moved it to a coaster.

"But I haven't done anything," the girl maintained, rolling her eyes. "There's nothing to get upset about. Jesus. I already told you, I see your game. You're trying to get me to cry on your shoulder, make me out to be the screwed-up one, like that's why I don't want to fuck you. I wasn't born yesterday, you know."

When Jeb was excited, his heart fluttered. "Like a pigeon in a burlap sack," he'd told the doctor.

"And what do you mean 'for free'?" the girl went on. "You think it's better to sell yourself? What is with you men, you always see everything as this and that? Like everything is for sale."

"Pardon?" Jeb said.

"Give and take. Like life is some bank account you're trying to fill up. And like every girl's a whore."

"My dear, I have no idea what you're talking about."

"No kidding," the girl said. She pursed her lips tight, wrinkling her chin. Jeb thought she looked rather ugly that way. She held her breath. She seemed somehow to be on the verge of combusting. Beneath the coffee table, her bare foot was jiggling like a bobblehead. A bolt of lightning cracked and flashed. "Is your nephew coming, you think?" she asked, her voice suddenly soft and innocent.

"No," Jeb said.

"Oh," she said.

But still the girl remained seated. She even adjusted her posture to make herself more comfortable, leaning forward so that her skin did not touch the rough fabric of the couch. He was quiet. He watched her lips tighten, then unfurl as she sipped her whiskey.

Jeb swallowed back some phlegm, moved stiffly to the couch, and sat down. His hand rested on the cushion between him and the girl. His pinkie finger grazed the soft fabric of her dress. If he'd wanted to, he thought, he could easily have pinched the flesh of her thigh.

"These are some photos," he said, turning to an old cigar box on the coffee table. He flipped the lid of the box open. The girl bent over to look at the photographs inside, slid them around in the box as though she were shuffling puzzle pieces. Jeb looked again at her tanned, dewy cleavage.

"What year was this?" she asked, picking up a photo. It was a small school portrait of Jeb as a boy. His face was fat, his eyes cold and tortured, his striped tie wrung tightly around his neck.

"Age nine," Jeb pronounced. He shook his head gruffly, as though to wake himself up. "If my age is an issue for you," he began to say.

"Why should I care how old you are? What's it to me?" She flipped another photo around, stuck it out so Jeb could see it. It was a photo of him as a young man, skulking beside his father, a dark, mean figure in a gray sacklike suit. In the photo Jeb had thick red hair. "Your hair's so *white* now," she said, looking at the photo again.

"They called me Red Jeb when I was young. Say that six times fast." He laughed. "People sometimes think I'm an albino, if you can believe that."

"Of course I can believe it," the girl said. "I'd believe almost anything in this world."

"And occasionally black folks think I'm an albino black, if you can believe *that*. I suppose it's a compliment. It isn't catching, my vitiligo. It's perfectly harmless. In some cultures it's considered a mark of the divine. If I went to those countries, people would stop and pray to me in the street, I guess. Saint Jeb." He said, and laughed again. "Nowadays, of course, I just look old. Children can be cruel—"

"Can I use your bathroom?" the girl asked, interrupting him.

Jeb looked down at her knees. The blue tint of her veins showed through her skin. He faked a cough, composed himself, then bent over the photographs again, wetting his finger not on his tongue but on the fat, spittley lip hanging down between his frown lines. "You know where it is," he said.

Jeb listened to her heavy step as she crossed the front hall to the bathroom beneath the stairs. In her absence, he looked at the photos and thought back to a failed romance from long ago. He'd thought he was in love, but after only one intimate rendezvous, the woman had sat on the toilet and dismissed him completely. "You're too uptight," she'd told him. "You have no imagination." His heart fluttered again as he remembered how her thighs had swayed when she rose to wipe herself. Then the toilet flushed. He listened for the sink faucet to run, but it didn't. The girl came back.

"I like the wallpaper in your bathroom," she said. "And the old sink." She sat down again. Jeb had placed a photo on top of the pile for her to see. It showed a skinny woman in a sun hat and a bikini sitting in a beach chair by a pool. "Who's she?" the girl asked.

"My wife, may she rest in peace."

"She's very pretty," the girl said politely. She leaned over to the end table and poured herself another tumblerful of Kenny May.

"She had a chipped tooth," Jeb said. "But she was pretty enough. A strange gal. Never could tell what she was thinking. Had strange habits, as do we all. And strange obsessions. She liked to buy all sorts of fancy things. Lace and silk stuff, you know? Lingerie. Tell you what," Jeb said, smiling now. "She left drawers full of that stuff upstairs. I'd be happy to show you. It's all very nice."

The girl put her glass down.

"Strange woman," Jeb continued. "Kept a diary every day of her life, made me swear I'd never touch it. When she passed, bless her dear heart"—he put his hand on his chest, sucked in air at a stutter for a moment, looked up at the ceiling—"I found the diary and I read it, and it was all about bowling. Bowling this and bowling that. Had me laughing and crying at once. That's love." He put his hand on the girl's knee, then looked out the window. The storm raged and clattered. The lights flickered, but they didn't go out. The pale, swollen, spotted hand on the girl's knee was inert, like a fat, sleeping lizard that could at any moment awaken and claw up her soft thigh.

"Get your nasty paw off my leg," the girl said flatly. She picked up his pinkie finger and craned his hand up and to the side. "You've got to be kidding me," she said under her breath, letting go.

Jeb ignored her. He swayed his head in painful reverie. "Oh, my sweet Betty Ann. She left a closet full of clothes, too. Great dresser," he said. "Real style. And you know me, so sentimental, I couldn't part with those nice dresses. I always thought maybe one day someone would have a use for them. Like you, for instance. Hey!" In a comic pantomime, he exhaled as though struck by lightning, sticking his arms out in front of him and letting his head loll and his tongue dangle from his mouth. "Here's an idea," he said. His face brightened. "Do you like old things? Vintage, as they say? I've got skirts, tops, and the dresses. Shoes too. You're welcome to try anything on. Just up the stairs." The fleshy wrinkles around his mouth deepened as he grinned.

The girl looked at her drink. "If the kid isn't coming, I should just go home."

"But you've only just arrived." Jeb opened his hands, flittered his fingers. He reached across her lap for the Kenny May, filled both glasses, although neither was empty. Outside, the storm paused for a minute. They sat listening, waiting to see if it was really over. Then the rain started up again.

"I don't believe you ever had a wife," the girl said after a while. "And this whiskey tastes funny." She set her glass on the coaster. "It tastes cheap," she said.

"Lie down for a bit," Jeb said, not getting up off the couch. "Take a load off. Stretch out if you like. *Mi casa es su casa*. I know a drop of Spanish. And French. *Voulez-vous? Comment ça va?*"

The girl yawned and shook her head. "I'm not lying down with you," she said.

"But these dresses," Jeb said. "They'd fit you perfectly. Let me bring one down so you can see it. My wife was quite the fashion plate. And just your size. Shall I bring one down? It'd be such a pity to throw them all away. You can come up and look through them yourself, if you like."

"No, thanks," the girl said. She was only pretending to be bored, it seemed, fingering the lid of Jeb's cigar box.

"It's all just sitting there, waiting to be revived," Jeb said. "Take whatever you want. It doesn't matter to me." A bolt of lightning flooded the room with pale blue light.

"If I wanted to be fooled into your bedroom, you wouldn't have to ask twice," the girl replied. "I already told you, I see your game."

Jeb looked up at the ceiling. The loose, spotted skin of his throat flapped as he ground his jaws. "So you're not interested," he said, crossing his arms. "You've gone and changed your mind."

"Changed my mind?"

"I was only trying to be courteous, neighborly. And here you come, wanting to be comforted."

"I'm sorry if I gave you the wrong impression," the girl

said sarcastically. Her mismatched eyes crinkled in derision, Jeb thought.

"You're lucky I'm not a creep," he continued. "I could do anything I wanted to you, you know. A young girl, drunk on my couch. You should be more careful. My wife—" Jeb gasped suddenly, dabbing pretentiously at invisible tears. "God bless her soul. She was a good woman. An honest woman. No tease or hussy like you find nowadays." He stared down at the girl's bare feet on the hardwood floor and licked his lips. Still the girl did not get up.

"I'm not feeling well," Jeb said, leaning back against the couch and closing his eyes. The girl turned and moved closer. The scent of coconut made him queasy. The hand she placed on Jeb's bony shoulder was warm and damp through his thin T-shirt. He froze. He felt her weight shift on the couch, heard the springs whine, and then she was on him, straddling him, her breasts shoved up against his chin. Jeb could barely breathe.

"Is this what you were hoping for?" she asked, watching his face for his reaction.

Jeb kept his eyes shut, licked his lips again. The girl could smell the stink of his breath, like a sick cat's. She sniffed his mouth, wincing happily. Their faces were only a few inches apart. "I was hoping . . ." Jeb began to say. The load of her body against him ground at his bones. He felt himself blush, harden. He lifted his hands.

The girl just laughed and hopped off him before he could touch her. Her dress had been hiked up in the maneuver. Jeb watched her thighs tremble with the impact of each step she took across the living room floor. In the hall she laughed to herself some more, put her boots on, and whipped her raincoat off the rack.

"Let me see you to your door," Jeb called out. But she was already gone.

An hour later, the nephew called again. "My whole damn building lost power," he complained. "I can't even watch TV."

"You could have spent the night here," Jeb chided him. "I had a fine time with the neighbor girl without you. But I don't think you'd like her much. Sort of a dud, if you ask me. A fish in a bucket, as they say. No fun for the hunt."

"I've got other girls," the nephew said and hung up.

In the morning, pale mist filled the air like smoke. The girl's house was obscured by the fog. Jeb awoke on the couch, got the Kenny May, and assumed his position in the basement once more. A small drop of water trickled from the crumbling concrete wall down to the floor. He drank. All he heard from the girl's house was drawers and cabinets opening and shutting, the faucet running, and then her radio dial crackling up and down, landing finally on bright, snappy pop songs. She listened to one after another, singing merrily along as though she were completely innocent, as though nothing at all had happened.

Days passed. Jeb spent them sitting at his kitchen window. He watched the girl carry cans of paint into her house, smoke cigarettes on the front steps, pick up debris from the yard, drag bags of trash to the curb. Her figure appeared now and then through the wispy drapes of her bedroom when she opened or shut the window. The mail came. The sun rose and fell. Jeb neglected the dead leaves that had blown from the girl's yard into his. He didn't want the girl to see him out there raking. She was a tramp, a tease, nobody worth his time, he told himself. He read the Sunday paper and fried his bacon while the girl painted and cleaned and hammered at her walls. Despite his neighborly instincts, he refrained from going over to offer his help or counsel.

"She's a plain Jane" is what he told his nephew when he came over for breakfast. "No substance, no depth. Full of herself for no good reason."

"Maybe I'll go over and say hello," the nephew said, but he didn't.

And then, a few days later, Jeb heard the thunderous squeal of a motorcycle peeling up the road. For hours, he listened at his basement window, nodding his head to the rhythmic tempo of the girl's headboard hitting the wall, the gasps and grunts and growls. When it was over, he took off on foot down the road into town and spent the whole afternoon ambling like a stray dog under the striped store-front awnings, dodging the daylight, lest his white skin burn and blister. He licked a vanilla ice cream cone and regarded his slumped silhouette in the shop windows. He straightened his posture as best he could, but he was stooped by nature. He could still be a god on Earth, however, if only he found the right tribe. That would be something—to be worshipped and beloved. Jeb whistled through the warm evening streets, imagining this wonderful new place and all the stupid people who would gasp and fall to their knees in ecstasy every time he shuffled past.

The friends met for dinner, as they did the second Sunday of every month, at a small Italian restaurant on the Upper East Side. There were three couples: Marty and Barbara, Jerry and Maureen, and John and Marcia, who had recently returned from a week-long island getaway to celebrate their twenty-ninth wedding anniversary. "Were the beaches beautiful? How was the hotel? Was it safe? Was it memorable? Was it worth the money?" the friends asked.

Marcia said, "You had to see it to believe it. The ocean was like bathwater. The sunsets? Better than any painting. But the political situation, don't get me started. All the beggars!" She put a hand over her heart and sipped her wine. "Who knows who's in charge? It's utter chaos. Meanwhile, the people all speak *English*!" The vestiges of colonialism, the poverty, the corruption—it had all depressed her. "And we were harassed," she told the friends. "By prostitutes. *Male* ones. They followed us down the beach like cats. The strangest thing. But the beach was absolutely gorgeous. Right, John?"

John sat across the table, swirling his spaghetti. He glanced up at Marcia, nodded, winked.

The friends wanted to know what the prostitutes had looked like, how they'd dressed, what they'd said. They wanted details.

"They looked like normal people," Marcia said, shrugging. "You know, just young, poor people, locals. But they were very complimentary. They kept saying, 'Hello, nice people. Massage? Nice massage for nice people?'"

"Little did they know!" John joked, furrowing his eyebrows like a maniac. The friends laughed.

"We'd read about it in the guidebook," Marcia said. "You're not supposed to acknowledge them at all. You don't even look them in the eye. If you do, they'll never leave you alone. The beach boys. The male prostitutes, I mean. It's *sad*," she added. "Tragic. And, really, one wonders how anybody can starve in a place like that. There was food everywhere. Fruit on every tree. I just don't understand it. And the city was rife with garbage. *Rife!*" she proclaimed. She put down her fork. "Wouldn't you say, hon?"

"I wouldn't say 'rife,'" John answered, wiping the corners of his mouth with his cloth napkin. "Fragrant, more like."

The waiter collected the unfinished plates of pasta, then returned and took their orders of cheesecake and pie and decaffeinated coffee. John was quiet. He scrolled through photos on his cell phone, looking for a picture he'd taken of a monkey seated on the head of a Virgin Mary statue. The statue was painted in bright colors, and its nose was chipped, showing the white, chalky plaster under the paint. The monkey was black and skinny, with wide-spaced, neurotic eyes. Its tail curled under Mary's chin. John turned the screen of his phone toward the table.

"This little guy," he said.

"Aw!" the friends cried. They wanted to know, "Were the monkeys feral? Were they smelly? Are the people Catholic? Are they all very religious there?"

"Catholic," Marcia said, nodding. "And the monkeys were everywhere. Cute but very sneaky. One of them stole John's pen right out of his pocket." She rattled off whatever facts she could remember from the nature tour they'd taken. "I think there are laws about eating the monkeys. I'm not so sure. They all spoke English," she repeated, "but sometimes it was hard to understand them. The *guides*, I mean, not the monkeys." She chuckled.

"The monkeys spoke Russian, naturally," John said, and put away his phone. The table talk moved on to plans for renovating kitchens, summer shares, friends' divorces, new movies, books, politics, sodium, and cholesterol. They drank the coffees, ate the desserts. John peeled the wrapper off a roll of antacids. Marcia showed off her new wristwatch, which she'd purchased duty free at the airport. Then she reapplied her lipstick in the reflection in her water glass. When the check came, they all did the math, divvying up the cost. Finally, they paid and went out onto the street and the women hugged and the men shook hands.

"Welcome home," Jerry said. "Back to civilization."

"Ooh-ooh ah-ah!" John cried, imitating a monkey.

"Jesus, John," Marcia whispered, blushing and batting the air with her hand as if shooing a fly.

Each couple went off in a different direction. John was a bit drunk. He'd finished Marcia's second glass of wine because she'd said it was giving her a headache. He took her arm as they turned the corner onto East Eighty-second Street toward the park. The streets were nearly empty, late as it was. The whole city felt hushed, focused, like a young dancer counting her steps.

Marcia fussed with her silk scarf, also purchased duty free at the airport. The pattern was a paisley print in red and black and emerald green and had reminded her of the vibrant colors she'd seen the locals wearing on the island. Now she regretted buying the scarf. The tassels were short and fuzzy, and she thought they made the silk look cheap. She could give the scarf away as a gift, she supposed, but to whom? It had been so expensive, and her closest friends— the only people she would ever spend so much money on— had just seen her wearing it. She sighed and looked up at the moon as they entered the park.

"Thank God Jerry and Maureen are getting along again," Marcia said. "It was exhausting when they weren't."

"Marty was funny about the wine, wasn't he?" John said.

"I told him I was fine with Syrah. What does it matter? *Que sera, sera.*" He unhooked his arm from Marcia's elbow and put it around her shoulder.

"It gave me such a headache," Marcia complained. "Should we cut across the field or go around?"

"Let's be bold."

They stepped off the gravel onto the grass. It was a dark, clear night in the park, quiet except for the sound of distant car horns and ripping motors echoing faintly through the trees. John tried for a moment to forget that the city was right there, surrounding them. He'd been disappointed by how quickly his life had returned to normal after the vacation. As before, he woke up in the morning, saw patients all day long, returned home to eat dinner with Marcia, watched the evening news, bathed, and went to bed. It was a good life, of course. He wasn't suffering from a grave illness; he wasn't starving; he wasn't being exploited or enslaved. But, gazing out the window of the tour bus on the island, he had felt envious of the locals, of their ability to do whatever was in their nature. His own struggles seemed like petty complications, meaningless snags in the dull itinerary that was his life. Why couldn't he live by instinct and appetite, be primitive, be free?

At a rest stop, John had watched a dog covered in mange and bleeding pustules rub itself against a worn wooden signpost. He was lucky, he thought, not to be that dog. And then he felt ashamed of his privilege and his discontentedness. "I should be happy," he told himself. "*Marcia* is." Even the beggars tapping on car windows, begging for pennies, were smiling. "Hello, nice people," the beach boys had said. John had wanted to return their salutations and ask what it was that they had to offer. He'd been curious. But Marcia had shushed him, taken his hand, and plodded down the beach with her eyes fixed on the blank sand.

Crossing the lawn in Central Park, John now tried to recall the precise rhythm of the crashing waves on the beach on the island, the smell of the ocean, the magic and the danger he'd sensed brewing under the surface of things. But it was impossible. This was New York City. When he was in it, it was the only place on Earth. He looked up. The moon was just a sliver, a comma, a single eyelash in the dark, starless sky.

"I forgot to call Lenore," Marcia was saying as they walked. "Remind me tomorrow. She'll be upset if I don't call. She's so uptight."

They reached the edge of the lawn and stepped onto a paved path that led them up to a bridge over a plaza, where people were dancing in pairs to traditional Chinese music. John and Marcia stopped to watch the dark shapes moving in the soft light of lanterns. A young man on a skateboard rumbled past them.

"Home sweet home," Marcia said.

John yawned and tightened his arm around her shoulder. The silk of Marcia's scarf was slippery, like cool water rippling between his fingers. He leaned over and kissed her forehead. There she was, his wife of nearly thirty years. As they walked on, he thought of how pretty she'd been when they were first married. In all their years together, he had never been interested in other women, had never strayed, had even refused the advances of a colleague one night, a few years ago, at a conference in Baltimore. The woman had been twenty years his junior, and when she invited him up to her room John had blushed and made a stuttering apology, then spent the rest of the evening on the phone with Marcia. "What did she expect from me?" he'd asked. "Some kind of sex adventure?"

"We can watch that movie when we get home," Marcia said as they reached the edge of the park. "The one about the jazz musician."

"Whatever you like," John said. He yawned again.

"Maureen said it was worth watching."

"It's unconscionable what they are doing to you, Eduardo," Marcia said to the doorman in the lobby of their building. The doormen were petitioning management to provide a proper chair for them to sit in. All they had now was a tall stool with no back. "To have to stand for that many hours, doesn't that constitute torture? John is going to have a word with them. They'll do something. They have to." Marcia pulled the silk scarf from her neck and folded it in her hands.

Eduardo leaned on his little podium, propped his chin in his hand. "How was the vacation?" he asked.

"Oh, it was wonderful, wonderful. Everything. I mean, the seafood was just beyond compare! The ocean was like bathwater," Marcia answered. "And now we're utterly exhausted."

"Jet-lagged," John said.

Eduardo tapped his pen on the podium. "When I go home to my country, it's the same. I don't sleep."

"Yes, it's rough. Well, good night," Marcia sang.

She and John climbed the wide marble stairs to their second-floor apartment. They'd lived in the building for twenty-six years. They could have navigated their way through the lobby and up the stairs in complete darkness, and had, in fact, done so during a blackout one summer when all of Manhattan lost power for a night. Marcia had enjoyed it. They'd lit candles, eaten the ice cream that was going to melt anyway, and talked.

Now they walked down the bright, wallpapered hallway, and John unlocked the door to their apartment. Inside, there was still a stack of unopened mail on the front table, a blinking red light on the answering machine, a smell of mothballs from the closet where Marcia had been looking for her squash racket earlier that day. "I want to get it restrung *now*," she'd insisted, "before it's too late."

"Too late for what?" John had asked. "For when someone asks me to play." John had stood and watched his wife's bottom wiggle as she stooped down into the depths of the closet. She was in remarkable shape for a woman in her fifties. She often teased John that he needed to start taking better care of himself. "I'm going to make it to a hundred and five. You don't want me to have to replace you, do you?"

"You'd have no problem, I'm sure," John answered.

It was true. People liked Marcia. All of John and Marcia's friends were really friends of *hers*. John sometimes felt as if he were just a strange appendage to his wife. Surely she could have done better—a brain surgeon, a lawyer, a physicist. Had he given her the life she deserved? They did take a trip every year, usually in late summer to celebrate their anniversary, but that was all. They'd never had children. John had never won any awards.

"I'm going to take a Tylenol for my headache," Marcia said. "Want to get the movie set up?" She shut the closet door and ran her fingers across the squash racket, which now lay on the table in the hallway.

"Will you eat popcorn?" John asked.

"I really shouldn't. But if you're making some . . ." Her voice trailed off as she walked down the hallway to the bathroom, flicking on the lights and rubbing her temples.

John went to the kitchen and got the jar of popcorn kernels down from the cupboard. He liked to make popcorn the old-fashioned way, in a big steel pot with a long metal arm that stirred the kernels. He lit the stove, melted the margarine, poured the popcorn in, and stood over the pot with his eyes closed, turning the handle slowly and feeling the warm air rise toward him, remembering moments on the island when the sun on his face had struck him as so hot, so intimate, it was like Marcia's breath on his cheek.

As the kernels began to pop, he brought his ear to the lid of the pot, closer to the heat and the noise. The irregular staccato made his pulse speed up. The heart fascinated him. Sometimes he liked to put his ear to Marcia's chest and listen. Her heartbeat was light and chatty, a rhythm that made you want to waltz around the kitchen. John could have been a cardiologist, but he'd pursued dermatology instead. At parties, he wowed people with descriptions of boils and rashes and growths, strange hair patterns, nasty scars, pus-filled cysts, bizarre freckles, cancers, moles. "Within six feet of this fellow, you could detect the distinct smell of porcini risotto," he'd say. "His armpit was filled with fungus." At the stove, John righted himself, continued to stir the popcorn with one hand, and took his own pulse with two fingers of the other, pressing on his throat and breathing slowly until his heart rate returned to normal.

Meanwhile, Marcia took two extra-strength Tylenol, splashed some cold water on her face, brushed her teeth, and went to sit on the leather sofa in front of the television in the living room. A sudden excruciating pain in her head made her vision blurry. It was as if she'd been plunged underwater, the room murky and muffled, and she couldn't breathe. She tried to call out to John. "Honey? John?" She could only gasp. Her throat gurgled, her hands trembled, and then she died. It was that simple. She was gone.

When all was quiet, John turned off the stove and poured the popcorn into a wooden salad bowl. He carried the bowl and the saltshaker into the living room, sat down next to Marcia's dead body, salted the popcorn, ate several handfuls, and turned on the television. "Which movie did you say?"

he asked her, scrolling through the pay-per-view listings. He looked at her downturned face. Her head hung to one side, resting on her shoulder. John smoothed her hair, put a hand on her knee for a moment, changed the channel to the baseball game, lowered the volume, ate the rest of the popcorn, then fell asleep beside her.

"I'm sorry, Mr. John," Eduardo said in the lobby, as the body was wheeled out early the next morning. John nodded, still in shock, having woken up and discovered Marcia, cold and limp, slumped across the couch beside him. He followed the EMTs out onto the street and watched them load her into the back of the ambulance and drive away, the siren blaring—but for what? "She's already dead!" John cried out after them. Eduardo took him by the arm and led him back inside and up to the apartment. A neighbor brought him some water from the kitchen. The glass, a souvenir from a cruise that he and Marcia had taken through the fjords of Norway, retained a faint smear of her berry-colored lipstick on its rim. John put his mouth on it and sipped.

The memorial service was a week later. The chapel ceiling at St. Ignatius was vaulted and painted a cornflower blue with spiky white stars. The carpet was dark red, with a jagged gold pattern that reminded John of shattered glass. Marcia's friends filled the pews. They moaned and wept. Maureen and Barbara embraced John and held his hands and babbled all at once, drowning out the few words he had to say as he took his seat in the front pew. He dabbed at his eyes with old tissues he found squirreled away in the breast pocket of his suit.

Several friends told stories, boasting about how much Marcia had meant to them, how deeply she'd touched their lives. Marcia would have liked it, John thought—all these people discussing her, pointing out her best qualities, remembering her finest moments. She'd have eaten it up. But what did these people really know about her? What *could* one know about a person? John had known her best of all, had been able to predict her every move, the arc of her sighs, her laughs, the twists of her shadow as it crossed a room. In the days since her death, he'd felt her drifting through the apartment. He'd done double takes the way you do when you think you see your own cat or dog begging for food under the table at a restaurant. Nobody would understand, John thought, how well he knew the sound of Marcia's coffee spoon hitting the saucer, how the sheets rustled around her when she turned over in bed. But were those things significant enough, he wondered, to boast about?

When it was his turn to get up, John spoke of their recent trip to the island. "She was so happy there," he said. "So *alive*." He paused, waiting for a laugh, but there was none. He looked out at the crowd, all those drawn, wrinkled faces wet with emotion. He could imagine Marcia sitting among them, already composing her opinion of the speech he was giving. "He was terribly overcome," he imagined her saying to her friends over coffee and cake at the reception. "You could see him really straining to get something across. To no avail, I'm afraid. Well, that's John. Not the best talker. But that's why we got along so well."

John leaned against the lectern for balance, trying to think of interesting memories to relate. "The seafood," he began to say, but stopped himself. It all seemed so trite. "Why tell stories?" he wondered aloud. "As soon as something is over, that's it. Why revive it constantly? Things happen, and then more things, inevitably, happen next. So?" He shrugged. His hands trembled. He tried to smile, but he was now, indeed, terribly overcome. He left the lectern, tripping down the shallow steps. He felt as he did when he was gassed at the dentist's office—disoriented, befuddled. "Eduardo?" John called out. He staggered drunkenly. His secretary came up and guided him back to his seat.

Maureen took the stage next and recited what she claimed was one of Marcia's favorite poems. John pulled the last crumpled tissue from his breast pocket. He found a tiny wishbone wrapped up inside it. He recalled a dermatology-conference dinner, where quail had been served, a few years earlier. He'd planned on bringing the wishbone home so that he and Marcia could make a wish together. John always wished for whatever Marcia wished for. "This way, we both win," he said. Now he pulled the bone from the tissue and held it in his hand as he dried his tears. Poor Marcia, he thought. She could have wished for everlasting life.

"We passed the fields of gazing grain, we passed the setting sun," Maureen was saying, her voice swelling and shaking in a way that she must have rehearsed for days, John thought. He'd always secretly hated Maureen. Her tireless obsession with rain-forest conservation confounded him. The woman was from White Plains, for Christ's sake. He would not miss Maureen, or any of Marcia's friends, for that matter. "Poor Marcia, she really *loved* you, you know," Barbara had told him before the memorial. Of course he knew that Marcia loved him. They'd been married for nearly thirty years. People feel so special, so wise, when somebody they know drops dead. "We'd just seen her at dinner," he'd heard Maureen telling someone. "And to think, just a few hours later, she was gone forever. Isn't life strange?"

But life wasn't strange at all. Marcia's sudden death was the strangest thing that had ever happened to John. And even that wasn't very strange. People died all the time, in fact. As he crushed the tiny wishbone in his fist, it cracked into pointy shards that poked into the skin of his palm like needles. "Since then 'tis centuries; but each feels shorter than the day," Maureen continued. John shook his head at this nonsense. Listening to the stupid woman revel in the spotlight made him ill. He held his bleeding hand over his heart, feeling it pound like an ax through a thick wooden door. His throat clenched with what—*sorrow*? Was that all it was? He scoffed at how small that seemed. Then something seemed to break inside him. His breath caught. He choked and coughed. The wild thumping of his heart stopped. He belched loudly, from the depths of his gut, as though releasing some dark spirit that had been lodged down there his whole life. His secretary laid a hand on his shoulder. "Excuse me," John said, wiping saliva from his mouth. When he looked up again, Maureen's poem was over. He straightened in his seat and felt his heart start back up. Its beat was now soft and aimless, like a baby's babbling. He was calm, he thought. He was fine.

Next, Marcia's choir group took the stage and began to sing an old Negro spiritual. They sang lifelessly, as though the song didn't mean anything to them. Perhaps it didn't. John rose and walked up the aisle to the bathroom at the back of the chapel. He blew his nose for a while in the stall, urinated, defecated, then flushed the broken wishbone down the toilet.

A week later, John still had not returned to work. He spent his days in silence, eating duty-free Ferrero Rocher chocolates and bouncing the strings of Marcia's squash racket against his skull. He paced the apartment, his mind empty but for the bits of music he heard from cars passing on the street outside. Or he sat on the leather sofa in front of the muted television, which was showing back-to-back episodes of true-crime docudramas. People liked to kill one another, it seemed, on speedboats. Aliases, disguises, offshore bank accounts—these notions began to pepper John's mind. With Marcia gone, perhaps he could fill his remaining years with criminal pursuits, he thought. He was too clumsy to be a cat burglar. But couldn't he stalk someone? Or vandalize something? Library books? The backseats of taxis? Easiest would be to send death threats to someone he despised—Maureen, perhaps. He could do that without even leaving the apartment. He winced at his cowardice. At every stage of his life he'd been reasonable, dutiful. He'd prescribed creams, lanced cysts, cut plantar warts out of the rubbery soles of smelly feet. Once, he'd pulled a seven-foot coil of ingrown hair from an abscess on the tip of a patient's tailbone. That was as wild as it got for John. He'd never been in a fight. His body bore no scars. The hands now folded in his lap were bland, beige, wrinkled in all the predictable ways.

The spot he'd chosen for the urn of Marcia's ashes was on a shelf in the kitchen, next to the coffee grinder and the mini food processor that she had used expressly for guacamole. "The secret is to freeze it first," he recalled her saying. Or was that something else? John didn't care. He'd had enough of what people said, tips and tales, theories, tidbits. If he could have it his way, nobody would ever say anything again. The entire world would go silent. Even the clocks wouldn't tick. All that mattered would be the beating of hearts, the widening and narrowing of pupils, the whirling of ties and loose strands of hair in the wind—nothing voluntary, nothing false. He opened the fridge and peeled back the tinfoil from a dish one of the friends had brought over. Fat from the chicken had congealed into a dun-colored jelly. He stuck his finger in it, just to feel the cold gunk.

Then the phone rang.

"And?" is how John answered. The voice on the line was

a recording from the local convenience store. Marcia's photos had been printed and were ready to be picked up. She'd used a disposable camera on their trip to the island. John hung up the phone. Marcia's purse was where she'd left it, on the table in the hallway. He rifled through and found the claim stub in her wallet. Without changing out of his pajamas, he put on a jacket and shoes and went down to the lobby.

"How are you, Mr. John?" Eduardo asked. He followed John to the door and opened it, his black rubber shoes squeaking on the polished marble floor.

John didn't answer. He had nothing to say. He let his head hang and plodded slowly down the block. He didn't care if people thought he looked forlorn or deranged. Let them judge. Let them entertain themselves with their stories, he thought.

At the convenience store, he went to the counter and pulled out the claim stub. When the shopgirl asked for his last name, he handed over his business card.

"Can you confirm the home address?" she asked.

John shook his head.

The girl rolled her eyes. "Are you deaf or something?" she asked.

"Maaa, haa," John said. He ground his jaws and pointed to his ears.

"OK," the girl said, softening. She held up a finger. "One minute."

John nodded. Why would she need to confirm his address, anyway? What kind of impostor would want someone else's photographs? Someone with a speedboat, perhaps. John laughed at himself. "Maaa, haa," he said again.

"I'm sorry, sir. I can't understand you," the girl said. She slid the packet of photos across the counter and pointed to the glowing numbers on the cash register's display screen. She held up her forefinger and thumb and rubbed them together. "Money," she said. "*Dinero.*"

"Gaaah," John said. He handed her the cash, then grunted. The girl waved good-bye cheerfully. If Marcia could see him now, acting like some kind of Frankenstein, she'd laugh, John thought.

He pulled the photos from their sleeve and shuffled through them on the way home. There were half a dozen shots of ocean waves, the horizon, and several street scenes, each interrupted by the splatter of bird shit on the car window through which they'd been taken. Nothing looked as beautiful as it had in real life. The people, the buildings, the beach—it was all flat and dull, despite the glossy finish of the photo paper. There was a close-up of cocktails served in coconuts and decorated with toothpick-speared chunks of pineapple and orange slices and Maraschino cherries, colorful paper umbrellas, curlicue straws. On either side of the frame were the brown, deeply lined hands of the server holding the raffia tray. There was a shot of Marcia's ankles, her feet plunged deep into the pale-gray sand. It had been gritty, soft, dry volcanic ash, like what was left of Marcia in the urn in the kitchen, John supposed. There were a few photos of the pool snapped from the balcony of their hotel room, a blurry shot of John on his cell phone in the lobby, one of John shaking hands with a tiny monkey in the forest, John shaking hands with the nature guide, John eating a platter of crabs. There was only one photo of Marcia, a self-portrait taken in the reflection of the vanity mirror in the hotel bathroom. She smiled coquettishly in her berry-colored lipstick, her face a floating mask above the white orb of the flash.

The final photo in the set seemed to be an extra, a half exposure at the end of the roll. The right side of the picture was gray, empty. A red line went down the center like a burn mark. The left side showed the grainy landscape of the beach at night, and, in the bottom corner, the top half of a face. It belonged to a local, a native. A beach boy, John presumed, one of those male prostitutes. The dark skin appeared almost black in the dimness of the picture. Only the whites of the eyes glistened, almost yellow, like hanging lanterns. Marcia had taken the photo by accident, John supposed. But when had she come so close to a beach boy? She'd made such a fuss about keeping her distance. During that first walk, when the beach boys had followed them, Marcia had hurried back to the hotel grounds and insisted vehemently that John look away. "If you make eye contact, it's like an invitation," she'd said.

"To what?" John had asked.

"To a party you wouldn't like," she'd answered, "and that you'd have to pay for."

"Would *you* like it?" he'd asked. He'd been joking, of course. Marcia had said nothing.

"Hello, nice people? Hello?"

At home, John found Marcia's magnifying glass in her bedside drawer. He sat down, turned on the lamp, and held the magnifying glass over the beach boy's eyes, hoping he might find some kind of explanation reflected in them. Had Marcia been unfaithful? Had she been pretending, as long as John had known her, to be a prude? He craned his neck and brought his own eye closer and closer to the photo, squinting, straining every muscle until he found something he took to be a sign, an invitation—a single red pixel in the darkness of the boy's right pupil.

Back on the island, John stood once again in the hotel lobby. The overnight flight had been bumpy. He hadn't slept at all. The radio in the hotel shuttle from the airport had warned of hurricane-force gales, possible flooding, thunder, lightning. A murky bank of clouds crept slowly but steadily across the sky.

"Will we have to evacuate?" John asked.

The desk attendant rubbed her eyes. "Maybe, sir. They don't tell us anything." She slid John's room key across the counter. Behind the check-in desk, the clerks were talking and yawning and sharing small cookies from a grease-soaked paper bag. John remembered the cookies from a tour of the market on the other side of the island. The guide had explained to him and Marcia that the cookies were made not from flour but from some native root vegetable, molasses, and butter that came from goat's milk. A sack of twenty cookies cost less than a dollar.

"Can you imagine?" Marcia had whispered.

John had hoped that the guide would arrange for them to try some, but they'd simply idled by the vendor's cart, Marcia covering her mouth and nose with a tissue, while the guide chatted with a passerby in the local patois. *Rife*, John recalled now. The sights and sounds and smells of the market came back to him. There were bowls of spices and beans of every hue, hot goat's milk poured from dirty metal teapots atop charcoal briquettes into small plastic cups like the ones John used at the dentist's to rinse and spit. Hot smoke from cauldrons of roasting meat roiled across baskets of nuts and fruits, stacks of woven shawls that the women used as slings to carry their babies on their backs, pyramids of pastel-colored toilet-paper rolls. In a dark corner of the market, they'd passed an old man, his eyes sky blue with cataracts. He sat behind a table full of empty Coke bottles and tin cans. Beside him was a rickety chest of drawers. When John asked what the man was selling, the guide answered "spiritual medicine," twirled his finger in the air, and widened his eyes, as though to make fun of the crazy old man. "People in the villages believe in that nonsense," the guide said. "They believe in magic. Evil." He crossed himself and laughed, then yelled at a young girl who had splashed dirty water on his shoes while rolling her bike through a puddle on the path. One of Marcia's photos had been of that market. The royal-blue plastic tarps covering the stalls appeared nearly black, like funeral shrouds. Recalling that image now gave John the chills. He'd told everyone back home that he was going to the island to scatter Marcia's ashes. That was the excuse he gave.

As John unlocked the door of his hotel room, a family passed by him in the hall—parents with three sleepy children.

"Last flight back to the mainland," the father said with a British accent, his arms full of gape-mouthed, plush toy monkeys.

John wasn't very worried. The beach boys would not get swept away in any flood, he knew. He had spotted a few of them already on the drive from the hotel. For prostitutes, he thought, they seemed so relaxed walking along the road, so casual in their sun-bleached striped T-shirts, their rubber sandals grinding over the gray dirt. His plan was to find the boy from Marcia's photo and do whatever she had done with him off in the dunes at night while he was sleeping. That would be revenge enough to set his heart at ease, he thought. It would be the strange thing that gave his life some meaning at last. It would be his life's one adventure.

He inspected his hotel room, approving of the lone queen-size bed, the flat-screen mounted on the wall, the small window that looked out onto the beach. The sky had an eerie, vapid whiteness. John could see the red-tiled roof of the hotel's al-fresco dining area and one corner of the fence that partitioned the beach. To get to a private spot where he could dump the ashes in the water, he'd have to go beyond that fence. A few beach boys sat perched in the dunes beyond the hotel, like exotic birds in their bright-colored shorts.

Even with no sun to reflect off their taut dark-brown skin, their bare backs gleamed. If only he had Marcia's opera glasses, John thought, he could see their faces.

The heavy-duty black plastic bag containing Marcia's ashes had passed through customs undetected. Of course, John had left the metal urn at home. He figured that if anyone asked what the bag contained he'd say that it was medicinal bath salts to soak his feet in. But nobody questioned him. He took Marcia's ashes out of his suitcase, carried the bag down to the empty dining room, selected a stale roll from the breakfast-buffet table, sat and ate it, and pocketed a knife from the place setting. He nodded and smiled at the hotel workers, who were busy shuttering the windows in preparation for the storm.

Outside, the wind whipped at John's face, forcing him to pitch his head forward as he walked along the fence. Sand pricked at his skin like needles. As he approached the waves, the sky flashed. A moment later, thunder pealed long and deep, and a few cold drops of rain fell on his back. He crouched by the water and took out the knife. It was a cheap knife, with dull, wide serrations. The plastic of the bag was so thick that he had to place it on the sand, hold it down with one hand, and stab at it repeatedly. To keep the sand out of his eyes, he shut them. He thought one last time of Marcia, pictured her clucking her tongue at this indecorous ceremony. He thought of all the wishbone wishes he'd wasted on her petty desires: good seats at the movies, a trip to Vermont to see the foliage, a sale on cashmere sweaters or towels. And, secretly, all along she'd been a whore, he thought, a deviant, a pervert, carousing with prostitutes right under his nose! Meanwhile, she'd shushed him every time he'd said anything remotely off-color, as if anyone were paying attention, as if it even mattered. John tore at the hole he'd made in the plastic bag, crawled over the sand on his knees, felt for the water, and dumped the ashes out.

A mere hour later, the storm was over. The sky was gray, but the rain had stopped. Little damage had been done to the island, though the hotel had lost electricity. John's room was dim. From his window, he watched the ocean pounding the beach in tall, floating waves, as the wind howled like a cartoon ghost in a haunted house, comically persistent. He stood and uselessly pressed the buttons on the TV remote, then stared at his reflection in the rectangular black screen. He was still wearing what he'd worn on the overnight flight: his gray summer-weight wool trousers and a white linen dress shirt. The shirt was now crushed and wrinkled, the collar warped around his neck. His face was swollen, his ears full of sand. His graying hair lay in waxy tendrils around his face. He laughed at his slovenly appearance and tried to smooth his hair back, but the rain and the salt air had dried it into straw. He didn't care. Marcia was gone for good now, and he felt like celebrating.

Downstairs in the empty restaurant, John took a seat on a bar stool. Outside, workers were unfolding the shutters from the dining-room windows. The clouds over the ocean were paler and thinner than before. He ordered a Glenfiddich, saluted the bartender, and drank. "How much for the whole bottle?" John asked. "No, don't tell me. Just charge it to my room." He flashed the number on his key. A whole bottle just for him, out from under Marcia's shaming gaze. Why had he let her control him like that? He'd lived his entire life on his best behavior, a slave to decorum. For what? John shook his head and poured himself more whiskey. He could do whatever he wanted now. He could buy a hundred goat-butter cookies. He could make all the crass jokes he liked. Through the windows, he saw the clouds part and the sun shine. The staff began to drag the lounge chairs and tables and umbrellas back onto the deck. A few large gulls coasted back and forth, low across the beach. John smacked his lips, slid off his bar stool, and took the bottle of Glenfiddich down to the sand, carelessly kicking off his salt-stained leather loafers and peeling off his socks on the way. He walked around the hotel fence and along the shoreline for several minutes, well past the spot where he'd dumped Marcia's ashes.

The sand was cool and hard under his feet. The waves were high and frothy still, but he could swim, he thought, chugging from the bottle. He looked around to see if anyone was watching. The beach was empty. He stuck the Glenfiddich in the sand, quickly removed his pants, and started sloshing into the warm, churning water. He waded in waist high, stiffening his body against the turbulent gushes, which seemed somehow gentle and powerful at once. He looked out at the horizon. This was what the beach was good for: staring out at the sea gave one the feeling of infinity. But it was an illusion, John thought. The sea wasn't infinite. There was land on the other side. Wasn't that always the truth about things? That they ended? How many more years did he have, at this point? Ten? Twenty? A powerful wave knocked him down, and when he righted himself and found his footing he was facing the shore. A beach boy in tiny, bright-red shorts stood on the sand, watching him. John waved and hollered "Hello!" just before the next wave pulled him under.

A few weeks later, telling the story over dinner, John would explain that the storm had kept him cooped up for days. "It barely made a dent, that storm. But everything shut down. You know these poor countries—there's no infrastructure. Even if you did try to intervene and make some order, the people are all so superstitious, it would take a hundred years, with all their spells and blessings."

"Well, I think it's beautiful of you," Maureen said, "to go back there, with Marcia."

"She said it was heaven, after all," Barbara said. "Didn't she say that? That it was heaven?"

"She did say that, yes," Maureen answered.

John put a hand over his heart, which was now broken by something he found far more interesting than a dead wife. His drunken jaunt on the beach had ended strangely. The beach boy, though not the one who'd appeared in Marcia's photograph, had indeed been young and beautiful, his eyes yellow, his lips thick and glossy. He'd spotted John flailing in the undertow, pulled him from the water, and dragged him to shore. John had rolled onto his side, sputtering and gagging on the salt water he'd swallowed. The boy stood over him, his strong brown legs just inches from John's naked body. "You saved me," John managed to say. As he reached a hand out to grip the boy's ankle, his fingers trembled. Some kind of force field seemed to surround the boy. He couldn't be touched. When John held his palm over the boy's foot, he could feel heat rising up. The boy took a step away. Perhaps he isn't even real, John thought. But there he was. "Come here," John demanded. "I need to ask you something." He got onto his hands and knees, tried to stand, but he was too exhausted. He was drunk. He collapsed on the sand. The boy stood and stared for a while, then yawned, turned, and walked away. It was clear to him and to the other beach boys watching from their perch in the dunes that the old man wasn't carrying any money.

The house was white stucco, ranch style, with tall hedges and a large semicircular driveway. There was a crumbling pool out back full of rust stains and carcasses of squirrels that had fallen in and slowly starved to death. I used to tan out there on a lawn chair before auditions, fantasizing about getting rich and famous. My room had green shag carpeting and a twin-size bed on a plywood frame, a little nightstand with a child's lamp in the shape of a clown. Above my bed hung an old framed poster of Marlon Brando in *One-Eyed Jacks*. It would have done me well if I'd prayed to that poster, but I'd never even heard of Marlon Brando before. I was eighteen. I was living in an area of Los Angeles called Hancock Park: manicured lawns, big clean houses, expensive cars, a country club. Walking around those quiet streets, I felt like I was on the set of a soap opera about the private lives of business executives and their sexy wives. One day I'd star in something like that, I hoped. I had limited experience as an actor in high school, first as George in *Our Town* and then as Romeo in *Romeo and Juliet*. People had told me I looked like a sandy-haired Pierce Brosnan. I was broke, and I was a nobody, but I was happy.

Those first few months in Los Angeles, I lived off powdered cinnamon doughnuts and orange soda, fries from Astro Burger, and occasional joints rolled with stale weed my stepdad had given me back in Utah as a graduation present. Most days I took the bus around Hollywood, listening to the Eagles on my Walkman and imagining what life was like for all those people way up in the hills. I'd walk up Rossmore, which turned into Vine once you hit Hollywood, and then I'd get on a crosstown local down Santa Monica Boulevard. I liked to sit with all the young kids in school uniforms, the teenage runaways in rags and leather jackets, the crazies, the drunks, housekeepers with their romance novels, old men with their spittle, whores with their hair spray. This was miraculous to me. I'd never seen people like that before. Sometimes I studied them like an actor would, noting their postures, their sneering or sleeping faces, but I wasn't very gifted. I was observant, but I couldn't act. When the bus reached the beach, I'd get off and run up and down the stairs that led from the street to the shoreline. I'd take off my shirt, lie out on the sand, catch some rays, look at the water for a minute, then take the bus back home.

In the evenings, I bused tables in a pizza parlor on Beverly

Boulevard. Nobody important ever came in. Mostly I brought out baskets of bread and carafes of box wine, picked up pizza crusts and grease-soaked napkins. I never ate the food there. Somehow that felt beneath me. If I didn't have to work and there was a game going on, I'd take the bus out to Dodger Stadium and walk around just to get a feel for the crowd, the excitement. Nearby, in Elysian Park, I found a spot on a little cliff where I could listen to the cheers from the crowd and watch the traffic on the freeway, the mountains, the pale gray and sandy terrain. With all those ugly little streets in the ravine down below, LA looked like anywhere. It made me miss Gunnison. Sometimes I'd smoke a joint and walk around the swaying eucalyptus, peek into the cars parked along the fire road. Sedate, unblinking Mexicans sat in jalopies in shadows under the trees. Middle-aged men in dark glasses flicked their cigarettes out their windows as I passed. I had some idea of what they were doing there. I did not return anyone's leers. I stayed out of the woods. At home, alone, I concentrated on whatever was on television. I had a black-and-white mini Toshiba. It was the first big thing I'd ever bought with my own money back in Gunnison and the most expensive thing I owned.

My landlady's name was Mrs. Honigbaum. When I lived with her, she would have been in her late sixties. She wore a short dark-blond wig and large gold-framed eyeglasses. Her fingernails were long and fake and painted pink. Her posture was stooped in the shiny quilted housecoat she wore when she walked around. Usually she sat behind her desk in a sleeveless blouse, her thin, spotted arms swaying as she gestured and pulled Kools from a tooled leather cigarette case. Her ears and nose were humongous, and the skin on her face was stretched up toward her temples in a way that made her look stunned all the time. Her makeup was like stage makeup, or what they put on dead bodies in open caskets. It was applied heavy-handedly, in broad strokes of blue and pink and bronze. Still, I didn't think she was unattractive. I had never met a Jew before, or anyone intellectual at all back in Gunnison.

Mrs. Honigbaum rented rooms in her house for forty-five dollars a week to young men who came to her through a disreputable talent agent—my agent. Forty-five dollars a week wasn't cheap at the time, but my agent had made the arrangements and I didn't question him. His name was Bob Sears. I never met him face to face. I'd found him by calling the operator back in Gunnison and asking to speak to a Los Angeles talent scout. Bob Sears took me on as a client "sight unseen" because, he said, I sounded good-looking and American over the phone. He said that once I had a few odd gigs under my belt, I could start doing ad work on game shows, then commercials, then bit roles on soaps, then small parts in sitcoms, then prime-time dramas. Soon Scorsese would come knocking, he said. I didn't know who Scorsese was, but I believed him.

Once I got to town, I called Bob Sears nearly every weekday morning to find out where to go for auditions and what time to be there. Mrs. Honigbaum let me use the phone in her bedroom. I think I was the only tenant to have that privilege. Her bedroom was dark and humid, with tinted glass doors looking out onto the swimming pool. Mirrors lined one wall. Everything smelled of vanilla and mouthwash and mothballs. A dresser was topped with a hundred glass vials of perfumes and potions and serums I guessed were meant to keep her youthful. There was a zebra-skin rug, a shiny floral bedspread. The ceiling lamp was a yellow crystal chandelier. When the door to the bathroom was open, I saw the flesh-colored marble, a vanity covered in makeup and brushes and pencils, a bare Styrofoam head. The lightbulbs were fixed along the edges of the mirror, like in backstage dressing rooms. I was very impressed by that. I went in there and studied my face in that lighting, but only for a minute at a time. I didn't want to get caught. While I was on the phone with Bob Sears, the maid sometimes flitted in and out, depositing stacks of clean towels, collecting the crumpled, lipstick-smeared tissues from the waste bin by the bed. The phone was an old rotary, the numbers faded and greasy, and the receiver smelled like halitosis. The smell didn't really bother me. In fact, I liked everything about Mrs. Honigbaum. She was kind. She was generous. She flattered and cajoled me, the way grandmothers do.

Bob Sears had said I'd need a head shot, so before I'd left Gunnison, my mother drove me to the mall in Ephraim to have my portrait taken. I had a lazy, wandering eye, and so I wasn't allowed to drive. She drove me resentfully, sighing and tapping her finger on the steering wheel at red lights, complaining about how late it was, how hard she'd worked all day, how the mall gave her a headache. "I guess in Hollywood they have chauffeurs to drive you around and servants to make your food," she said. "And butlers to pick up your dirty underwear. Is that what you expect? Your Highness?"

"I'm going to Hollywood to work," I reminded her. "As an actor. It's a job. People really do it."

"I don't see why you can't be an actor here, where everybody already knows you. Everybody loves you here. What's so terrible about that?"

"Because nobody here knows anything," I explained. "So what they think doesn't matter."

"Keep biting the hand and it might slap you across the face one day," she said. "Boys like you are a dime a dozen out there. You think those Hollywood people will be lining up just to tie your shoes? You think you're so lucky? You want an easy life? You want to roller-skate on the beach? Even the hairs on your head are numbered. Don't forget that."

I really did want an easy life. I looked out the window at the short little houses, the flat open plains, the sky purple and orange, blinding sparks of honey-colored light shooting over the western mountains where the sun went down. "Nothing ever happens here," I said.

"You call fireworks over the reservoir nothing? How about that public library you've never once set foot in? How about all those teachers who I had to beg not to fail you? You think you're smarter than all them? Smarter than teachers?"

"No," I answered. I knew I wasn't smart back then. Being an actor seemed like an appropriate career for someone like me.

"You're running out on your sister, on Larry," said my mother. "What can I say? Just don't get yourself murdered. Or do. It's your life." She turned up the radio. I kept quiet for the rest of the drive.

My life in Gunnison really wasn't that bad. I was popular and I had fun, and pretty girls followed me around. I'd been like a celebrity in my high school—prom king, class president. I was voted "most likely to succeed" even though my grades were awful. I could have stayed in Gunnison, gotten a job at the prison, worked up the ranks, married any girl I chose, but that wasn't the kind of life I wanted. I wanted to be a star. The closest movie theater was in Provo, an hour and a half away. I'd seen *Rocky* and *Star Wars* there. Whatever else I'd watched came through one of the three TV channels we had in Gunnison. I didn't particularly like movies. It seemed like hard work to act in something that went on for so long. I thought I could move to Hollywood and get a role on a show like *Eight Is Enough* as the cool older brother. And later I could be like Starsky on *Starsky and Hutch*.

I explained all this to the photographer at the mall. "People say I look like Pierce Brosnan," I told him. He said he agreed, handed me a flimsy plastic comb, told me to sit down and wait my turn. I remember the little kids and babies in fancy clothes in the waiting room, crying and nagging their mothers. I combed my hair and practiced making faces in the mirror on the wall. My mother went to Rydell's and came back with a new rhinestone belt on. "Discount," she said. I suspect she lifted it. She did that when she was in a bad mood. Then she sat down next to me and read *People* magazine and smoked. "Don't smile too much," she said when it was my turn with the photographer. "You don't want to look desperate."

Oh, my mother. A week later she drove me to the bus stop. It was barely five in the morning and she still wore her burgundy satin negligee and curlers in her hair, a denim jacket thrown over her sunburned shoulders. She drove slowly on the empty roads, coasted through the blinking red lights as though they didn't exist, stayed silent as the moon. Finally she pulled over and lit a cigarette. I watched a tear coast down her cheek. She didn't look at me. I opened the car door. "Call me" is all she said. I said I would. I watched as she pulled a U-turn and drove away.

Gunnison was mostly empty fields, long gray roads. At night the prison lights oriented you to the north; dark, sleeping wolves of mountains to the east and west. The south was a mystery to me. The farthest I'd ever gone down Highway 89 was to the airport, and that was just to see an air show once when I was a kid. I had never even left Utah before I moved to Los Angeles. I fell asleep on the bus, my little Toshiba under my feet, and woke up in Cedar City when a fat man got on and took the seat next to me. He edged me against the window and chain-smoked for three and a half hours, his body roiling and thundering each time he coughed. In the dim bus, flashes of light bounced off the mirrored lenses of his sunglasses, smudged by fingers greasy from the dough-nuts he was eating. I watched him pick out the little crumbs from the folds of his crotch and lick his hands. "The Garden of Eden," he said. "Have you been to Vegas?" I shook my head no. All the money I had in the world was folded up in the front pocket of my jeans. The bulge there embarrassed me. "I go for poker," the man gasped.

"I'm going to Hollywood to be an actor," I told him. "On television, or in movies."

"Thatta boy," he replied. "The slimmest odds reap the highest payouts. But it takes balls. That's why I can't play roulette. No balls." He coughed and coughed.

This cheered me to hear. I was bold. I was courageous. I was exceptional. I had big dreams. And why shouldn't I? My mother had no idea what real ambition was. Her father was a janitor. Her father's father had been a farmer. Her mother's father had been a pastor at the prison. I would be the first in a succession of losers to make something of myself. One day I'd be escorted through the streets in a motorcade, and the entire world would know my name. I'd send checks home. I'd send autographed posters from movies I starred in. I'd give my mom a fur coat and diamonds for Christmas. Then she'd be sorry she ever doubted me. We crossed into Nevada, the blank desert like a spot on a map that had been rubbed away with an eraser. I stared out the window, imagining, praying. The fat man caressed my thigh several times, perhaps by accident. He got off in Las Vegas, at last, and a black lady got on and took his seat. She batted the smoky air with a white-gloved hand. "Never again," she said, and pulled out a paperback Bible.

I put on my earphones and busied my mind with the usual request: *Dear God, please make me rich and famous. Amen.*

Mrs. Honigbaum was a writer. Her gossip column, "Reach for the Stars," ran in a weekly coupon circular distributed for free in strip malls and car washes and Laundromats around town. The gossip she reported was unoriginal—who got engaged, who had a baby, who committed suicide, who got canned. She also wrote the circular's monthly horoscopes. She said it was easy to steal predictions from old newspapers and switch the words around. It was all nonsense, she told me.

"You want voodoo? Here." She pulled her change purse from a drawer and fished out a penny. "The first cent you've earned as an actor. I'm paying you. Take it, and give me a smile." Once she even made me sign one of my head shots, promising that she wouldn't sell it, even when it was worth millions. "Don't get too attached to who you are," she said. "They'll make you change your name, of course. Nobody's name is real out here. My real name was Yetta," she said, yelling over the clamor of her TVs. "Nobody here calls me that. Yetta Honigbaum, can you imagine? First I was Yetta Goslinski. Mr. Honigbaum—" She pointed to a small golden urn on top of her filing cabinet. "Now I have no family to speak of. Most of them were gassed by the Nazis. You've heard of Hitler? He had the brains but not the brawn, as they say. That's what made him crazy. I was lucky. I escaped to Hollywood, like you. Welcome, welcome. I learned English in six days just reading magazines and listening to the radio. That's brains. And believe it or not, I was a very pretty girl once. You can call me Honey. It's a lonely life."

She said she didn't believe in fate or magic. There was hard work and there was luck. "Luck and hard work. Good looks and intelligence. In this city, it's rarely a two-for-one." I remember her telling me that the day I moved in. "Any fool can see you're handsome. But are you smart at all? Are you at least reasonable? That counts for a lot here. You'll catch on. Did you see this?" She held up the cover of a flimsy magazine showing Jack Nicholson picking his nose. "This is good. This is interesting. People like to see celebrities at their worst. It brings the stars back to earth, where they belong. Listen to me. Don't go crazy. I should warn you that there are cults in this city, some better than others. People ask you to open a vein, you walk away. You hear me?" She made me fill out a form and sign my name on a letter stating that if anything happened to me, if tragedy struck, she would take no responsibility. "I don't know what they teach you in Utah, but even Jesus would get greedy here. The Masons, the satanists, the CIA, they're all the same. You can talk to me. I'm one of the good ones. And call your mother," she said.

I had no desire to speak to my mother. I took a mint

candy from the crystal bowl on Mrs. Honigbaum's desk. "My mother and I don't really get along," I said.

Mrs. Honigbaum put down her pen. Her shoulders slumped. I could see the fringe of her real hair poking out from under her wig in short gray tufts across her forehead. Tight bubbles of sweat, murky with makeup, studded the deep lines of her wrinkled cheeks. "You think you're the first? My mother was a terror. She beat me black and blue, made me chew on bars of soap any time I mouthed off. She forced me to walk miles in the rain to get her plums from a tree, then beat me because they were full of worms. And yet I mourn her passing. I'm a grown woman, and still I cry. You only have one mother. Mine got starved to death and thrown in a trench full of rotting corpses. You are lucky yours is still living. If I were a Christian I would cross myself. Now go call her. You know she loves you." And still I didn't call.

I felt safe at Mrs. Honigbaum's house. I trusted her. She said there'd been an incident only once. A girl had stolen one of her rings. "It was a ruby, my mother's birthstone," she told me dolefully. Because of that, it was forbidden to bring guests into the house. I had a lock on my door but I never used it. There was a guest bathroom all the tenants shared. We had to sign our names to book shower time on a piece of paper taped up in the hallway. Mrs. Honigbaum never gossiped about the tenants, but I had the sense that I was the one she liked best. One tenant was a voice actor for some cartoon show I'd never heard of. He walked around barefoot and shirtless, perpetually gargling and speaking in a falsetto, to keep his vocal cords from seizing, he explained. There was also a man in his thirties, which seemed ancient to me at the time. He was always widening his eyes as though he'd just seen something unbelievable. He had deep creases in his forehead as a result. I saw him carrying a painting to his car once. It was a portrait of Dracula. He said a friend was borrowing it for a music video. Another guy was an aspiring makeup artist. He always wore flip-flop sandals, and I could hear him flapping up and down the hall at odd hours. Once I caught him without any clothes on, thrusting his genitals into the cold steam of the refrigerator. When I cleared my throat, he just turned around and flapped back down the hall.

My room was next door to Mrs. Honigbaum's office, so from morning to night I could hear celebrity news blaring from her six or seven televisions. The noise didn't really bother me. Every morning when I passed her open doorway on the way to the shower, her maid would be spraying the carpet where the poodle had shit. Stacks of old tabloids flapped in the breeze from an industrial-sized fan. The poodle was old and its hair was yellowed and reddish in spots that made it look like it was bleeding. It was always having "bathroom mishaps," as Mrs. Honigbaum called them. Whenever Rosa, the maid, saw me without a shirt on, she covered her eyes with her hands. Mrs. Honigbaum sat at her desk and stared at her television screens, sweating and taking notes. It seemed like she never went to bed.

"Good morning," I'd say.

"A sight to behold," exclaimed Mrs. Honigbaum. "Rosa,

isn't he beautiful?" Rosa didn't seem to speak English. "Ah!
My menopause," Mrs. Honigbaum cried, shoveling barium
supplements past her dentures. "Thanks for reminding me.
Look at you." She shook her head. "People will think I'm
running a brothel. Go get yourself some lemonade. I insist.
Rosa. Lemonade. *Dónde está la* lemonade?" With all the
rejection I got at auditions, it was nice to be home and be
somebody's favorite.

One afternoon, as I was coming in from tanning, Mrs. Honigbaum invited me to dine with her. It was only five o'clock.
"Someone was going to come, so Rosa cooked. But now he's
not coming. Please join me, or else it will go to waste." I had
the night off from work, so I happily accepted her invitation.
The kitchen was all dark wood, with orange counters and a
refrigerator the size of a Buick. The white tablecloth was
stained with coffee rings. "Sit," said Mrs. Honigbaum as she
pulled the meat loaf from the oven. Her oven mitts were like
boxing gloves over her tiny, knobby hands. "Tell me everything," she said. "Did you have any auditions today? Any
breaks?"

I'd spent most of the day on a bus out to Manhattan
Beach, where Bob Sears said a guy would be expecting me
at his apartment. I arrived late and rang the doorbell. When
the door opened, a seven-foot-tall black man appeared. He
plucked my head shot out of my hands, pulled me inside,
took a Polaroid of me without my shirt on, gave me his card

and a can of 7UP, and pushed me out the door. "It was a quick meeting," I told Mrs. Honigbaum. "I didn't have many lines to read."

She slid a woven-straw place mat in front of me, plunked down a knife and fork. "I'm glad it went so well. Others have a harder time of it. They take things too personally. That's why I know you're going to make it big. You've got a thick skin. Just don't make the same mistake I made," she said. "Don't fall in love. Love will ruin you. It turns off the light in your eyes. See?" Her eyes were small, blurry, and buried under wrinkled, blue-shadowed lids and furry fake lashes. "Dead," she affirmed. She pointed upward to the ceiling. "Every day I mourn." She cleared her throat. "Now here, eat this." She returned to the table with a dinner plate piled high with meat loaf. I hadn't eaten a home-cooked meal since Gunnison, so I devoured it quickly. She herself ate a small bowl of cottage cheese. "That is kasha," she said, pointing to a boiling pot on the stove. "I would offer you some, but you'll hate it. It tastes like cats. I make it at night and eat it for breakfast, cold, with milk. I'm an old lady. I don't need much. But you, you eat as much as you can stomach. And tell me more. What did Bob say? He must be very proud of you for all you're doing. I hope you're going to call your mother."

I still hadn't called my mother. By then I'd been in Los Angeles for several months.

"My mother doesn't want to talk. She doesn't want me to be an actor. She thinks it's a waste of time."

Mrs. Honigbaum put down her spoon. Under the harsh

light from the hanging lamp over the kitchen table, her fake eyelashes cast spidery shadows on her taut rouged cheeks. She shook her head. "Your mother loves you," she said. "How could she not? Just look at you!" she cried, raising her arms. "You're like a young Greek god!"

"She'd be happier if I came home. But even if I did, she wouldn't love me. She can't stand me most of the time. Everything I do makes her angry. I don't think she'd even care if I died. There's nothing I can do about it."

"It's impossible," cried Mrs. Honigbaum. Her rings clanked as she clasped her hands together as if in prayer. "Every mother loves her son. She doesn't tell you she loves you?"

"Never," I lied. "Not once."

"She must be sick," said Mrs. Honigbaum. "My mother nearly killed me twice, and still she loved me. I know she did. 'Yetta, forgive me. I love you. But you make me mad.' That's all. Is your mother a drinker? Does she have something wrong with her like that?"

"I don't know," I answered. "She just hates me. She kicked me out," I lied some more. "That's why I came here. I just figure acting is a good way to make a living, since I can't go home. And my dad's dead." That was true.

Mrs. Honigbaum sighed and adjusted her wig, which had fallen off center with all her gesticulating. "I know what it means to be an orphan," she said gravely. Then she stood up from her chair and came to me, the sleeves of her housecoat skimming the table, knocking over the salt and pepper shakers shaped like dancing elves. "You poor boy. You must be so scared." She cradled my head in her thin arms, squishing the side of my face against her low-slung breasts. "I'm going to make some calls. We're going to get you on your way. You're too handsome, you're too talented, too wonderful to be squandering your time working at that pizza place." She leaned down and kissed my forehead. Then I cried a little, and she handed me a chalky old tissue from her housecoat pocket. I dried my tears. "You'll be all right," said Mrs. Honigbaum, patting my head. She went and sat down and finished her cottage cheese. I couldn't look her in the eye for the rest of the night.

The next day I picked up a copy of the coupon circular where Mrs. Honigbaum's columns were published. I found one at the pawnshop across from the bakery where I bought my cinnamon doughnuts. Then I boarded an express bus going east on Melrose. I took a window seat and laid the circular across my lap. Mrs. Honigbaum's columns ran side by side on the last page. I found my horoscope. "Virgo: You will have trouble with love this week. Beware of coworkers talking about you behind your back. They could influence your boss. But don't worry! Good things are in store." It was nonsense, but I considered it all very carefully. The gossip column was just a list of celebrity birthdays and recent Hollywood news items. I didn't know anybody's name, so none of it seemed to be of any consequence. Still, I read each and every word. Suzanne

Somers is suing ABC. Princess Diana has good taste in hats. *Superman II* is out in theaters. As I watched the people of Los Angeles get on and off the bus, I felt for the first time that I was somebody, I was important. Mrs. Honigbaum, who cared so much about me, wrote columns in this circular that traveled all across the city. Hundreds if not thousands must have read her column every week. She was famous. She had influence. There was her name right there: "Miss Honey."

Oh, Mrs. Honigbaum. After our fourth dinner together, I found myself missing her as I lay on my bed, digesting the mound of schnitzel and boxed mashed potatoes and JELL-O she'd prepared herself. She made me feel very special. I wasn't attracted to her the way I'd been to the girls back in Gunnison, of course. At eighteen, what excited me most was a particular six-inch length of leg above a girl's knee. I was especially inclined to study girls in skirts or shorts when they were seated beside me on the bus with their legs crossed. The outer length of the thigh, where the muscles separated, and the inside, where the fat spread, were like two sides of a coin I wanted to flip. If I could have done anything, I would have watched a woman cross and uncross her legs all day. But I'd never seen Mrs. Honigbaum's legs. She sat behind her desk most of the time, and when she walked around, her thin legs were covered in billowy pants in brightly colored prints of tropical flowers or fruit.

One morning, I stopped off at Mrs. Honigbaum's office on the way to the shower, as usual.

"Darling," she now called me, "I have something for you.

An audition. It's for a commercial or something, but it's a good one. It could put you on the map quick. Go wash up. Here, take this." She came out from behind her desk and handed me the address. Her handwriting was large and looping, beautiful and strong. "Tell them Honey sent you. It's just a test."

"A screen test?" I asked. I'd never been in front of a real movie camera before.

"Consider it practice," she said. She looked me up and down. "What I wouldn't give," she said. "That reminds me." She went back to her desk and riffled through her drawers for her pills. "To be young again! Well, go shower. Don't be late. Go and come back and tell me all about it."

It took me several hours to get to the studio in Burbank. The audition was held in a small room behind a lot that seemed to be a place where food deliveries were made. The whole place smelled faintly of garbage. Two slender blond girls sat in folding chairs in the corner of the room, both reading issues of *Rolling Stone*. They wore tight jeans and bikini tops, huge platform sandals. The director was middle-aged and tan, his chest covered in black curls, eyes hidden behind dark sunglasses. His beard was long and unruly. He sat with a script open in front of him on the table and barely lifted his gaze when I walked in. "Honey sent me," I said. He didn't stand or shake my hand. He just took my head shot and flicked his cigarette butt at the floor.

He must be doing Mrs. Honigbaum a favor by allowing me to audition, I thought. He could have been a former tenant of hers. If he'd be reporting back to her, I wanted to perform better than ever. I had to be perfect. I slowed my breathing down. I focused my eyes on the blue lettering on the cameraman's T-shirt. GRAND LODGE. The cameraman had huge shoulders and hair that flopped to one side. He winked at me. I smiled. I chewed my gum. I tried to catch the eyes of the girls, but they simply sighed, hunched over their magazines.

It turned out to be the longest and most challenging audition I'd ever had. First the director had the cameraman film me while I stood in front of a white wall and gave my name, my age, my height and weight. I was supposed to say my hometown and list my hobbies. Instead of Gunnison, I said, "Salt Lake City." I had no real hobbies, so I just said, "Sports."

"What do you play—tennis? Basketball? What?"

"Yeah," I said. "I play everything."

"Lacrosse?" the director asked.

"Well, no, not lacrosse."

"Let's see you do some push-ups," he said impatiently. I did ten. The director seemed impressed. He lit another cigarette. Then he told me to mime knocking on a door and waiting for someone to answer it. I did that. "Be a dog," he said. "Can you be a dog?" I sniffed the air. "What does a dog sound like?" I howled. "Not bad. More wolf than dog, but can you dance?" he asked. I did a few rounds of the electric slide. The girls watched me. "Needs work," the director said.

"Now laugh." I looked around for something funny. "Go. Laugh," he said, snapping his fingers.

"Ha-ha!"

He made a mark on the paper in front of him. "Now be sexy," he said. "Like you're trying to seduce me. Come on, like I'm Farrah Fawcett. Or some chick, whoever, some girl you want to lay. Go." He snapped his fingers again.

I'd never had to do anything like that before. I shrugged and put my hands in my pockets, turned to the side, pursed my lips, winked at him. He made another note.

"Come in for a close-up," the director said to the cameraman. "Stand straight, dammit," he told me. "Don't move." The camera came about six inches from my face. The director stood up and came toward me, squinted. "You always got zits up there between your eyebrows?"

"Only sometimes," I answered. I tried to look at him, but the lights were too bright. It felt like I was like staring into an eclipse.

"Your eye's messed up, you know that?" he asked.

"Yeah, it's a lazy eye."

"Work on that," he said. "There's exercises for that." He sat back down. "Now be sad," he said.

I thought of the time I saw a dead cat on the street in Gunnison.

"Be angry."

I thought of the time I slammed my thumb in the car door.

"Be happy."

I smiled.

"Be brave. Be goofy. Be stuck-up." I tried my best. He told me to stick out my tongue. He told me to close my eyes, then open them. Then he told me to kiss the two girls. "Pretend they're twins," he said. He clapped his hands.

The girls stood up and came toward me.

"You. Stand on the line," the director said to me. "That line." He pointed to a length of black tape on the concrete floor. The girls stood on two Xs marked in red tape in front of me. They looked young, maybe sixteen, and pretty in a way girls hadn't been back in Gunnison. The skin on their faces was orange and as smooth as plastic. Their eyes were huge, blue, with wide black pupils, white liner drawn across their lids like frost. Their heads were big and round, necks and shoulders narrow and bony. I chewed my gum and put my hands in my pockets.

"What are you chewing?" one of the girls asked.

"It's gum," I said.

"Get in the shot," said the director. "On the line. Jesus."

"That's rude," the other girl said to me.

"Take out the gum!" the director yelled. "Let's do this. We haven't got all day."

I took out my gum and held it on the tip of my finger and looked around for a place to throw it out. The girls sighed and rolled their eyes. The camera came closer.

"Action!" the director cried.

The girls lifted their chins.

I just stood there holding my gum, looking down at the

legs of the table where the director was sitting. I was paralyzed. The girls laughed. The director groaned.

"Just kiss," he said.

I couldn't do it.

"What, you don't like blondes? You've got a thing?"

I waved my finger around helplessly. I suddenly felt I couldn't breathe.

"I'll count to ten," said the director. "One, two, three . . ." I looked into the lens of the camera and saw my upside-down reflection. It was like I was trapped in there in the darkness, suspended from the ceiling, unable to move. I looked at the girls again. Their lips were frosted in pale pink, mealy and shimmering, nothing I'd ever want to kiss. Then one of the girls bent down to my finger and sucked my chewed-up wad of gum into her mouth. I took a step back. I was shocked. I tripped on a cord. The girls tittered. "Ten!" the director shouted.

I did not get the part.

On the way home, I boarded two wrong buses, going east all the way down through Glendale and Chinatown. I walked through downtown Los Angeles, past all the bums and garbage, then finally found a bus on Beverly back to Hancock Park. At home, I walked straight into Mrs. Honigbaum's office. I could have been irate that she'd sent me there. I could have blamed her for my humiliation. But that didn't occur to me. I just wanted to be soothed.

"It was bogus," I told her. "The director was some hippie. There wasn't even a trash can to throw my gum out in."

"You win some, you lose some" is all Mrs. Honigbaum said.

"I'm a good kisser, too," I told her. "Do you think Bob Sears will be mad?"

"Bob Sears doesn't know his face from his armpit. Let me see your mouth." She got up from her desk and pointed to a chair. "Sit. I promise I just want to take a look. Now open up." I did as I was told. I closed my eyes as she peered inside. I could smell her breath, acrid from cigarettes and those harsh mints I'd grown fond of. She hooked a finger into my gums and pulled my bottom lip down, her long nail tapping against my two front teeth. "All right," she said finally. I opened my eyes. "You have nothing to worry about." She removed her finger, turned, and went and sat back down at her desk. I took a mint. "I'll tell you a secret," she said, sharpening her pencil. "Teeth are what make a star. Teeth and gums. That's the first thing they look at. That director is a fool. Forget about him. You?" She shook her head. "You're too good for that guy. Good gums. Good mouth. The lips, everything. My teeth are fake, but I know a thing or two, and you've got the proportions." She turned back to her pad of paper, flicked a page of a magazine, lit a cigarette. I stood. It was a relief to hear I wasn't doomed for failure, but I was still all torn up inside. If I failed to make it as an actor, where would I go? What else could I do with my life? Mrs. Honigbaum looked up at me as though she'd forgotten I was still sitting there. "Are you going to cry, darling?" she asked. "Are you still upset about the kissing?"

"No," I answered. I wanted her to embrace me, hold me tight. I wanted her to rock me in her arms as I wept. "I'm not upset."

"Is that what you wore to the audition?"

I was in my usual getup: leather loafers, tight jeans, and a loose Indian shirt that I thought made me look very open-minded.

"Stuff the crotch next time," she said. "You'll feel silly but you won't regret it. Half of a man's power to seduce is in the bulge of his loins."

"Where's the other half?" I asked. I was completely sincere. By then I'd kissed half a dozen girls in closets at parties back in Gunnison but had never gone all the way. I never had enough enthusiasm to do all the coaxing and convincing it seemed necessary to do. And I was too anxious, too attached to my dreams of stardom to get tangled up in anybody's private parts. Of course, I thought about sex often. I kept a condom in my wallet, like an ID card. My stepfather had given it to me on my last night in Gunnison. "Don't go and pierce your ears or anything," he'd said, and punched me in the arm.

"Power is in the mind," Mrs. Honigbaum was saying, patting her head, jangling her bracelets. "Read an hour a day and you'll be smarter than me before you turn twenty. I used to be too smart, and it made me miserable. So now I spend my time on soft stuff, like gossip." She held up a copy of the coupon circular. "It's all fluff, but I'm good at what I do. So-and-so is retiring, this one has cancer, that one is going crazy. *The Love Boat,* can you believe it?"

"Believe what?"

"It's nothing. Go have a cry, then come back and I'll tell you a story."

"But I'm not going to cry," I insisted. I flashed her a big smile to prove it.

"You go. Have a cry. If you want to talk after, come back. Have another mint."

I retreated to my room to smoke a joint out the window and listen to the Eagles for a few hours. And I did cry, but I never told Mrs. Honigbaum. In the evening, I went to work and tried to get those blond girls out of my head. Women left lipstick smears on their pizza crusts and the rims of their wine glasses, cigarette butts rattling in their cans of diet soda, phone numbers scribbled on cocktail napkins, smiley faces, Xs and Os. Their winks and tips did nothing for my low spirits, however. At home, I stared at my head shot and tried to pray for solace: *God, make me feel good.* I cried some more.

In the morning I called Bob Sears. He mentioned nothing of my failure from the previous day. "I received a call from your mother earlier this morning," he said instead. He told me that she'd threatened to call the Los Angeles police. If I didn't call her that day, she'd open a missing-persons case. "She seemed very upset and inquired as to my qualifications as a talent agent. I told her, 'Madam, I've been doing this work for forty-seven years and none of my boys has ever gone missing. Not under my watch.' I'm not going to send you out into the lion's den, now, am I? How could I profit? How?"

He gave me the addresses for two casting calls that day, neither of which I went to. I still didn't feel good. My head hurt. My face was swollen from crying. I spent the rest of the morning in front of the Toshiba, watching *Hollywood Squares, Family Feud,* all the while imagining my mother's rage. "It was Larry's birthday last week. What, now you're too good to call? You think you're better than us, than me, your own mother?" I knew she'd be furious. I had nothing to say for myself. I had promised to call, and I hadn't called. Maybe I wanted to make her worry. Maybe I wanted her to suffer. "I've been scared to death," I imagined she'd say. "How dare you do this to me. What have you been doing? Ballroom dancing? Champagne and caviar? Fooling around with who—whores?" I walked back and forth to the doughnut shop, feeling like a criminal. I didn't go out to the beach. I just crawled back home into bed, under the covers and listened through the blanket to *Days of Our Lives, Another World, Guiding Light.* Again I cried. At six o'clock, Mrs. Honigbaum knocked on my door.

"I just got off the phone with Bob Sears," she said. "It's time to call your mother. See if she still hates you. Use the phone in the bedroom. Follow me."

Mrs. Honigbaum led me down the softly carpeted hallway and ushered me into her chambers, which I'd never seen at night before. The poodle scurried under the bed. Mrs. Honigbaum turned on the chandelier, and suddenly everything was cast in dappled yellow light. The perfume bottles and crystal decorations glinted and winked. She slid open the heavy glass door to the backyard to let in some air. "It gets stuffy," she said. The room was filled with a fragrant breeze. It was nice in there. She pointed to the bed. "Have a seat," she said. Just then the phone rang.

"Who's calling me now?" she murmured. She plucked off one earring, handed it to me, and lifted the receiver. "Hello?" I held the large golden earring in my open palm. In its center was an opalescent pearl the size of a quarter. "All right. Thank you," she said quickly and hung up. "It's my birthday," she explained. She took the earring and clipped it back on. "Now, sit here and call your mother. I'll be your witness. It'll be fine. Go ahead."

She stood there watching me. I had no choice but to pick up the phone.

"Very good," said Mrs. Honigbaum after I'd slid the tip of my finger into the number on the rotary. "Go ahead," she said again.

I dialed.

The phone rang and rang. Nobody was answering. It was a Saturday night.

"See, no one's home," I said to Mrs. Honigbaum, holding the receiver out toward her.

"Leave a message," she said. She lit a cigarette. I nodded and listened to the brassy bells dinging on the line, ready to hang up if my mother answered. Mrs. Honigbaum exhaled two huge plumes of smoke through her flared nostrils. "A good message."

Finally the machine picked up. I heard my mother's voice for the first time in months. I held the phone out to Mrs. Honigbaum again. "That's her, that's what she sounds like," I said. "She always sounds so mad."

"Never mind," said Mrs. Honigbaum.

After I heard the beep, I started my message: "Hi, Mom, it's me." I paused. I looked up at Mrs. Honigbaum.

"I'm so sorry I haven't called," she whispered. She waved her hand at me, smoke dotting the air, as though to spur me ahead.

"I'm so sorry I haven't called," I repeated into the phone.

"My life out here is fabulous. I am making some major progress in my acting career." Mrs. Honigbaum widened her eyes, waiting for me to proceed.

I repeated what she said.

"And I'm meeting lots of fascinating characters."

"I'm meeting fascinating characters."

"I'm safe and eating well. There's nothing you need to worry about."

I delivered these lines word for word.

"Please don't call Bob Sears again. It's not good for me, professionally."

"Please don't call Bob Sears again. It's not good for me, professionally."

"I love you, Mother," said Mrs. Honigbaum.

"I love you," I said back to her.

"Now hang up."

I did as I was told.

"There, that wasn't so hard, now, was it?" Mrs. Honigbaum extinguished her cigarette and sat down beside me on the edge of the bed.

"She's not going to like it," I said.

"You've done your duty. She'll sleep better now." My heart was racing. I bent over and put my head in my hands. "Take some deep breaths," Mrs. Honigbaum said, a hand rubbing my back. I sat and breathed with her and I felt better. "Now listen. I have something I've been meaning to show you," she said. "I don't show this to many people. But I think you deserve it. It's something to make you smarter."

Then she reached across my lap and opened the drawer of her bedside table. She pulled out a sheaf of index cards. "It's a special deck of cards I made myself," she said. She shuffled through them. They were blank on one side, and on the other side they bore strange symbols—mostly shapes, solid or outlined or striped or polka-dotted, in different colors. Mrs. Honigbaum had drawn them all in Magic Marker. One card had three green diamonds. Another had two empty red circles. A solid black square, a striped purple triangle, and so on. The point of the game was to set the cards down in rows and find patterns between the shapes and colors, what have you. "This game is a metaphor for life," Mrs. Honigbaum explained. "Most people are dumb and can't see the pattern unless it's obvious. But there is always a pattern, even when things don't make sense. If you build your brains up, the people here will think you're a genius. Nobody else is going to teach you how to do this. You'll see what I mean."

She laid out three rows of three cards each on the bed-spread.

"The pattern here is easy. Three of the cards have wiggly lines on them."

I nodded.

She collected the cards, then laid out three more rows. "This set is a little more mysterious. You see these three?" She pointed to three of the cards. One was an empty blue square. One was a solid red rectangle. The other was a striped green star. "Sometimes the pattern is that they're all different. Do you see that? These three have nothing in common, and that's exactly what they have in common. Understand?"

I said I did.

"This is how to succeed as an actor. Point out the hidden pattern. Find meaning in the mess. People will kiss your feet." I watched her pick up the cards again. I didn't understand what she meant at the time, but I could tell that what she was saying was true. "Practice, practice, practice. You've got the brawn, now work on the brain. You want the big time, don't you? The big roles?"

"Yes," I answered, though by then I really didn't. When she looked up at me, I stared deep into her small, blurry eyes. "Thank you," I said.

"No need to thank me," she replied. She shuffled and laid down more cards, pointed to three circles. "Easy," she said and clucked her tongue.

Then she was quiet. She shuffled the cards. She looked at me and shook her head. I thought maybe she was lost in her own reveries and would tell me a story about her dead husband or something funny that happened when she was young. But instead, she put down the cards, placed one hand on my knee, the other over her tanned, bony sternum. "Your mother is a lucky woman to have such a boy," she said, exhaling as though it hurt her to admit such a painful truth. She lifted her hand from my knee and caressed my face, lovingly, reverently, and shook her head again.

Nothing ever happened under the covers of Mrs. Honigbaum's bed, but from then on, each night before I fell asleep, she recited some prayers in Hebrew and put her hands on my face and shoulders. Whatever spells she cast, they didn't work. Neither of us was very surprised.

met her two days before Christmas at a holiday pop-up market on the Lower East Side. This was 2006, and she was selling refurbished antique furniture, which she'd placed around her taped-off space like someone's fancy living room. She wore tight red trousers and a black shirt that looked like the top of a ballerina's leotard. Her hair was frizzy, bleached blond, and she had a lot of makeup on—too much, I'd say. Her face was pinched, as though she'd just smelled someone farting. It was that look of revulsion that awoke something in me. She made me want to be a better man.

While she was busy with customers, I sat on a chaise longue for sale and pretended to be fascinated. I pushed at the springs with the palms of my hands. I lay down like a patient in analysis, then sat up again. The thing was priced at $2,750. I took out my cell phone and pressed some buttons, pretending that I wasn't staring at the girl. Finally she noticed me and came over.

"King Edward, home on the range" is the first thing I ever heard her say. I had no idea what she meant by this. "It's all mahogany. Late Edwardian. Only that panel has the inlay missing." She pointed. I turned around to look at the wood. "The festoon there?" she was saying. "But I like it without the mother-of-pearl. Mother-of-pearl would look chintzy, I think, with this shade of leather." I could only clear my throat and nod. She told me she had reupholstered the chaise in leather from an old armchair she'd stripped on the side of the road. "It was like skinning a deer," she said. "This past summer in Abilene."

I turned back around to face her crotch—a tender triangle swollen and divided by the thick protuberance of her zipper fly, thick thighs pulling at the weave of the red wool. A tiny key hung from a coiled loop of white telephone cord wrapped around her left wrist. She fingered the coils with long, chipped black nails. I had to marry her. If I couldn't, I would kill myself. I broke out in a sweat as though I were about to vomit.

"Field dressing," I blurted. And then, "Field dressing?" I looked up at her face for some kind of validation. Her eyes were a dark, watery blue.

"Oh, are you a hunter or something?" Again, her face like someone had farted—fragile and strangely condemning, like a queen's.

"No," I answered. I went back to pushing on the springs.

"But there's a new book about hunting by this guy in Montana, I think, who says you should smoke weed when you hunt because it attracts the animals. Apparently they're attracted to it, to your energy and, like, the vibrations in your brain. I don't totally remember. Not that I smoke weed. I mean, I did in college. I'm thirty-three," I added, as if this explained something.

"You're reading a book about hunting?"

She folded her arms. Her mouth, as she waited for my answer, was a heavy, wilted rose.

"No," I told her. "I was just reading *about* the book. Online."

"Oh, okay." She scratched her head and started to walk away. "The springs are all new," she said, not bothering to turn around.

I got up and followed her. I asked if she did custom work. "I have this ottoman," I lied.

"Any custom work would have to wait until after the New Year," she told me. But I could e-mail her photos in the meantime and let her know what I had in mind.

"I'm definitely going to think seriously about the couch," I said. I was scared I'd mispronounce the words "chaise longue." She gave me her business card and smiled falsely. "Gee, thanks," I said. She said nothing. And so I left, stumbling over the legs of a wicker rocking chair and waving back at her like an idiot. I went straight home and lay in bed, moaning in ecstasy, over and over, each time I read the letters of her name: Britt Wendt.

"That's not a name, it's the beginning of a sentence," Mark Lasky said over coffee the next day when I told him I was in love. It was Christmas Eve. "And you met her where? Working at a furniture store? Nick, you went to Yale, for Christ's sake."

Mark was my oldest friend, the first of many to suddenly quit smoking, lose his hair, get married, and buy a brownstone in a part of Brooklyn he wouldn't have set foot in five years earlier. Some of these friends had even conceived children already, which seemed preposterous to me at the time. I was nearly thirty-four, approaching the end of my "Jesus year," as it's often called. In Christ's honor, I'd grown my hair out past my ears. I had to use a rubber band and bobby pins to keep loose strands out of my eyes when I went running.

"She makes the furniture herself," I explained to Mark. "She *refurbishes* the furniture herself, I mean. She has her own business. She's an artist."

"An artis*an*," Mark corrected me. "Did you sleep with her already? Has she seen your apartment—excuse me— your *room*?"

"Well, no."

"I don't see why you can't date Becky or Elaine or Lacey Freeman," Mark said.

"Gross," I said. "Lacey Freeman?"

"Okay, not Lacey. But Jane? Jane Germeroth is perfect for you. Jane Germeroth is smart *and* she has good boobs.

Listen to me, Nick. Cut your hair. You look like a drummer in some shitty band. You look like a fucking bartender. Also, your scarf is gay."

My scarf was gay indeed. It had cost several hundred dollars, but it was beautiful—red and white checkered silk with long tassels.

"And it's offensive," Mark went on. "It's supposed to look like what Yasir Arafat wears on his head. Now teenagers are wearing polyester versions like it's some hip-hop thing."

"This is *silk*," I protested. "From Barneys."

"You know you can buy that shit on the street in Chinatown for ten dollars?"

"Well, you look like a gynecologist," I said. Mark was wearing a monogrammed cable-knit sweater and khakis.

"What does that even mean?"

"It means you look old," I told him. "And, you know, perverted."

"What do you want me to do? Wear tight jeans and roll my own cigarettes? I'm a grown man."

"Rolling your own is better for you," I said quietly, collecting the last crumbs of my cinnamon scone. "Less tar."

Mark groaned and finished his coffee. "You're not *in love*," he said. Then he paused to watch a girl in a short skirt bend over to tie her shoe. A few days earlier I would have clung to the image for weeks—the lines of her panties under the opaque black tights, the soft dimpling down the backs of her thighs. When she stood back up, her thick brown hair seemed to undulate around her shoulders in slow motion. Her face was irreverent, almost pug-nosed, mean and adorable. But I was unaffected. I had Britt Wendt now. Other girls meant nothing to me. "So are you going to buy the couch?" Mark asked finally. "Where would you even put it?"

For the past year I'd been renting a room month to month for $350 cash in a flophouse owned by a Hasidic slumlord. I had to myself an eight-by-eight, windowless corner of the building, which had once housed a plant that manufactured little tongue-colored erasers. The place still smelled vaguely of burning rubber. My room was on the top level. The other tenants up there were all hip young people. I didn't know anyone's name. Downstairs, Middle Eastern gypsy cab drivers slept in shifts on bunk beds, their black sedans parked outside like a presidential cavalcade. Streetside, there was a soaped-up storefront full of car parts and broken computers. The building should have been, and probably was, condemned.

The only furniture I had was a twin mattress and a low glass coffee table, on top of which I piled my shoes, each pair in a Ziploc freezer bag to keep the vermin and roaches out. The walls between the rooms were single sheets of gypsum board. Hand-drawn signs in the crumbling hallways read: NO BEDBUGS! NO STREET MATTRESS! NO HOMELESS! The place had two communal bathrooms full of silverfish and a shared kitchen full of mice. I was constantly looking for a sublet or a room in an apartment or a cheap studio, but nothing seemed good enough. I couldn't commit. Plus, I was always broke. I kept spending all my money on clothes.

Christmas morning, I was woken up by my neighbors having sex. Usually I'd pound on the gypsum, but that morning, in the spirit of the holiday and in honor of true love, I let the grunting slide. I stayed under my comforter with my laptop on my crotch, listening to the sex sounds and Googling Britt Wendt for the thousandth time. The Britt Wendt I found on Myspace was twelve years old, lived in Deering, New Hampshire, and posted inspirational photos of nature scenes with captions about how to be your best self, jokes about periods, links to articles about Olympic skating and beauty pageants. The only other Web pages that came up for "Britt+Wendt" were Swedish genealogies. *My* Britt Wendt was a mystery. I looked at her business card again. It was minimal, just her name and e-mail address and the words "redesigned antiques." The font was generic, Arial bold. The card stock, flimsy. It was like she just didn't give a shit. After my neighbors finished, I heard them walking down the hall to the showers. I considered visiting my go-to site for porn but chose not to. With Britt Wendt to pine for, watching videos of strangers having sex felt sacrilegious, like squirting a mayonnaise packet into your mouth while riding the elevator up to Per Se.

"Hi Britt" is how I decided to begin my e-mail.

It took thirty minutes of Google image searching to find a photo of an ottoman that conveyed what I wanted to convey: I lived in an expensive converted loft, had a very high-quality camera, and was an organized and broad-minded music aficionado and reader of literature. The photo was perfect—sunlight streaming in through a wall of opaque factory windows, neat shelves of books and records, the corner of an electric guitar leaning against the exposed brick wall in the background. The source of the photo was the for-sale section of craigslist in Providence, Rhode Island. The ottoman itself was just a lame, gray, fabric-covered cube. The legs were short, angular, blond wood stubs. I could tell it was a factory piece from the 1950s and worth more than the fifteen dollars the seller was asking, but not much more. I understood that I'd be deceiving Britt Wendt by claiming ownership of this ottoman, but I reasoned that as soon as she fell in love with me—perhaps she already had—the existence of furniture or lofts, any trite reality, would become laughably irrelevant. So I downloaded the photo, adjusted the levels in Photoshop, attached it to my e-mail, and wrote, "It's the dude about the stoned hunters and the chaise longue from the other day. Would love your ideas and a rough quote on reupholstering this ottoman (attached) in vintage leather from your Texas roadkill or other source. Merry Xmas?" I signed my name "Nicholas (Nick) Walden Darby-Stern" and added my phone number. "P.S. Did the chaise longue sell? Still pondering . . ." How could she not love me now? I wondered.

I spent the rest of the morning in bed, eating steel-cut oats with maple syrup out of my mini slow cooker and watching DVDs on my computer. I checked my e-mail every two minutes. Each time I saw that Britt Wendt hadn't written back yet, there was disappointment, but also great relief. In the infinite realm of possibilities, I felt I still had a chance. That was the last dreg of youth, I suppose, that hopefulness. I watched *Face/Off* and *Con Air* and a few episodes of *Fawlty Towers.* I took a shower and put a sheet down on my floor and did sit-ups and push-ups in front of my space heater. Then I watched the first ten minutes of *Marathon Man* and the first five minutes of *Hoffa,* clicking back to my e-mail all the while. My neighbors through the gypsum had gone out. Everyone was out, it seemed. The flophouse was strangely quiet.

At such times, it was my habit to buy things online. But I had resolved to try to cut down on my spending. All I had to show for my earnings as a graphic designer were my computer and a rack of expensive clothes, each item safely sealed in a clear plastic garment bag. Despite my refined taste, I blended easily into the rank and file; my clothes were just high-end versions of the crap everyone else was wearing. My workday uniform usually consisted of black jeans from MDR; a plain, handpicked-pima-cotton T-shirt from Het Last; a washed-linen button-down and a heather-gray hoodie, both from Deplore; and white leather high-top limited-edition Chucks, or my perforated wingtip leather miner boots from Amberline, if there was snow on the ground. At home, I wore satin pajamas—burgundy and blue striped top and bottom from Machaut—and a heavy Peruvian parka

I'd won on eBay. I had recently splurged on rabbit fur–lined deerskin gloves at Modo and a custom-ordered cashmere hat from an atelier in Tokyo that I'd read about in *Mireille*. I'd had to measure the circumference of my head for it. I rationalized these expenditures easily: luxury accessories were better investments than, say, the seventy-five-dollar goat-milk soap from the Swiss Alps, which had taken a month to get through customs and lasted me exactly twelve showers. For the previous six months, I'd been working part time without benefits at *Indent,* a lifestyle magazine for rich intellectuals. It did not pay well. My bank account was empty. My credit-card debt by this time was in the five figures. I'd even cut up my cards in an effort to curb my spending. Until Christmas money from my father arrived, I would have a hundred dollars cash in my wallet, plus a fifteen-dollar gift card to Burger King that Mark had given me for Hanukkah as a joke. He had gone off to Vermont with his wife to be with her family. Everyone else was home with their parents, or on glamping trips in Joshua Tree or sunning themselves in Maui or Cabo or Puerto Rico with their girlfriends. My father was skiing in Tahoe with his new wife. He hadn't invited me along. Without the funds to buy anything, I could only drift through online stores and put things into virtual shopping carts. It was all so futile. It was all just trash. What I really wanted was to run the tip of my tongue across Britt Wendt's pale, trembling throat, then suck each of her ears until she begged me to fuck her. "Tell me you love me, or I'm pulling out," I'd demand. "Oh God," she'd say as I

entered her. "I love you, I love you," she'd pant at every
thrust.

In the afternoon, Lacey Freeman texted to invite me to
Christmas dinner at her apartment. This kind of last-minute
invitation was typical of Lacey. "Herding all the strays over
for my annual Xmas feast, so stop by if you're lonely ☹ 6–11
p.m." Every time I saw Lacey, she'd gained five more pounds.
She was turning into the kind of obese girl who does her hair
like a forties pinup and wears bright red lipstick, a blue polka-
dot dress with a white doily collar, colorful tattoos across
her huge, smushed cleavage, as if these considerations would
distract us from how fat and miserable she had become. In a
few years she'd get her eggs frozen, I predicted correctly, and
the rockabilly thing would disintegrate into Eileen Fisher
tunics and lazy, kundalini yoga. Any man interested in Lacey
would have had to be seriously self-loathing. I knew this because I'd made out with her when we first met at Mark's birthday party five years earlier. I got drunk and went back to her
place, came to with my face buried in her back fat, about
to consummate my desperation. I left quickly and rudely. I
never told Mark about it. The next time I saw Lacey she
acted unfazed, like we were chums who had merely shared a
funny moment. "That Scotch!" But having held my dick in
her hand, she seemed to feel she'd earned the right to belittle
me as much as possible. "Are you getting by okay?" she liked
to ask me. She was a sad person, sheltered and confused and
ineffectual, et cetera. She'd recently become obsessed with
canning and baking and making her own bitters. The last

thing I wanted for Christmas was her homemade eggnog and gin-pickled okra. "Merry Xmas! I'll try to make it!" I texted back. But I had no intention of giving her the satisfaction. Mark texted me a photo of his father-in-law's model replica of a World War II battlefield. I did not reply.

For the rest of the afternoon I watched more DVDs, checked my e-mail, and pined for Britt Wendt. I fantasized about our life together. We'd get a one-bedroom in Flushing, fill it with her furniture, cook roasts, and drink expensive wine bought with the money we saved by living in Queens. Our repartee would be rich with subtlety and sarcasm, as smart and funny as midcareer Woody Allen. Our fucking, like Werner Herzog, serious and perplexing. I could imagine Britt Wendt lying beside me in bed, her frothy blond hair flattened into a fuzzy halo. We'd be like dope fiends for each other, reaching out our swollen hands for one more hit, her body pale and freckled, nipples pink as sunsets. "The worse your morning breath, the more I love kissing you," I'd say, slipping my tongue into her hot, bitter, velvety mouth.

I think by then I'd been single longer than is healthy for a young man. I'd had just one serious girlfriend since graduating from college. Postbreakup, there was a consequent jag of failed sexual reprisals (including the one with Lacey), a two-year dry spell, then a single and only semi-interesting encounter with a completely hairless Taiwanese girl I met at Bloomingdale's. Next came a few standard Brooklyn bar hookups with insecure twenty-five-year-olds, then three more years of nothingness, not a drop, not a cloud on the

horizon. By my Jesus year I was practically a virgin again.
My father told me to focus on my career. "Women are attracted to money," he had said over the phone before leaving
for Tahoe.

"I'll die alone," I told my father. "I don't care." This was
all before I'd met Britt Wendt, of course.

"There are plenty of girls who would be interested in
you," my father said. "You're a long-term investment, they'll
think. Women are good about the future. They can see further down the line. I'll mail you a check when I get back
from Tahoe."

When the sun went down, I checked my e-mail one more
time, found nothing, got dressed, pinned my hair back,
jogged through the snow, bought a can of soup and beef jerky
from a bodega, and walked back in the dark feeling heroic
and despondent. Mine was not the usual self-pity, but the
kind of fearful admiration one feels watching footage of
young tribal boys performing dangerous rites of passage.

I passed by Schoolbells and Soda, a bar where all the young,
hip gentrifiers of the neighborhood congregated and, as they
tended to do, ignored one another every evening, taking
advantage of the Tecate-and-tequila special and the plein air
seating with fire pit out back. The interior was all old, weath-
ered wood sourced from Navy Yard scrap, the lamps Edison
bulbs hanging from thick ropes, the glasses jam and mason
jars. At the time, this was considered innovative design. I'd
been a regular there until mid-November, when I got caught
refilling my beer glass from the tap myself. I'd actually been

stealing beer for weeks and could refill my glass one-handed by then. All I had to do was rise slightly from my barstool, get my glass under the spout, hold the rim with my fingertips, and lower the tap with my thumb. It took two seconds. When the bartender, in his suspenders and bow-tie neck tattoo, caught me in the act, he turned red, shut his eyes, and began to inhale and exhale dramatically, his lips moving as he counted each breath. I recognized this practice as an effort to reduce violent rage. I couldn't imagine him beating anybody up. He looked like one of those portly, nebbish types who if you shaved him and scrubbed him and dressed him in Van Heusen, you'd discover your cousin Ira, a tax attorney in Montclair. The whole bar hushed. Joanna Newsom yodeled and harped from the speakers. After ten breaths had gone by, I felt I had to do something. So I pulled three dollars out of my wallet and waved them in the air. "I'm happy to pay for the extra beer," I said. The bartender simply shook his beard and pointed to the door.

Mark loved to convict me of being an alcoholic. The Schoolbells story in particular seemed to arouse him. I made the mistake of recounting it a few days later. He listened attentively, said, "I feel like an opportunity has presented itself," then made a big fuss about silencing his phone. He went on to explain how embarrassed he'd been at his bachelor party two years ago when I'd made a joke of calling his cousin Daniel "Herr Schindler" in front of all the groomsmen.

"I'm Jewish, Nick. That means something to some of us. And why Schindler? How is that even funny? Do you even know what Schindler looked like? Or were you thinking of the actor in *Schindler's List*? Ralph Fiennes?"

"It's pronounced like 'rape,' but with an *f*," I said.

"Fuck you," said Mark.

I nodded. "It wasn't a great joke, okay? But Dan had been making a big deal about paying for the stripper, blabbing every chance he got, being a Schindler," I said. "It was a joke about self-interested generosity, the glove-on-the-invisible-hand thing."

"What invisible-hand thing?"

"Like when people tell you they gave money to a home-less person. The invisible hand of selflessness, only it's wearing a glove so everyone can see it."

"You could have called him Queequeg or Alyosha," Mark said. "But did Schindler really brag? Was he blabbing? Is that the takeaway, that he was a blabber?"

"I'm sorry," I said. "It was insensitive. I get it. Who is Queequeg?"

"The cannibal from *Moby-Dick,* idiot." Mark turned the ringer on his phone back on. "In all seriousness," he said, "please get a grip on the drinking. Have some self-respect."

For the six weeks since the incident at Schoolbells, I'd limited my drinking to Fridays and Saturdays, and only beer from bottles, and only alone in my room, safely cast away in my dark corner of the flophouse. As a result of this discipline, I was sleeping better. My morning jogs were faster. My small talk at work was funnier and more enjoyable. When I met Britt Wendt, I wasn't bloated or burpy. My eyes were clear. I was in prime condition. Such self-improvement was worthy of reward, I thought. And it was Christmas, after all. I stopped in front of Iga, a Polish bar across the street from Schoolbells. I'd passed by it countless times, but I'd never been inside. A buzzer sounded. I pushed on the door.

The place was bigger than I thought it would be. There were a dozen tables with red checkered tablecloths and worn metal chairs with black vinyl seats. The floor was parquet, and my footsteps squeaked as I walked haltingly toward the bar. There was no music on, nothing. A small cat slunk by, then rubbed itself against a stack of old newspapers. A radiator hissed and sputtered. The only light came from neon signs on the walls, and an old light-up beer advertisement with a broken clock. The back wall of the room was covered by a dark curtain. In the corner by the door to the toilet sat a large potted plant and a statuette of Adonis or David or Hercules or somebody, a Santa hat on its head. A middle-aged woman stood behind the bar, smoking a cigarette. Otherwise the place was empty.

"Jewish?" asked the woman, waving her cigarette smoke around with a thick, grubby hand. She seemed a little drunk to me. She asked again. "No Christmas for you. So, Jewish?"

"Well, half," I said.

She put a cocktail napkin on the bar. Her face under the strange pink light was yellowish and waxy, her hair purple, slightly bouffant, but she was not unattractive for a woman her age. "Half is good. You have both sides. What will you? Beer?" She lowered her voice mockingly. "Ho ho. You are a beer man?" I sat on the stool, put my plastic bag from the bodega on my lap. "Or for your Chrystus half, maybe we celebrate tonight. You know slivovitz?" She didn't wait for an answer. She poured out two shots from an old water bottle. "This is coming from Warsaw. Homemade," she said, sliding my glass toward me. "The best."

"Thank you," I said, smelling it.

"Very good. *Na zdrowie.* Ha!" She swallowed hers in one gulp, then coughed and belched. Her eyes filled with tears. "Now you," she said, pointing her thumb at me.

I drank mine and coughed and cried, too. The stuff was like perfume mixed with battery acid and lighter fluid. She gave me a pint glass of water and offered me a cigarette. I took one. We sat quietly, smoking, me fingering the plastic bag in my lap, her tapping a finger on the bar in time to nothing. After a few minutes, she blew her nose and stared into the crumpled tissue. "I see blood," she said softly, then tucked the tissue into the cuff of her sweater.

"Are you okay?" I asked.

She snorted and poured out two more shots. We drank and coughed and cried again, the woman eyeing me comically, her gaze distant and soft now in the weird light. My eyes paced the shiny surface of the bar. The cat purred. Then the woman went to the bathroom. A few minutes passed. I thought to leave, to go home to check my e-mail. If Britt Wendt had written to me, I'd have to be careful not to write back too quickly. The last thing I wanted to do was send her a drunken e-mail. Then I pictured Lacey Freeman's buffet spread—roasted suckling pig with an apple in its mouth, whiskey-laced yams, German chocolate cake. I was hungry. I ate a piece of jerky and listened as the woman flushed the toilet and blew her nose again. When she returned, she poured out two more shots, and this time when we drank them we winced and moaned, but we didn't cry.

"You like it here?" she asked. "Nobody comes here. But you? You like it?"

"It's great," I said.

She nodded, folded her arms, and rested her elbows on the bar. Swaying absentmindedly, she started singing an out-of-tune folk song, then caught herself and laughed. She seemed deep in thought for a while. I can't really say what her deal was. It was like I had walked into some kind of cosmic warp zone. Then all of a sudden she looked up at me. We locked eyes. When I blinked, she smiled cruelly and squinted, as though calling me a coward. What nerve, I thought, to try to take me down, her only customer. I felt insulted by her bravado. And so we had a staring contest, like a game of chicken, to see who was the least penetrable, whose mind would conquer whose. I cleared my throat and stared long and hard. I felt my face go cold, my teeth clench. Her face remained relaxed, eyes open wide. Even when she puffed on her cigarette and the smoke rose up, she didn't blink. She was amazing. There was nowhere to hide in the eyes of this woman. I could see that she was reading me, and my challenge was to resist her taunting expressions and try to read her even more deeply, with even more scorn and disgust than she had found for me. I tried as hard as I could, but all I came up with was my own foolishness. I blushed. It was like I was naked before her, holding my own limp dick in my hand.

She sucked her teeth and stubbed her cigarette out in the ashtray, still staring. It was clear that she had beaten me. But I didn't want to look away. Nor did I want her to. I enjoyed the attention, the scrutiny. So much of my life I'd been faking my reactions, claiming to myself and others that I liked what I liked because I believed it was good for me, while in fact I didn't like that shit at all. This woman could see that I wanted to be ruined. I wanted someone—Britt Wendt, maybe—to come and destroy me. "Murder me" my eyes said to the woman. She laughed, as though she heard my thoughts and found them ridiculous. I laughed back at her, a false, triumphant laugh, as though she were a bitter ex-lover come to dance on my grave and mine was the zombie hand rising up out of the earth to strangle her.

"Psss," she said, and looked away finally. She poured two more shots. We drank. Wordlessly, we mended our rapport. Then she offered me another cigarette and I lit the wrong end. That did it. "You waste," she said and clucked her tongue. She put the bottle away. When I took out my wallet, she just waved her big fat hand. "It's nothing," she said. In perhaps my first genuine expression of gratitude, I leaned over the bar and tried to kiss her cheek. She moved out of the way and laughed at me again, this time with great satisfaction, like a rare, wondrous beauty, arrogant and magical. She pointed to the door.

Later that night, leaning against the crumbling, mildewed tile of the shower stall back home, I looked down at myself. I was beautiful, I thought. Legions of curious fingers should be reaching out to touch me. My arms were thick and strong. A spurt of wiry black hair rose from my wrist, trembling in the warm spray like a delicate morning tendril in the dew. There I was, spectacular and alive, and the whole world was missing it. Britt Wendt was missing it most of all. I thought I heard someone call my name, some sweet angel descending from heaven just to appreciate me—I was that great. But of course, when I stumbled out into the dark hall, there was nobody. No one in that flophouse even knew my name. The only faces I could ever hope to recognize were of the lovers on the other side of the gypsum. I'd seen them entering their room once on my way back from the toilets. Where were they now? I wondered. Dancing in the fucking moonlight? I stumbled back to my room, lay on my bed, checked my e-mail, and, finding nothing, cried a little with loneliness, and then a little more with hope. I fell asleep naked in front of my space heater.

"what are dimensions"

All lowercase, no punctuation. These were the words Britt Wendt had e-mailed back to me on December 26, seven minutes past midnight. I read them in the early dawn, my eyes still crossed with slivovitz, but the meaning was clear:

she was interested. I rubbed my eyes, read her e-mail again, praised Jesus, then ran to the toilet and vomited with joy.

By noon I was on a Chinatown bus to Rhode Island. My message to the anonymous Craigslist-generated e-mail address had resulted in a tense and flurried correspondence with one "K Mendez" who would happily meet me at the Providence bus station to exchange the ottoman in question for fifty dollars cash, a sum more than three times the original amount listed. "There are other interested parties," he'd threatened. My e-mail at the crack of dawn, "IS THE OTTOMAN STILL FOR SALE???????!!!!" might have come across as a bit desperate. I had to pay him what he wanted. After spending twenty dollars on my round-trip bus ticket, I'd have only five dollars and change through the New Year. I'd never been that broke before. I'd have to live off ramen, give up a few days of cappuccinos, but it was worth it. "What are the dimensions?" I'd e-mailed K Mendez. He answered that it was about a foot high and weighed around twenty pounds. "I'll take it!" I replied. I figured I could go to Providence, buy the ottoman, turn around, get on the next bus home, and e-mail Britt Wendt back by nine. I closed my eyes as the bus veered out of town. I would have no book, no earphones, nothing to distract me from my thoughts and thirst and hunger and headache for three hours and seven minutes. I could live on cold, potty-scented air for as long as it took, I told myself. Soon, Britt Wendt would be safe in my arms forever.

Halfway to Providence, the bus stopped at a McDonald's

outside New Haven. It had been more than a decade since I'd set foot in that town. In the bathroom, I studied myself in the mirror. If my twenty-two-year-old self could see me now, I wondered, what would he think? What would he say? I wore my double-breasted cashmere peacoat from Junetree, a two-ply cashmere turtleneck from Boxtrot, a vintage Fendi belt, my usual black jeans, my Amberline boots, the hat from Japan, my Yasir Arafat scarf, the rabbit fur–lined gloves. "You look like a tool" is what I imagined Nick at twenty-two would say. "But my hair," I'd protest. "Would a tool have Jesus hair?" I debated back and forth at the urinal. My piss smelled like toxic waste. "Yes," Nick said in the mirror on the way out. I imagined what I must have looked like to the woman at Iga the night before. She must have thought I was one of those rich jerks ruining the neighborhood.

I got back on the bus.

In Providence, I waited, paced, and fumed, and when K Mendez turned up at the bus station thirty-six minutes late in a taxi, I was ready to crumble. The kid appeared to be in his early twenties, tall and thin, wearing baggy jeans, a Thrasher T-shirt, and an unzipped ski jacket with a fake fur–lined hood. He barely looked at me as he set the ottoman down and straddled it between his Vans. I worried that the upholstery would get stained from the dirty, salted layer of slush on the ground, but I was too stunned by his pluck and swagger to air that concern. I held out his money. He turned away and spit and lit a cigarette and told me, in a passionless monotone, "It's two hundred bucks now. Plus the cost of the taxi."

"That's insane," I argued. "I have fifty-five bucks. And a fifteen-dollar Burger King gift card. It's all I've got."

"Fuck Burger King," he answered. Without another word, he picked up the ottoman and headed back to the taxi stand in front of the bus station.

"Wait!" I cried out, shuffling after him. He was a fool, a punk, privileged and greedy, but he had what I wanted. "I'll give you this!" I said, pulling the scarf off my neck as an offering. K Mendez paused and turned back to face me. His cheeks were riddled with soft, red acne scars. His teeth were like fangs. His eyes, indecipherable. He was probably selling his furniture for drugs. What else?

"Yeah, okay," he said, surprising me. "Plus your hat. And your coat. That should do it."

"This coat is worth twelve hundred dollars." I laughed. I held out the scarf and waved it around. "Here. And the money." He turned his back and got in line for a cab, looking at me surreptitiously now and then, like a dog. It was a bizarre standoff, and I probably would have won out if I'd stood my ground. But I was impatient. My future was at stake. I came away barely clothed. He even took my Burger King card. The ottoman was a piece of shit, but that didn't matter in the end.

○——○

Back in Brooklyn that night, walking home from the subway with my ottoman, I couldn't help but smile at all the nice, happy people. Each face seemed spectacular in its originality, like a walking portrait. Everyone was beautiful. Everyone was special. It was cold and windy, and I had just a T-shirt on, but the moon was full, the sidewalks cleared of snow and sparkling with salt. A fleet of fire trucks blared by, deafening and cheerful. When I turned onto my street, there they were again. The flophouse billowed with smoke. Firemen strutted around the area, looking, I guessed, for a hydrant. My neighbors, the lovers from through the gypsum, stood together across the street from the blaze, naked but for towels, watching as flames leaped from an open window like a red flag. As I approached them, I could see that the girl's eyes were pink and teary. She was thin and short, nose warped like she'd been punched, shoulders concave and white and goose-pimpled in the frigid air. Her skinny legs were plunged into mammoth black motorcycle boots, presumably belonging to the boyfriend, who stood beside her in the snow. He was perversely tall and lanky, his sinewy torso spattered with black moles like flecks of mud. He coughed and reached an arm down around the girl. The vertical disparity between their bodies made me wonder how they'd managed to have so much effective intercourse. An EMT came and gave them each a thick gray blanket. I wished for one myself but was embarrassed to ask.

"They think someone left their heater on," the girl said to me, arranging the blanket over her shoulders, trembling.

My heart sank, but not completely.

"Was it you?" asked the boy. His mouth was like a horse's mouth, frothy and shuddering with plumes of white vapor and spittle in the frozen air. "Did *you* start the fire?"

"Come on," the girl said gently. "Don't get feisty. It's just a bunch of crap burning up. Who cares?"

The boy spit and coughed again and hugged her, his wide nostrils flared and dribbling with mucus.

I set the ottoman down in the snow and considered the boy's question.

"I didn't start the fire," I said, like the dumb man I'd become. "This is an act of God."

"This suit will be your costume." Lao Ting pointed to the black skirt and jacket hanging from the coatrack in the corner of his office. "You will tell people you are the vice president of the company. They may see you as a sex object, and this will be advantageous in business negotiations. I have noticed that American businessmen are very easy to manipulate. Has anyone ever told you that you resemble Christie Brinkley, the American supermodel of the nineteen eighties?"

I said a few people had. I did look like Christie Brinkley, and like Jacqueline Bisset and Diane Sawyer, I'd been told. I was five foot nine, 116 pounds, with long, silky light brown hair. My eyes were blue, which Lao Ting said was the best color for someone in my position. I was twenty-eight when I became the surrogate vice president. I was to be the face of the company at in-person meetings. Lao Ting thought American businessmen would discriminate against him because of the way he looked. He looked like a goat herder. He was short and thin and wore a white linen tunic and a belt of rope around his beach shorts. His beard was nearly white and hung down like a magical tail from his chin to his pubis. My previous job had been as a customer-service representative for Marriott Hotels, taking reservations over the phone at home. I'd been living in a studio apartment above a Mexican bakery in Oxnard. The view out my window there was a concrete wall.

"Your last name will be Reilly," Lao Ting told me. "Would you like to suggest a first name for your professional entity?"

I suggested Joan.

"Joan is too soulful. Can you think of another?"

I suggested Melissa and Jackie.

"Stephanie is a good name," he said. "It makes a man think of pretty tissue paper."

The company, called Value Enterprise Association, was run out of the ground floor of Lao Ting's luxurious three-story family complex on the beach in Ventura. It was a family business and had an old-fashioned quality that put me at ease. I never understood the nature of the company's services, but I liked Lao Ting. He was kind and generous, and I saw no reason to question him. The job was easy. I had to memorize some names, some figures, put on the suit, makeup, use hair spray, perfume, high heels, and so forth. Everybody at the office was very gracious and professional. There was no gossip, no fooling around, no disrespect. Instead of a watercooler, they had a large stainless-steel samovar of boiling-hot water set up in the foyer. The family drank green tea and Horlicks malted milk from large ceramic mugs. Lao Ting's wife, Gigi, gave me my own mug to use, like I was part of the family. I spent a lot of time sitting on the deck, looking out at the sea. It felt good to be out during the day, and to be appreciated. Lao Ting assured me that he would never expect me to engage in unprofessional activities with clients or vendors, and I never did. Everything was handled very honorably.

The surrogate position paid six times what I'd been making answering phones for the Marriott. I quickly paid off my credit-card debt and moved into a converted loft in an industrial area of El Rio. I furnished it with rentals and little decorations from gift shops. I was relieved to sell my car, a huge white Cadillac that had been on the brink of engine failure. Lao Ting employed a service to drive me everywhere I needed to go for work, and when I went out to clubs and parties on the weekends, I called cabs. I could afford it. I mostly went to the underground clubs and after-parties downtown or out in the desert. It was a weird crowd—freaks edged out of the LA scene, kinks from the valley, middle-aged ravers, tech rats on acid, kids on E, old women, the usual hustlers. I got dressed up special on the weekends. I liked to wear a trench coat, an old hat like a detective's, and large, tinted eyeglasses. Underneath my coat I wore a lacy red teddy. I'd snipped at the fabric around the crotch to accommodate my genitals, which were abnormally swollen due to a pituitary situation. Underneath the teddy, there were pennies taped over my nipples and a cutout photo of Charlie Chaplin's face taped across my pubis. I felt good wearing all that. Even before I got the job as the surrogate, I felt like normal clothes were all just costumes.

I'd been ashamed to bring men back to the studio in Oxnard because it smelled like a deep fryer, and there was no place to sit but on the grubby carpeted floor or on my bed, which felt too intimate. When I took men home to my loft in El Rio, which I didn't do often, they looked around at my stuff and asked me what I did for work.

"I'm the surrogate vice president of a business enterprise," I'd say. I'd sit them down on the rented couch and give them a clear plastic bag to put over their heads if they so desired. When my swelling was particularly bad, I got a little uptight. "I do not want to make love," I said to one man I remember. He was handsome and tan. He wore white clothes for dancing the capoeira, which is what drew me to him.

"'Do not want,'" he repeated, chortling under the plastic, his eyes sparkling.

"I don't do sex," I explained. "I just want to strip."

During the long cab ride from the club, he'd talked like this: "My work pays for everything—drinks, meals, travel, hotels. I go to Canada all the time. Coffee shops, theater tickets, everything. I get reimbursed," he was saying. "Quote unquote," he said over and over. His hands twitched and his eyes were hot-wired and roving, like there was lightning trapped inside of his eyeballs.

"Tell me something secret," I said to him, unknotting the belt of my coat.

"I have pet bunnies," he said. He sat up straight on the edge of the couch. "White with red eyes. I feed them meat. I feed them tuna." Then again, "While I'm in Canada, quote unquote, a neighbor babysits them, my little babies," and so forth.

Being watched was the only erotic pleasure I could really enjoy. After I removed my trench coat, I took off my shoes. Next, I undid the snaps of the teddy and let it fall to my feet. "I do not want to make love," I reiterated, as I plucked the pennies from my nipples.

"'Do not want'?" the man repeated. "Why do you talk that way?"

"For emphasis," I said. I told him to peel the photograph of Charlie Chaplin off my pubis. He flicked at the Scotch tape with his long, brown fingers. He wasn't in any rush. It was like he had enough excitement happening inside his eyeballs. Maybe, to him, the rest of life was just so-so.

"Who's this guy?" he asked.

"Hitler," I said.

He gasped, and I pulled the plastic bag from his head.

"Limos, dinners, dance clubs," he was saying. He yanked at the photograph and my labia tumbled out against my thighs. "Ha-ha," he said, poking. "You have more than meets the eye."

Gigi was the operations manager. She helped me with my hair and makeup and prepped me for meetings with the businessmen. We got to know each other pretty well. One time, I told her about my troubles in romance. "I can't engage with normal people," I explained. "When I go to the grocery store, or out for dinner at a normal restaurant, I am frightened. I don't understand how to act. Men pay me attention because of my looks. But I feel it is a mistake to look for love in these normal people. They're too neurotic. They aren't capable of love, only of comfort and equanimity."

Gigi said, "Don't worry about finding a husband. When the woman is the hunter, she can only see the weak men. All strong men disappear. So you don't need to hunt, Stephanie Reilly. You can live on a higher level. Just float around and you will find someone. That is how I found Lao Ting. It was as if there were a spotlight on him and he walked on air about two feet off the ground. I saw him from a mile away, floating down Rego Boulevard. Funny to imagine now, but he was once a very handsome man."

"That's beautiful, Gigi," I said.

"It's a beautiful love story. I will tell you more about it another time."

Value Enterprise Association employed another surrogate to act as my attorney at important meetings. He and I would sit at long glass tables in office buildings in LA, drink ice water, and give the businessmen contracts to sign. Apart from these meetings, communications between the family and business-men were conducted in writing and over the telephone. Lao Ting and others used the name Stephanie Reilly in their cor-respondence. Gigi spoke as Stephanie Reilly on the phone. She had a perfect American way of talking and laughing. When the businessmen met me in person, they said, "It's a pleasure to put a face to the name. I didn't expect you to be so young!"

"Please, call me Stephanie," I'd say, crossing and uncross-ing my legs, sliding the contracts across the glass.

"Well, Stephanie, can we go through the numbers one more time? Because there seem to be a few items here that maybe none of us anticipated."

"By all means. I don't want there to be any surprises." Lao Ting taught me how to speak this way.

I would walk them slowly through the revisions, refuting their objections before they could even raise them. "Keep them nodding," Lao Ting taught me. I worked the older ones against the younger ones.

"You see, I told you that was the issue," one would say to the other while I smiled.

"Don't predict your needs based on past performances or, for that matter, the Chinese expectations," I liked to add. "Our services don't work that way, which is what makes us so attractive. Most companies that coordinate American and Chinese contracts can't navigate those waters. Still, if you'd like to speak directly with the Chinese . . ."

"No, no. Of course, of course. We understand," the businessmen would say, and I'd stand and lean across the desk to point at where Gigi had stuck all her colored arrows.

If their pens still wavered, Robbie got nervous in the silence. He said, "Everything is underwritten, of course. We have bonded insurance, blah-blah. But please, don't sue us!"

"Let them think," I said. "Let the men think." The businessmen signed everything I gave them. They were always eager to please me, eager to show that they were on my side. Nobody ever sued Lao Ting.

Robbie was a handsome homosexual from Arroyo Grande and very talented, I thought. He was a health nut. Every morning he jogged twelve miles barefoot on the beach. He took frequent trips to Hawaii to meet with a medicine healer to repair his spirit. In a past life, Robbie was a mule and horribly brutalized by his master. Robbie said he was starved to death in a stall the size of a small closet.

"What country were you a mule in?" I asked him once.

"Russia," he said. "About twenty miles from Finland. The summers were the worst because the sun was up all day and night, and my master had insomnia. He suffered from psychosis and nobody understood him. He'd ride me out into the forest where nobody could hear him, and then he'd beat me, screaming and crying. God, it was awful. I felt for him, too. It's not that I didn't feel for him. I just can't get over how he put me in that stall. He was too cowardly to cut my head off, I guess."

"Did he abuse you sexually?" I asked.

"Just emotionally," Robbie said. "My healer is having me take this ancient lava ash. It makes my tongue gray, so I have to suck on red candy." He stuck his tongue out to show me how red it was. "For when I have auditions."

"Looks good," I said.

"All natural ingredients. But it still rots your teeth. Any sugar will do that. Even fruit. But I'm feeling a little more grounded now, I think, taking the lava ash."

Robbie didn't eat meals with the family. He lived mostly on vegetable juices, nuts, and herbs. The family didn't judge him for that. They supported him unconditionally. For his birthday, they gave him a little almond tree. For my birthday, they gave me a white silk robe with a pink dragon embroidered on the back. Lao Ting and Gigi were the kindest people on Earth. They were the most tender souls one could ever hope to find.

"You're going to get over what happened to you, I'm certain of it," Gigi said to Robbie. "I had a dream last night you were a white stallion, running free across the tundra."

"Yes, you will come out a winner. And dear, dear Stephanie Reilly," Lao Ting said across the table. "You and Robbie are doing such a good job. We feel happy to have you two in our lives. Our beautiful American son and daughter. We are so proud of you. Look at you both! So handsome! So pretty!"

Lao Ting had a digestive issue that restricted his diet to shrimp and boiled yams. The digestive issue seemed to be well managed by this diet, and by his daily regimen of swimming and stretching and Ping-Pong. Because he was the patriarch of the family and the boss of the business, and because the family was disciplined in their loyalties, shrimp, yams, and rice were all that was offered at meals. I once asked Lao Ting whether he ever grew tired of eating the same foods again and again each day.

"I never grow tired of food," he answered and slapped at his narrow torso.

I wasn't keen on cooking for myself. I had fancy flatware and some cast-iron pots at home, but I preferred taking party drugs to making food and eating it. During the workweek, all that I ate I ate with the family. I liked the rice they made. It was cooked in an enormous bamboo steamer and tasted of old wood, like the way an antique store smells. The shrimp were boiled whole, then slathered in butter and Chinese spices. The family ate the shrimp by first biting off the heads. They'd spit the little antennae and black spidery eyes out on the ground between their plastic footstools, which they used as chairs around a low table in the dining room. Then they'd put the whole shrimp in their mouths, chew them up, and spit out the exoskeletons. The eldest son, Jesse, swept and mopped the dining room after every meal. There were four children— three boys and one girl. All but Jesse were still in high school. When they came home, they helped their parents with paper-work and tidied up. The complex was always very clean and smelled of burning incense. All the floors were flesh-colored marble. The walls were decorated with big crosses woven out of red silk ropes. "These are from China," Gigi told me. "They're good luck. They signify birth and prosperity."

Once Gigi showed me on a map where the family's ancestors were from. "My mother's mother's father is from this city. Lao Ting's mother's father's mother was born here, on this river. My father's mother's mother is from this village. You see that dot? It's so beautiful there. You know mist? There's so much mist in that place. It's like a big ghost, the whole village is one big, happy ghost."

"I would like to go there sometime," I said.

"You can go anytime. There are all kinds of magic stuff there. Maybe you can go there and go crazy. You need to go a little crazy sometimes, have a little fun. Sometimes I think you look sad too often. But I think you're going to be happy soon. Here, let me say a blessing."

I never told Gigi about my pituitary situation, which was the source of all my sadness. Anytime I had a cold or a rash or an upset stomach, Gigi would make a tincture from Chinese herbs she kept in a locked wooden chest in the master bedroom on the second floor. Each tincture had a different flavor, and it usually made me well again. I am sure that if I'd told Gigi about my situation, she would have made me a special tincture for that, too. And then every day after, she'd be asking, "Is it better? Is the flesh smaller now, or still so swollen? Poor Stephanie Reilly. You are so pretty. We need to get your gah-gah healthy again."

One night I had a dream that Gigi told me to make a radio program out of the demon voices inside of me. I did so, and when I put the program on the air, the world heard the evil things the demons were saying, and everybody went crazy and killed themselves. In bed, as I dreamed, I became paralyzed. The ceiling opened up and an alien spaceship lasered down a powerful ray of vacuous light and exorcised all the demons out through my chest. It took about ten seconds.

"I wonder if they're really gone," I told Gigi. "If they are, I wonder what I'll do. I wonder if I'll be different from now on."

"I had a dream last night, too," Gigi said. "I met a young woman in a little shop somewhere. It was just a small mom-and-pop, dirty, not very nice. This young woman took a drink from the shelf and broke the bottle on the floor. Then she started eating the little shards of broken glass. I tried to pull her off the floor. 'Don't do that, sweet child!' I was yelling, but she used the shards to cut my arms. Her hair became tangled in her face. She had hair like an African American woman when they get it ironed. It was like ribbons tied in knots across her face. When I woke up from this dream, I was thinking people could try wearing their hair like that, tied in knots across their faces. If it were done well, it could be very decorative and beautiful." She turned to her daughter, who had long, straight black hair. "Maybe you'll let me try some designs on you later." The girl chewed her food and waved her chopsticks back and forth. "No?" said Gigi. "You'll be sorry." She laughed. "I hope your demons are gone, sweet Stephanie Reilly. But please don't change too much. I'd miss you. We would all miss your warm, fragile spirit."

○———○

The demons didn't leave me, though. They were always there, taunting me, filling my pituitary with poison. One day, after a successful business meeting, I told Robbie about my pituitary situation as we drove back to the complex.

"I can understand your frustration," he said. "My healer says that the body erupts from the mind. Everything is emotional. Ideas and feelings. Is there some emotion you are storing up in your pituitary, some negative feeling that makes your genitals so big and gross?"

"I guess I have a lot of emotion stored up. But it's nothing bad. It's love. It's just love rotting up inside of me."

"I've never heard of such a problem."

"That's it," I said. "I have too much love, I think, and nobody to give it to."

"What a conundrum," Robbie said. "I can give you the number of a magician I know. He converts energies so they can be purged and donated to people in need."

"It would be nice," I said, "to help somebody out."

"When I had tendonitis, he transferred the inflammation onto a dying mosquito, he told me. And then later that day a mosquito bit me. It was wonderful. I don't know if it was the same mosquito, but my wrist felt better almost instantly."

"That's amazing, Robbie," I said.

"Life is amazing, Stephanie Reilly. We won the jackpot, getting to live on this beautiful Earth. When I can keep that kind of positive attitude, a madman can beat me all he wants. He can break every bone in my body. There is no pain," said Robbie. "Experiences are just time passing in different ways. Time passes and continues on and on. It has nowhere else to go. Call him." He wrote down the magician's phone number on the back of a business card.

"You know what happens when you jump off a bridge?" This was another man I remember. He had a scar across his forehead like a third eye. I found him panhandling outside the liquor store in Saticoy. He was intense and perturbed and smelled like motor oil and vomit, which is what drew me to him. I told him he could sleep on my couch if he promised not to touch me, and I took him home to the loft. He was just a kid, it turned out, only nineteen years old. He'd run away from his home in Nebraska and was thumbing rides down to Venice Beach. "Basically you bleed to death," he told me. "Your bones turn into knives inside your body when you hit the water. Or your heart explodes under the pressure. And you break your neck. Can I use your bathroom?"

"Sit down," I said, pointing at the couch.

In the cab, he'd talked like this: "You know how many murdered bodies never get discovered? You know how to tell if a person's soul has left its body? You know that guy back there outside the liquor store? I think he's possessed or something."

"I'm possessed," I told him. "Many people often are."

"What's it like? Do you speak in tongues? Do you ever do things you regret but can't take back?"

"It's not like that," I said. "It's more of a medical issue."

"Do you know that there are people in India, if you cut off their hands, they'll just grow back new ones? Some people have special powers. I wish I could go to India. I like your apartment. Is your husband home? Is he down for whatever?"

I did not strip for the boy. I gave him what little I had in my fridge to eat: an apple, yogurt, chocolate-covered almonds, a frozen samosa. We sat together on the couch, discussing all the different ways to die. By sunup, I had my pants down, asking for his opinion on the situation, hoping he'd say he'd seen so much worse. But he had not.

"You should come to India with me," he said. "Gurus, special doctors, chanting."

"There's always surgery," I began to say.

"Yeah, but that won't get to the root of the problem. The demons, right? You're still really pretty, though," he said. "You have that going for you."

Life can be strange sometimes, and knowing it can be doesn't seem to make it any less so. I know I don't have any real wisdom. I don't have any wonderful ideas. I am lucky to have found a few nice people here and there.

Lao Ting went swimming in the ocean one morning

and never came back. They sent boats out there to try to find him, but he was gone. He was probably eaten up by sharks, the family said. There was no funeral or missing-person report. But there was a memorial service, just a family meeting in silence on the patio at sunset. I came for the last few hours. Robbie was away, filming an exercise video with his medicine man in Hawaii. When the sun went down, Gigi gave everyone a cup of special tea, and when I drank it, I fell asleep on the white leather love seat and dreamed of nothing, not a sound, just whirling gray air in an infinite space. In the morning, the children packed up all of Lao Ting's belongings. A Goodwill truck came to collect the boxes. It broke my heart to see how tidy everything was, how neatly Lao Ting could be put away.

There were no more meetings, no more businessmen, no shrimp, no yams, no rice. Gigi ordered fried chicken and let it sit out in the dining room, orange oil seeping through the paper buckets and staining the white tablecloth. But she was strong. I never saw her shed a tear. The sons went down to the beach and lit paper documents on fire and stared out into the water and screamed out their sorrow. The daughter stayed in her room, listening to twinkling music on her computer. Without Lao Ting, the company could not function.

"It is the best thing," Gigi said, signing my last paycheck. "We will sell the complex. We don't need all this luxury. You know, Stephanie Reilly, when I met my husband, I was a teenage prostitute. I did things I hope my daughter never does, not for money, nor for free. When Lao Ting first saw me on the street, I was just a skinny Chinese tramp in a bikini top—can you imagine? All my dreams were nightmares back then. Nothing good. Nowhere safe to sleep. Lao Ting gave me this." She unbuttoned the top of her black mourning gown and pulled out a tiny bloodred stone hanging from a gold chain around her neck. "He told me this stone would mend my broken heart. Fancy words, romance—I know how silly it sounds. But it worked. It made me strong. That is not the whole story. Just to say, Stephanie Reilly, we all need to have composure. We need some solid stuff to hold on to. When I look at you, I see fine loose threads, like a silk cushion that has been rubbed for a hundred years, poor girl."

A few years later, when I was desperate and wanted to end my life, I called Robbie's magician. By then I was living in a rented room in Van Nuys, taking the bus down to Tijuana every month to buy special hormones a doctor had said might balance the situation out a bit. It wasn't working. On the phone with the magician, I explained my situation. I cried.

I said, "On a good day, every small thing is enchanting. Everything is a miracle. There is no emptiness. There is no need for forgiveness or escape or medicine. I hear only the wind in the trees, and my devils hatching their sacral plans, fusing all the shattered pieces together into a blanket of ice. I have found that it's under that ice that I can feel I am just another normal person. In the dark and cold, I am at 'peace.'"

"What is your name?" the magician asked.

So I moved here to Vacaville to be with him. It is good to have someone to turn to late at night, when the voices in my head are loud and there are no drugs to dull them. The magician doesn't mind my swelling. He blossoms like a tree in front of my eyes, a man of seventy-five years, revitalized by my pain and sadness. It makes me feel good to see him thrive.

Takashi dressed in long black rags, ripped fishnet stockings, and big black boots with long, loose laces that splatted on the floor when he walked. He smelled strongly of old sweat and cigarette smoke, and his face was scabbed from tearing his pimples open and squeezing the pus out with dirty chewed-up fingernails. He covered the scabs with makeup that was too pale for his skin. He used scissors to cut off all his eyelashes. Sometimes he drew a French mustache on with black felt-tip pen. He was very intelligent and preoccupied with death and suffering. He had a way about him I really liked. His hair was long and bleached and dyed rainbow colors. Occasionally he bit into his lip and dribbled blood down his chin. Sometimes he vomited in public just to make a scene. Strangers would rush to his aid, offering handkerchiefs and bottles of water. People even stopped to take his picture when we walked down the street. Takashi's taste in classical music was just like mine: Saint-Saëns, Debussy, Ravel. He was talented on the violin. He said his instrument was worth more than his father's car. He chewed licorice gum sometimes, his favorite flavor, but his mouth still tasted like excrement when we kissed each other. Takashi was my first real boyfriend.

Last spring, we got locked in a practice room above the large concert hall at the music school where we both took lessons on Saturday afternoons. This happened during a rehearsal of the youth orchestra, in which Takashi played violin. At first I thought Takashi might have arranged the entrapment to take advantage of me sexually, but that was not the case. How it happened was so funny: We went up a secret spiral staircase behind the concert hall while the orchestra was tuning. We just wanted to explore a bit before Takashi's rehearsal started. In the practice room, we closed the door behind us and then we couldn't open it again.

The locked room contained a couch, a radiator, several chairs, and music stands but no piano. As a pianist, I was never part of any orchestra. I was mostly studying composition then, and that kept me from having to perform very often. I was not as outgoing as Takashi. Everything made me nervous, in fact. It was partly why I liked Takashi so much. He seemed fearless, like he could do anything he wanted to do, even if it was disgusting. In the corner of the room was a rack of costumes that I recognized from the student production of *Figaro*. The opera had been part of the holiday festival in which my first composition for violin and harpsi-chord had been debuted. Takashi had played the violin part very well. The harpsichord part was so difficult, and I was so nervous, that my piano teacher, Mrs. V, had to fill in for me at the last moment.

We banged on the locked door and yelled but nobody could hear. We heard the conductor shouting, and then the orchestra began to play. I tried picking the lock with one of my barrettes. Takashi had a small knife he carried around for mutilating himself, and we each tried using it as a screw-driver to dismantle the lock or take the door off its hinges, but it was impossible. The other door was a fire door of rein-forced steel, bolted shut. Behind that door was another secret staircase that only maintenance workers used, we learned later. The room had one window looking down onto an alleyway. Across the alley was a concrete parking structure. We were on the fifth floor.

"We should knot these costumes together, make a rope, tie one end to the radiator, and throw the other end down to the alley. Then you can climb down and come back up and let me out," I told Takashi.

He scratched at the veins on his wrist. "Let's just stay here forever," he said. "Anyway, you should be the one to climb down. You're lighter. You're the girl."

We were quiet for a while after that. Then I took a few cos-tumes off their hangers and tried them on. I could see my re-flection in the window. I looked like a tiny clown in the big blouse and vest. Takashi found a short gray wig and tried it on.

"You look great in that wig," I told Takashi. He took it off and held it in his hands, petting it like it was a kitten he loved so much.

I took off my costume and tied all the garments on the rack together with double knots. Takashi held up a blue cotton undershirt, sniffed it, and threw it on the ground. "If we have to pee, we can pee into it," he said. Luckily, I didn't have to pee. We tied the makeshift rope to the radiator. We opened the window and threw the rope out. The end of the rope did not reach the ground, but if one of us climbed down to the end of it, the remaining distance to the sidewalk was only one or two stories. I didn't think it would be a lethal jump.

A thought came into my mind. It was a question: "Do you see this, God?" God seemed like a fly on the wall, like a hidden camera. I mentioned the thought to Takashi. He told me that he was an atheist, but that he believed in hell. I leaned out through the open window and looked down. A homeless man was pushing a shopping cart of garbage up the narrow alleyway.

"Hey!" I shouted. Takashi grabbed my arm and told me to be quiet. "We're trapped up here!" I squealed. When Takashi clamped his hand over my mouth, it tasted like baby powder from the wig, and excrement.

I bit down on Takashi's finger, not very hard, but hard enough for him to let me loose. I picked up the blue undershirt for peeing into and threw it out the window, hoping it would get the homeless man's attention. It simply drifted off to the side of the alley and disappeared behind a Dumpster. I spoke to God in my mind. *Please, open the door,* I said. I tried both doors again. Of course, they were still locked. And then I felt very stupid.

I tried to express the idea of mind over matter to Takashi. "If you believe something, really and truly, it becomes reality," I said. "Don't you think?"

"I believe in death," was Takashi's reply. He leaned out and spat blood down into the alleyway. Some blood and spit bubbled down his chin. Then he sat down on the couch and petted the wig again.

I had to try to escape from the locked room. I tugged at the rope. It seemed to be tied securely enough to the radiator. So I wrapped it around my arm and held on and began to step out onto the window ledge. Takashi sat on the couch and picked at the scabs on his face and watched me. I told him that I was not afraid of falling. And for a moment, I wasn't nervous. Not at all.

What happened next is absolutely true. Once I was all the way out the window, I gripped the rope, lowered myself a little, and put the soles of my shoes flat against the side of the building. Then a car came squealing up the alley. It was copper colored and very shiny. The motor was very loud. The car screeched to a halt below me. I froze. Takashi threw the gray wig past me, out the window. I screamed and pulled myself back up and crouched on the ledge of the window. I looked down, though it made me dizzy. It was windy up there in the sky. A man got out of the car. His movements were violent and angry as he pointed up at me and yelled, "Young lady, you better get back inside this instant!" I'd never seen anyone so angry. Even my mother had never seemed so angry. "Young lady!" the man repeated. He swung his finger up at me, stabbing at the air. In my mind now, I picture him in a black suit and shiny black shoes, but I couldn't make out his pants or shoes from so high up in the air. I think he was actually wearing a white T-shirt and dark sunglasses. Of course, I did what he told me to do. I grappled with the rope, hoisted myself over the windowsill, and climbed back inside the room. I hid by the couch. It was so warm and quiet inside the room. I could hear my heart pounding. Takashi got up to look out the window. He said he saw the man shake his head and get back in the car. I could hear the door slam and the car drive away.

"We should put the clothes back on the hangers," Takashi said, lazily pulling up the rope.

I was pretty shaken up. I wanted to talk about the man with Takashi, but Takashi wouldn't look at me. I helped pull the rope back in, and we untied the garments and put them back on the rack. I wanted Takashi to tell me that he was happy I was safe inside the room, and that he'd have been sorry if I'd died. I wanted to discuss the angry man. I wanted to say I believed in guardian angels, but I was scared Takashi would roll his eyes. He blew his nose into a white dress shirt and pinched a pimple on his neck. We sat on the floor with our backs against the couch and watched the sky darken behind the parking structure across the alleyway. The orchestra rehearsal had ended hours since. I knew my mother would be angry that I wasn't home in time for dinner. Takashi pulled a cigarette from his purse and lit it. We passed it back and forth, blowing the smoke at the sliver of moon visible from where we sat on the floor by the window. Finally, Takashi told me his theory about the man in the car. "He was a hallucination. We're in a vortex. We're in a black hole. We've always been in it. Nothing we've ever seen has been real. Only this room is real." He ashed his cigarette onto his tongue. "You shouldn't have thrown that blue shirt out the window," he said. "Now our reality has been punctured. And I have to pee."

"You shouldn't have thrown out that gray wig," I said. My heart raced again when I thought of how that gray wig had flown past me, a tiny kitten pawing through the air. I don't know what happened to that gray wig. Maybe the man in the car caught it and brought it home.

I told Takashi I didn't want to be his girlfriend anymore. He said nothing.

I felt very depressed after that. All of eternity seemed to be laid out in front of me, and there was nothing but the couch and chairs and music stands, the wrinkled costumes, the radiator, and Takashi. That was hell there, in that locked room. When the cigarette was finished, Takashi tried to kiss me. I just turned my head away.

Not long after, a janitor came and let us out. "I smelled smoke," he said, eyeing the crust of blood around Takashi's chapped lips.

I cried as we walked down the secret staircase and through the dark, quiet hallways of the music school. Takashi found his violin and I found my composition notebook in the place we'd left them, under a table in the concert hall where the orchestra had rehearsed.

Outside it was a warm and pleasant evening, like nothing was wrong. Takashi waved good-bye at the bus stop and I walked to the tram. At home, I sat in the kitchen and my mother gave me a cold boiled potato, black instant coffee, and a small container of diet yogurt.

"You should try harder to please me," she said. "For your own good."

"I'll try harder," I told her. "I promise."

But I never did try very hard to please my mother. In fact, I never tried hard to please anybody at all after that day in the locked room. Now I only try hard to please myself. That is all that matters here. That is the secret thing I found.

come from some other place. It's not like a real place on Earth or something I could point to on a map, if I even had a map of this other place, which I don't. There's no map because the place isn't a place like something to be near or in or at. It's not somewhere or anywhere, but it's not nowhere either. There is no *where* about it. I don't know what it is. But it certainly isn't this place, here on Earth, with all you silly people. I wish I knew what it was, not because I think it would be great to tell you about it; I just miss it so much. If I knew what it was, maybe I could make something like it here on Earth. Waldemar says it's impossible. The only way to get there is to go.

"Waldemar," I say to my brother. "How do we get back to the place, to the thing, whatever?"

"Oh, you have to die. Or you have to kill the right person."

That's his answer now. For a long time he

thought only the first part was true, but over time he's thought long and hard and figured out that there is a second way. The second way is much harder. I don't know how he figured it out, but thank God for Waldemar, who is so much wiser than me, though only a day older. I took some extra time to come out of the woman. I had doubts, even so early on, about this place here on Earth with all the dumb things everywhere. It was Waldemar who persuaded me to come out finally. I could hear his cries and feel his little fists poking through the woman's skin. He is my best friend. Everything he does, it seems, he does because he loves me. He is the best brother ever, of all brothers here on Earth. I love him so much.

"Well, I don't want to die," I tell him. "Not yet. Not here."

We talk about this from time to time. It's nothing new.

"Then you've got to find the right person to kill. Once you've killed the right person, a hole will open up in the Earth and you can just walk straight into the hole. It will lead you through a tunnel back to where we came from. But be careful. If you kill the wrong person, you'll get into trouble here. It wouldn't be good. I'd visit you in prison, but chances are slim that the right person will be sitting beside you in your prison cell. And the prisons they have for little girls are the worst. There, the only way to the place would be to die. So you've got to be really sure about the person to kill. It's the hardest thing to do, to be so sure about something like that. I've never been sure enough, and that's why I'm still here. That, and because I'd miss you and I'd worry if I left you all alone."

"Maybe I'll just die after all," I say. I get so tired of it here, thinking of how much better it is back there, in the place we came from. I cry about it often. Waldemar always has to soothe me.

"I could kill you," he offers. "But I'm not sure you're the right person. But wouldn't that be great? If you were?"

"That would be ideal!" I say.

I don't know what I'd do without my brother. I'd probably cry even more than I do now, and take poisons that make my brain weak and my body tired so I wouldn't even have the strength to think about the other place. I'd try to poison the place out of my mind. But I doubt that's even possible. Some nights I hate it here so much I shake and sweat and my brother holds me down so I won't start kicking the walls or breaking things. When I kick the walls, the woman gets angry. "What's going on up there, children?" She thinks we're fighting and threatens to separate us. She doesn't know about the other place. She's just a human woman, after all. She gives us food and clothes and everything, as human mothers like to do. My brother says he's sure the woman is not the person he could kill to get back to the place. I'm not so sure she's not my person. Sometimes I think she is. But if I killed her and I was wrong, I'd be sorry. Mostly I'd be sorry for Waldemar.

One morning as we lie in our beds, I say to my brother, "Waldemar, I think I know who my person is." I don't really know. I am still sort of dreaming. But then I think up a name to say. "His name is Jarek Jaskolka and I'm going to find him and kill him, mark my words."

"But are you sure?" my brother asks.

"I think so," I say. And then, suddenly, I am sure. Jarek Jaskolka is the person I have to kill. I know it in my bones. I am as sure about Jarek Jaskolka as I am about the place, and about me and Waldemar being from there.

"You must be completely sure," my brother warns me. He rises from his bed and lifts the blanket over his head like an old lady going to the market. His face becomes dark and his voice suddenly low and frightening. "If you aren't sure, you could get in trouble, you know."

"You look like a witch, Waldemar. Don't make me laugh at you," I say. Waldemar doesn't like to be ridiculed.

"If you kill the wrong person . . ." he begins.

But I am sure now. I can't go back and pretend I'm not. I have to return to the place somehow. I miss it too much. My brain hurts and I cry all the time. I don't want to be here on Earth for one moment longer.

"It's that damned Jarek Jaskolka!" I cry. It is just a name I've made up, but it is the right name, that I am sure of. I jump from my bed. I pull the string to lift the curtains. The room where Waldemar and I sleep looks out into the forest. Outside, soft gray clouds hang between the trees. Some silly birds sing a few nice notes. I miss the other place so much, I want to cry. But I feel brave. "I will find you, Jarek," I say to the window. "Wherever you are hiding!"

When I look at Waldemar, he has gone back under his covers. I can see his chest rising and falling. My brain hurts too much to try to comfort him. And anyway, there is no comfort here on Earth. There is pretending, there are words, but there is no peace. Nothing is good here. Nothing. Every place you go on Earth, there is more nonsense.

For breakfast the woman gives us bowls of warm fresh yogurt and warm fresh bread and tea with sugar and lemon, and for Waldemar a slice of onion cooked in honey because he has been coughing.

"Jarek Jaskolka," I whisper to remind myself that I will soon be far away from this place and all its horrors. Every time I say the name out loud, my head feels a little better. "Jarek Jaskolka," I say to Waldemar. He smiles sadly.

The woman, hearing me say Jarek Jaskolka's name, drops her long wooden spoon. It skitters across the kitchen floor, dripping with the tasty yogurt. She comes at me.

"Urszula," she says. "How do you know this name? Where did you hear it? What have you done?" She isn't angry, as she so often is. Her face looks white and her eyes are wide. She holds her lips tight and frowns, holding me by the shoulders. She is scared.

"Oh, he is just some person," I say, batting my eyes so she cannot see the murder in them.

"Jarek Jaskolka is a bad, bad man," the woman says, shaking me. I stop blinking. "If you see him on the street, you run away. You hide from him. Jarek Jaskolka likes to do bad things. I know because he lived on Grjicheva, next door to my house before they tore it down for the tramway when I was little. Many girls came away from his house black and blue and bloodied. You have seen my marks?"

"Oh no, Mother!" cries Waldemar. "Don't show her those!"

But it is too late. The woman pulls her skirt up past one knee and points. There they are, marks like swollen earthworms, enough of them to make a lump from the side, the poor woman.

"Jarek Jaskolka will do the same to you," she says. "Now go to school and don't be stupid. And if you meet that bad man on the street, run away like a good girl. And you, too, Waldemar. Who knows what Jarek Jaskolka is up to now?"

It is usual for the woman to get in the way of good things I want to do.

"Jarek Jaskolka made those marks on the woman, but so what?" I ask Waldemar on the walk to school. "What's so bad about some measly marks?"

"You don't want those marks," Waldemar answers. "You'll end up like Mother, always angry. She only has bad dreams."

"But I have bad dreams already," I say. "All my dreams are about this place here and all the boring, stupid things and people."

"You take it too hard," Waldemar says. "Things here aren't so bad. Anyway, what if the other place is no better? You could go back there and be just as troubled."

"Impossible," I say. But I wonder. "What do you think

Jarek Jaskolka did to the woman? How did the marks get there?"

"There are things men do. Nobody knows. It's like a magic act. Nobody can solve it."

It doesn't sound so bad to me. Magic acts are easy to solve. There is an old man in the town square who eats fire and makes the crows that mill under the big tree there disappear in a puff of smoke. Any fool can see that they've just flown up into the branches to hide.

"Will you help me find Jarek Jaskolka?" I ask Waldemar. "I really want to get out of here. Even though I'll miss you when I'm gone."

"I'll try," he answers and frowns. He is angry at me, I can tell. When my brother is angry, he plucks the poison berries from the bushes on the road and puts them up his nose. Everybody knows that's where the brain is, up the nose there. Waldemar likes to poison his brain that way. It makes him feel better to do that. I myself like to swallow the poison berries like tablets. So because Waldemar is plucking berries, I pluck berries, too, and swallow them one by one. They are soft and cold. If I snag one on my fang, goop spills out and tastes bitter, like the poison that it is.

At school we sit at different tables. At chorus I can see Waldemar's mouth moving, but I know he isn't singing the song. When we file out of the big stone church, I ask Waldemar again. "Will you help me find him? Not just for me, but for the woman. Maybe if I kill him, the woman won't be so angry all the time. It seems she holds quite a grudge."

"I won't help you," says Waldemar. "And don't try to cheer me up. You'd better think of a way to kill him when you find him. I'm not going to help you do that."

Waldemar is right. I'll need some kind of knife to kill Jarek Jaskolka with. I'll need the sharpest knife I can find. And I'll need poison. The poison berries from the bush make our brains just a little sleepy, but that is all they do. If I make Jarek Jaskolka eat many poison berries, maybe he will fall asleep, and then I can kill him with the knife, step into the hole, and go back to the place at last. This is my plan.

On the walk home with Waldemar that day after school, I fill my skirt with poison berries. I look like a farmer girl holding my skirt up like that. I tell Waldemar to fill his pockets with berries, but he says they will get squished, and anyway, I have picked enough to kill Jarek Jaskolka already.

"Really? This is enough to kill him?" I ask my brother.

"Oh, I don't know. Don't ask me." Waldemar is still so angry. I don't blame him. I try to sing a funny song as we turn the corner and cross the town square, but Waldemar covers his ears.

"Sorry, Waldemar," I say. But I don't feel sorry. Sometimes Waldemar loves me too much. He thinks it is better I stay with him on Earth, rather than be happy in the other place without him. "When you die, we'll be together again," I say, trying to console him. "Or maybe you'll find your person to kill. Don't give up." My legs are cold as we walk the rest of the way home. But I have so many poison berries.

I am happy. "I'll make poison berry jam," I say. "I've seen the woman do it with cherries."

"She will never let you use her pot," Waldemar says. He looks at me. I know I could persuade Waldemar to help me make the jam, but I don't want to. When he is angry with me, I feel he loves me even more, and that feels good to me, even though it also feels so bad.

When we get home, the woman is outside hanging wet clothes on the line of rope between the trees. I imagine the marks on her thighs again. They are like welts, like slugs crawling up her leg. My thighs are like my arms. They are just skin and flesh with no marks. They are clean blank skin and flesh. Nothing is ever going to crawl up them, not ever, I decide. I'd die before I let anyone give me marks like the woman's, I decide. Even if they are just marks of magic. I hide my skirt of poison berries behind Waldemar as we pass and wave to the woman. We go inside the house. I pull a big black pot from the cupboard and fill it with the poison berries.

"How do you make jam, Waldemar?" I ask my brother.

"Add sugar and cook it for a long time."

"Oh, I love sugar," I say. "I'll do it tonight while the woman is sleeping."

"You better not taste too much of it. Don't forget, when you cook it, the poison gets stronger."

"Will you help me remember, Waldemar?"

"No," he says and puts a few more poison berries up his nose. "I have to sleep at night. If I don't sleep, I feel sick during the day. I don't like feeling sick at school."

"Oh, poor little Waldemar," I say, mocking him. I swallow a few of the berries and drag the pot into our bedroom and hide it in the closet.

When the woman comes back in from hanging the clothes, she says, "Go play outdoors, children. Waldemar, go run around while the sun is still shining. Urszula, go and be energetic. You look so serious. You look like an old lady. Go out and have fun. It's good for you."

"I don't like fun," I say.

Waldemar snorts and goes outside to play. I want to play with Waldemar, but I have to stay in my room to guard my pot of poison berries in the closet. If the woman finds it, she'll start asking questions. She'll get in the way of my killing Jarek Jaskolka, and then I'll be stuck here on Earth with her forever. I can imagine what she'll say if she discovers my plan. "There is something wrong with you, Urszula."

"No," I will tell her. "There is something wrong with this place. There is something wrong with you and everybody here. There is nothing, nothing, nothing wrong with me."

And anyway, I still have to find Jarek Jaskolka. I can't kill him if I don't know where he is, after all. While Waldemar is still outside playing, I go to the kitchen. It smells like cooking rice and parsley.

"Hello," I say to the woman. "Jarek Jaskolka, does he still live on Grjicheva?"

"Of course not. Unless he lives in a hole in the ground. All the houses got torn down there. I hope he moved very far away. His sister is the lady in the library."

"That big fatso?"

"Don't be cruel."

"I think I need a book to read," I say.

"Then go, go," the woman says angrily. "I don't know what you're up to, but remember what I said about Jarek Jaskolka. Remember the marks. But go, do what you want, as if I care."

"You're angry at me now because I want to read a book?"

"Urszula is Urszula," is all she says. She leaves the kitchen, wiping her hands on her apron, and goes outside to watch Waldemar build a tower of pinecones. The woman is mean and stupid, I think. The entire world is stupid. I find a sharp butcher knife in the drawer and take it to my room and hide it in my satchel. I kick at the walls for a while. Then I start off for the library to find the fat sister of the man I am going to kill.

"Jaskolka?" the fat woman asks. "I don't use that name any-more. What do you want? Why are you asking?"

"I'm just curious. What happened when they tore your house down for the tramway? My mother lived on Grjicheva once, too."

"Whose daughter are you?" the fat lady asks.

"My name is Urszula" is all I say.

"Those houses on Grjicheva were all poor and ugly and it's a good thing they're gone now or else they'd just crumble down over our heads and kill us."

"Kill you?" I ask.

"We moved to a small apartment near the river, if you must know."

"You and your family? And your brother?"

She puts down the rubber stamp in her hand and closes the book on the counter. The sunlight through the windows falls on her face as she leans toward me.

"What do you know about my brother? What is it? Why are you asking me these questions?"

"I'm looking for Jarek Jaskolka," I say. The lady is so fat and lazy looking, it seems not to matter what I tell her. "I have to kill him."

The lady laughs and picks up her rubber stamp again. "Go right ahead," she says. "He lives up the street in the house across from the cemetery. He'll be pleased to have a visitor. You can't imagine how pleased he'll be."

"I'm going to kill him," I tell the lady. She just laughs.

"Good luck. And don't come running back here full of tears," she says. "Curious girls get what they deserve."

"What do you mean?"

"Don't listen to me."

"I will kill him dead, you know," I say. "That's why I'm curious."

"Do what you can," she says. "Now be quiet. People are trying to read."

On my way home, I walk through the cemetery, past my father's grave, and I look through the windows of what I guess is Jarek Jaskolka's house. The sun is setting, and the sky is beautiful colors and I wish Waldemar were there with me, holding my hand. "Why is it, Waldemar," I would ask him, "that when something here is so beautiful, I just want to die?"

"Because it reminds you of the other place," Waldemar would say to me. "The most beautiful place of all."

Jarek Jaskolka's house is clapboard painted cloudy green like pond water, and the windows facing the road are covered by a dark curtain. The front steps are missing, and in place of the steps there are big broken pieces of cement piled on top of one another. There are dry bushes around the house full of orange meadowlarks. I pick up a little rock and throw it at Jarek Jaskolka's window, but the glass doesn't break. The rock just makes a little *ding* sound against the glass. The meadowlarks start to chirp at me, whining like babies crying. I don't care. I could throw rocks at them if I wanted. I could crush them with the heel of my shoe. I wait, hiding in the bushes, waiting to see if anything will happen. Then I throw another rock. This time, Jarek Jaskolka comes to the window. I watch him pull the curtain back. His big wrinkled hand grips the dark cloth, and just for a moment, I see his face. He looks like any normal grandfather, eyes drooping, white beard, wrinkled cheeks, and a nose like a melted candle. When he moves away from the window, his fingernails tap against the glass.

They are long and yellow like an ogre's. But it's clear he's just a feeble old man. It will be easy to feed him the jam, then hack him up with a knife, I figure. Old men are easy to hack. Their flesh is like an old limp carrot. But if Waldemar is right about the black hole opening up, and if Jarek Jaskolka is really my right person, then I don't have to worry about hacking him up all the way. Maybe one hack will be enough to kill him and I can just jump down into the hole and go back to the other place.

When the curtain falls back across the window, I run away, back through the cemetery, kicking at the stones that mark whatever silly people have come and gone, and I wonder where they've gone off to, if there are other places for each of us, and whether my father is really, as the woman has always told us, in a better place than this.

That night the woman is angry at me again. She wants to know what I was reading at the library. "I hope you didn't get some book that's going to fill you up with crazy notions."

"I didn't find any good books at the library," I say. "They were all boring. They were all dumb."

"Ach, Urszula," the woman says. "You think you're smarter than all the rest."

"But aren't I? Who is smarter than me? Show me the person. Don't you always say—" The woman has always said not to mind other children at school when they tease me, and that I am the smartest, and the best, forever and ever, amen.

"Forget what I always say," says the woman. "You need to learn respect."

"Respect for what? For you?"

"God forbid!" She turns her back and hacks at a loaf of bread with a butcher knife. It isn't as big as the butcher knife I've stolen, though. I can't wait to kill Jarek Jaskolka and leave this place, I think. Again I wish that the woman would be my person to kill. But she isn't. I am pretty sure of that by now.

"And you, Waldemar," the woman says when she turns around. "Who stole your candy? Why are you frowning like a lost little child?"

Waldemar looks sad with his soupspoon in his fist. He won't look at me. He takes a chunk of bread from the woman and doesn't answer.

"Did you do something?" the woman asks me. "Did you hurt my special boy?"

"I would never do anything to hurt Waldemar. Why would I? I love him the most."

"Sometimes you can be rough, Urszula. You don't show love the best way. When was the last time you did something nice for me? When was the last time you said 'thank you'?"

Waldemar stands and leaves the table.

"Waldemar, come back, please. Your soup will get cold," the woman says gently.

"Let him go," I tell her. "He's crying because of those marks you showed us. He thinks it's his fault. But it's yours."

I really think I am just so smart.

The woman sits and lowers her face so that it is dark and sad and I can see her spirit rise up a little from her body, like it doesn't want to be here either, like it has some better place to go.

"Jarek Jaskolka," I say softly, reaching my hand out to touch the woman's soft knee under the table.

"Ach!" she says, flinching. The legs of her chair scrape on the floor as she pushes herself away. "Pest," she calls me and stands up and goes around the kitchen, opening and closing cabinets. I think she might be looking for the iron pot I've hidden in the closet. But she doesn't ask if I've taken it. Nor does she notice her big butcher knife is gone. She puts the bread in the bread box and takes my bowl of soup away, spills it in the sink, unties her apron, and goes and stands by the window, staring out at nothing, it seems, just the darkness between the trees.

That night I have a dream about the old magician in the town square. He is showing me his tricks. "Like so," he grumbles and shakes into my hand a pile of little pellets. When I drop them on the ground, they explode into puffs of smoke. "These are made from moonstones," he says. He points up into the dark night sky. "You see that darkness? And you see the moonlight? There isn't one without the other." I guess I say something to show an interest in how his magic is possible, even though I know it's just a sham. "You're just a little child," he says. "Why are you so concerned with what you don't yet know?"

I wake up, and there is Waldemar sleeping in his bed beside me. It is very dark and quiet in the room. The woman is asleep in her bed on the other side of the wall. I can hear her snoring. At night, the noise from her nose is like a locomotive chugging. We are used to it. I think the noise from her nose is so enormous because her brain wants to take a train far away from here. I know she isn't happy. She likes Waldemar but she doesn't like me. It seems well enough that I leave this place. It will make her happy, I feel, if I leave. But it will make Waldemar so sad.

As quietly as I can, I drag the big pot of berries from the closet and take it to the kitchen. I light a fire on the stove and set the pot on the flame and drag a chair to the stove so I can stand on it and stir the berries. I pour a cup of sugar in and stir and listen to the berries singe and steam. The only light comes from a few lone stars through the darkened windows and the blue fire from the burner. "Jarek, this is for you," I say under my breath and inhale the poison-berry smell. My brain is comforted a little by the smell. My eyes are drowsy. But I keep stirring. I feel sad there all alone in the dark kitchen. I wish Waldemar were here to help me. This is my last night on Earth, I think to myself. And here I am, toiling over the stove like the woman does all day. "Ha." I laugh. Because my cooking seems funny suddenly, like I am making fun of the woman and her stupid life. I keep stirring. When the berries are all melted and smashed and mixed with the sugar, I spoon them up into one of the old glass jars the woman keeps on the shelf for her own jams and jellies. I switch off the stove, put the chair back by the kitchen table, take my jar in one hand, and drag the dirty pot back to my room, where Waldemar is still sleeping. In all that ruckus, nothing can be heard in the house but the locomotive engine, the woman snoring her way far away from here. I hide the dirty pot in the closet again. The jar of poison jam in my hands is hot. I get back into bed and let the jar cool on my nightstand. I sleep a little, but I don't have any more dreams.

In the morning, I put the jar of poison jam in my satchel. I act like everything is normal.

"Good morning, Waldemar," I say. I try to pretend I am normal, but Waldemar knows that I am not.

"What is it? What's that smile for?"

"Oh, nothing, just that I'm going to kill Jarek Jaskolka today and go back to the other place. Sorry you can't come with me." I try to sound cheerful, like I don't know that Waldemar's heart is broken. He can see right through me. He has that ability, as my brother.

"I don't like this idea, Urszula. I think Jarek Jaskolka won't eat the jam. I think he'll hurt you instead. You'll get those marks like Mother, and turn into an angry woman just like her."

"But I'm angry already," I say. "Marks or no marks, it makes no difference. I need to get out of here. And if I go through the hole and arrive back to the other place, whatever that is, what will I care if my legs are full of worms?"

"Worms?"

"Worms."

My thoughts go suddenly to the cemetery, the rich black dirt that was dug up to make room for our father to be buried in. I wonder, once I go through the hole back to the place, will my body be left behind? Later, will Waldemar stand in the cemetery and watch the dirt get dug up for me to be buried in? Will worms want to eat my flesh? Will they chew my flesh and spit out mud, which the teacher says is good for planting things? I can't discuss this with Waldemar now. It would upset him too much to answer such questions. We get dressed for school and go to the kitchen for breakfast. The woman is slicing an onion, crying. I can't look at her. I am worried she can tell I've used the stove the night before. The air, I worry, still smells like poison jam.

"You look tired, Urszula," she says. "You look sick. Maybe you should stay home today. Maybe you're getting Waldemar's cough."

"Yes," Waldemar says. "You should stay home. Don't go anywhere. Just stay in bed and read a book. I'll bring your schoolwork home for you. Don't go doing anything crazy."

"You sound just like the woman," I say to Waldemar.

"Call me Mother," the woman says.

The woman gives us our bread and yogurt, Waldemar's onion cooked in honey, and one for me, too.

"Thank you, Mother," Waldemar says.

I roll my eyes.

We eat in silence, Waldemar sniffling and clearing his throat. I keep my eyes on the worn wooden floor. "Good-bye, stupid floor," I say to myself. "Good-bye, ugly, stupid, old wood floor." But what do I care about that floor? A house can be full of life one day, then torn down into rubble the next. Tramways can be laid out. Millions of silly people can walk across a bit of Earth and never know what was once built on that place. We don't even know who's buried beneath our feet. So many people have come and gone, and where are they now? I think of the better place. "Jarek Jaskolka," I say to myself, but not out loud. I don't want Waldemar or the woman to hear me. I don't want any more trouble. I feel that I am ready to leave them both behind.

My satchel is heavy now, the jar of poison jam and butcher knife sagging down under my schoolbooks. Waldemar offers to carry my satchel for me.

"You look tired," he says. "Why not let me take that off your back?"

"Oh, you think you can solve things? You're just a little boy. You might have more muscles than me, but you're only a day older. You think you're smarter than me for that? You think you have all the answers, do you?"

Waldemar doesn't say anything. I am very excited with the thought that very soon, I'll be gone. I'm finally going

home, I think to myself. I try to hate Waldemar, but I can't.
I try not to think about how much I really love him. It is
hard to do.

We continue on our way up the road. I am breathing like
a crazy person breathes. My heart is beating like a crazy
person's heart beats. "Don't do anything crazy," Waldemar
had warned me. What is crazy about what I'm doing? What
does "crazy" even mean? There is one person everyone calls
"crazy." She is an old lady who lives between the cans of garbage behind the market. She covers herself in cabbage leaves
and fronds from carrot tops and old wax paper smeared with
animal fat, and she talks to herself and smokes the dirty tips of
cigarettes men toss to her where she lies during the day, bask-
ing in the sunshine, underneath the monument to the martyrs
in the town square. But even she doesn't seem so crazy. She is
probably just sad, like me, and from another place entirely. She
seems to be making the most of her time on Earth, though,
doing as she pleases. She doesn't work or have a crying baby
to tend to. Nobody is going to get near her. Nobody is going
to make her black and blue and bloody. She smells like so
many toilets. But she does as she pleases. She is a grown
woman. If I can't kill Jarek Jaskolka, I think to myself, I'll be
like that crazy lady and cover myself in garbage.

"Are you mad?" Waldemar asks, kicking a little rock
across the road.

"I'm sorry," I say. "I didn't sleep well. I'm all testy. My
brain is like a bug bite I scratched bloody. Sorry," I say again.

Waldemar puts his arm around my shoulder, plucks some

berries from the bush as we walk past. He puts one up his nose and hands me the rest.

"Thanks," I tell him, but I don't swallow any berries. I don't want to be poisoned anymore. I want to be awake and ready to jump and dive down into the hole when it opens up for me. I don't want to be sleepy and miss my chance, in case the hole is only open for a second. And I want to be on my toes for when I kill Jarek Jaskolka. Waldemar puts another berry up his nose. I feel I have more courage than Waldemar now. He seems like the sad lost child the woman had said he'd looked like the day before. I let the poison berries in my hand drop to the ground. When we reach the square, I turn in the direction of the cemetery. Waldemar turns to the road that leads to school. We stop and look at each other.

"Are you really doing it?" Waldemar asks.

"It's worth a try," I shrug. I am just pretending to be easy-going. Inside, I am determined.

"I'll come with you," Waldemar says. "I mean that I'll walk to Jarek Jaskolka's house with you, just to see what happens. If he is really your person, and you kill him and the hole opens up, maybe I can jump through with you."

Somehow I don't believe what Waldemar is saying. I feel like he's just giving an excuse to follow me. I worry that he might sabotage my plans. But then I look into his eyes. No. He won't get in my way. He is my brother. He will never keep me from being happy.

So I allow Waldemar to follow me on the road to the cemetery. We are quiet as we walk. I don't ask what he's

thinking. I don't want to know. When we get to Jarek Jaskolka's house, we stand and watch the dark, curtained windows for a while. A meadowlark comes and taps its beak
on the glass and hovers. Then another comes and flies right
into the glass and breaks its neck. Its body falls to the ground.
The first meadowlark flies away. This seems like a good
omen.

The sun comes out from behind a cloud. The shadows of
my body and Waldemar's body lie out in front of us like
holes in the ground. I carefully lay my satchel down and put
my arms around my brother.

"I'm sorry," I say. "I have to go in there alone. You know
the hole will only be big enough for one. You know that,
right?" I ask.

Waldemar nods. All our lives, we've understood each
other. Even when we are angry, there is too much love to
pretend to think that what we know to be true is only a
made-up story. That's the cruel way of all those silly people:
they tell you that what you believe is just some silly story.
That's why I hate it here. Everybody thinks that I am crazy.
I let go of Waldemar and pick up my satchel and start up
the big broken concrete slabs to the door of Jarek Jaskolka's
house.

"Will you come back for me?" my sweet brother asks.
There are tears in his eyes. He looks so small and lost and sad
from where I stand up high above him. I tell him I wish I
could stay with him, but not here, not on Earth. Earth is the
wrong place for me, always was and will be until the day I die.

"Just try, if you can, to send me a letter from the place. And if there's some way you can come back, come get me."

"Okay, Waldemar. I'll try," I say, but I will never come back. Even if I can come back, I won't. I drop my satchel down into the dirt below. The books land hard like the sound of "good-bye." I hold my arms behind my back, and with the butcher knife in one hand, the jar of poison jam in the other, I kick on Jarek Jaskolka's door. Waldemar cries and hides against the wall of the house, holding the dead meadlowlark in his hands. He pinches his eyes closed.

"I'll miss you, Waldemar!" I whisper.

I wait for the bad man to let me in.